Dedication

To my husband. May you always be so good-natured about being a role model for my fictional heroes; along with the Lord, you are my life's hero.

1

In search of the yellow sticky with her ideas for today's meeting, Cisney Baldwin sifted through papers on her desk. She had a choice: honor her rash commitment to spend the Thanksgiving holiday with Nick LeCrone and his family, or lie and join her friends on the Colorado ski slopes.

Biting cold air and exhilarating speed might keep her mind off slime-ball Jason. And, she'd need her Richmond friends nearby to nurse her self-esteem after she told Daddy she'd lost his pick for her future.

She planted fists on her hips and stared at the papers sprinkled with yellow stickies that covered her workspace. Minutes before her meetings with Nick, she could never put her fingers on her notes. Why did this always happen?

How was she going to face him today, after he'd stood in her office doorway last week and watched her disintegrate during Jason's dump-Cisney phone call? If only she'd stopped there, but no, she hung up and blubbered about the end of her six-month relationship and having nowhere to go for Thanksgiving.

She splayed her arms over her paper-covered desk and knocked her head on the piles. This was all Jason's fault. Jason needed space? Right. What he needed was freedom to date that woman with a waist the size of his muscular neck.

"Hi."

She shot erect, raking her hair from her face.

Nick stood in her doorway. He didn't have a greasy mop of hair or wear button-down shirts two sizes too small, but he carried a calculator loaded with countless complicated functions. The joke around Marketing was that actuaries were accountants without personalities.

Nick came from a long line of actuaries, several still kicking. And unlike go-getter, snap-decision-maker Jason, built like a football tackle, lean Nick was analytical, reserved, and deliberating.

Daddy would eat him for lunch.

She peeled a yellow sticky from her arm and stuck it back on her desk. "Hi. Come in and have a seat." She moved aside a stack of company summaries. Her new marketing strategy would turn the profiled companies into customers for Virginia National Health Insurance—if Nick approved the financial risks.

As he eased into the chair beside her desk, she fiddled with her pen. She needed to back out of the weekend now, before he had a chance to give her holiday details. Which of her excuses would avoid hurting his feelings?

He hooked his arm over the back of the chair and rested his ankle on his knee, as if he had no upcoming trips on his mind. "Did you come up with an alternative to shortening the pre-existing period?"

Happy day! Could he have forgotten he'd invited her to spend Thanksgiving with his family? Oh, yeah, he never chitchatted before getting down to business. Didn't he want to know how she was holding up the week after her boyfriend had dumped her? He must know her heart still hurt like a triple bypass.

She lifted a legal pad. None of the yellow stickies

beneath it had miraculously morphed into the one she needed since the last time she'd checked. "Yes, I do have a couple of new ideas that came out of our focus groups." If she could find them. She picked up an empty foam cup hinting of French vanilla and threw it into the trashcan. Maybe this was a good time to renege on their trip south.

Nick leaned over and removed a yellow sticky adhering to the side of her desk. "Is this what you're looking for?"

She squinted. Yep, that was the sticky. "How'd it get there?"

The knowing smile on the tight-lipped man's face probably meant he thought she'd resorted to using other surfaces of her desk, now that no space existed on top. What next, her forehead?

"Let's see..." She turned over a memo and drew boxes, circles, squiggles, and lines, labeling them while she pitched her proposal. His gaze kept up with her scurrying pen, until the paper filled with shapes and words, and she stopped.

He studied her pen scratches.

Was he entering one of his endless deliberations of her great ideas? Cisney didn't need this right now. Boyfriend problems and Thanksgiving among a family of actuaries still loitering on her calendar was enough. She would not nudge Nick for his opinions. Today, she'd let him sit and think. She'd bring blood to her lips before she'd say a word. She tapped her toe under the desk.

He didn't move. Not a comment. Not a question.

Would it be impolite to ease her new phone from her pocket and set the stopwatch? She put down her pen and bit her lip. *Cisney Ann, do not open your mouth.*

3

She sat back and crossed her arms. Did Nick have a girlfriend? He wasn't bad looking. Hair, ho-hum brown. Decent nose. Maybe turned slightly to the right? Lips…kissable, if actuaries knew how to kiss. Eyes…whoa. Nice job, Mr. and Mrs. LeCrone.

Why, in the year she'd professionally known this man, hadn't she noticed how his abundant lashes framed and gave life to his gentle brown eyes? Probably because of the get-down-to-business glasses he always slipped on as soon as he sat.

Nick punched numbers on his calculator and jotted figures next to her drawings.

Ah, movement from the actuary. *Come on, Risk Man, bless my proposal.*

Who'd have thought this analytical man of few words would sympathize with her falling-apart moment and tell her she'd spend Thanksgiving with his family in some small town in North Carolina? Who'd have…?

Ha! He hadn't asked her, he'd told her. She'd nodded, while she blew her nose, but her nod was ever so slight. So insignificant it didn't count as a commitment.

"Sounds doable and the risks are manageable."

She startled. "What?"

"They're good ideas, Cisney."

She sat up straight. "Really? I mean, that's great." She jetted her hands upward. "Hurray! I can move forward with actuarially sound ideas."

He smiled while removing his glasses. "I knew you'd come up with something workable."

Was that a second bona fide compliment? "Thanks, Nick."

"Anything else?"

She rose as he stood. Time to weasel out of Thanksgiving with the LeCrones. Her heart hammered and her hands trembled. Could she deliver her spiel without her voice betraying her twist of the truth? She swallowed. She could do this. The words were simple: She was so sorry. When she'd accepted his kind offer during her stressful moment, she'd forgotten about the ski trip with her friends.

"Um..." Her tongue sought saliva, but finding none, ran over her lips like a dry cotton swab.

Let your yes be yes and your no be no.

But she needed the companionship of the other singles in Marketing. Marketing people were outgoing and fun. With Mom and Daddy in Germany, wasn't a ski trip with her friends the balm for her wounded heart? Angela and the others were her safety net after she told Daddy his ideal future son-in-law had bolted.

Let your yes be yes and your no be no.

OK. Fine. She'd go with Nick.

He collected his calculator and legal pad. Wasn't he going to give her trip details? After all, they would leave for his hometown in less than three days. She needed to know the Thanksgiving dress code and what time he'd pick her up.

He put his pen in his shirt pocket.

If he still wanted her to spend four days with his actuary infested family, why didn't he act like it? She widened her eyes and arched her eyebrows. "Well...?"

He met her gaze. "Yes?"

She refused to drag trip information from him. He needed to learn to communicate. Before she'd met Jason's parents, Jason told her to wear her royal blue dress, bring a homemade dish to wow his mother, and remove her shoes on the welcome mat.

She shrugged off her comment.

He moved to the door.

Lord, aren't you going to prod him, as you so rightly did me?

Nick stopped.

Ah. Now he remembered he'd invited a guest who needed particulars.

He nodded at the paper she'd used to pitch her proposal. "As soon as you turn your collage into a document, get it to Julie, and she'll run the official numbers."

She stared at him, speechless.

He held up his hand in farewell and left.

She sank to her chair and thrust her hands toward the drop-ceiling tiles. "Actuaries! They should be forced to take remedial communication classes."

⮞⬧⬧

Cisney hunched over the kitchen counter in her apartment, her stocking feet resting on the rungs of the barstool. While she crunched her second bowl of fruit-flavored cereal, she stared at her phone. Nick hadn't called, and probably wouldn't. She rolled her eyes and pushed her cell to the other side of the counter.

"Your plan to show him the consequences of poor communication backfired on you, didn't it?" she said between munches. "He's not suffering. You are."

If she'd asked him about the Thanksgiving Day dress code while he stood in her office, life would be simpler now. But, no, she had to punish him for the way God wired him.

She swirled her spoon through the cereal. Why did she always create trouble for herself? Maybe Jason wouldn't have dumped her if she were more refined and less headstrong. If she'd nurtured his ego more. How would she ever find another man like Jason?

Daddy had banked on Jason rescuing her from spinsterhood. She couldn't visit Mom and Daddy without him voicing how proud he'd be to call Jason his son-in-law. Now, jilting Jason was gone. Would she ever find her forever man? A man Daddy would be proud to have in the family? One who'd sweep her heart up to where the angels harmonized?

She loved Jason for his charm, but had the charismatic skunk ever taken her heart to heavenly heights?

She raised her spoon like a sword. "Forever Man, where are you?"

Hopefully, he'd show up someday, but for now, she needed to know what to pack for the holiday. She shouldn't have to beg information from Nick, when she didn't even want to go. Calling him would only encourage his substandard communications skills. But, giving him another opportunity to bring up the trip might be a fruitful alternative. She needed a strategy.

He ate lunch in the cafeteria with other actuarial types a half hour before she usually went to lunch. Tomorrow, she'd go down early, and when he dumped his flatware in the utensils bin, she'd happen to bump into him.

Was she twenty-nine going on thirteen? She slurped the milk from her bowl. But what a crafty twenty-nine-year-old teen she was. Her plan would work.

る⌒⌒

Nick laid out all the ingredients on the kitchen counter to create the perfect hamburger: grilled medium rare sirloin patty, cheddar cheese slice, dill pickles, Dijon mustard, ketchup, onion, lettuce, and tomato. The aroma of hickory seasoning lingered in the kitchen, making his mouth water.

His cell vibrated. He glanced at its screen, wedged the cell between his shoulder and jaw, and built his burger.

"Hi, Mom. What's up?"

"Is everything set for your trip Wednesday night?"

"Uh-huh," he said around a bite of his burger.

"Is Cisney still coming?"

"Why wouldn't she?" He licked ketchup from his fingers.

"I'm setting the table now, and I need to know whether to set a place for her."

"If she's changed her mind, I think she would have told me. That'd be the polite thing to do."

Strange, after only one week, Cisney hadn't seemed depressed today over losing her boyfriend. Short mourning period. But a good thing for him. With Dana bailing on him, he understood Cisney's pain, but four hours in the car with her lamenting her breakup would be torture—the half hour in her office last week had been bad enough.

"Why is Cisney all alone for Thanksgiving?"

"Her parents are visiting her brother's family in Germany." His family needn't know Cisney's ex-boyfriend had abandoned her.

"I'm so glad you invited her to join us."

Why would Mom be so glad? She'd better not be getting any ideas about Cisney being daughter-in-law material. Cisney wasn't.

The clink of china sounded.

"Why are you setting the table now? It's Monday."

"I always set the table on Monday night. I need Tuesday and Wednesday to make rolls, stuffing, gelatin salad, and so forth."

"You realize they sell rolls ready to bake at the grocery store, don't you?" He smiled, waiting for her expected retort.

"Did I hear you right, Mr. Gotta-Have-Mom's-Snowflake-Rolls?"

He laughed. "Just ribbing you. Won't the plates get dusty sitting out for three days?"

"Are you saying my house is dusty, young man? What's Cisney's last name?"

"Baldwin. Dust in the air is a constant."

"Let me write that down."

"You're going to be tested on home air quality?"

"I'm writing down her name, smarty-pants. I turn the glasses and plates facedown until Thursday. What kind of soft drinks does she like?"

"I don't know."

"You've never had a soft drink with her?" He pictured Mom's raised eyebrows accompanying her shocked tone.

"No." During their weekly meetings, he'd seen only fancy foam coffee cups on Cisney's desk. Several.

"I'm not going to ask why not. Please find out what soft drinks she likes and get back to me."

"Mom, before you hang up, I have a favor to ask."

"Sure."

"I have business to take care of Friday and Saturday in Charlotte for a couple of hours each day. Will you entertain Cisney while I'm gone?" He prepared to mouth her response.

"Business during Thanksgiving?"

"As much as I'd like to see you and Dad again the week after Thanksgiving, this saves me the drive." And if everything went as planned, he'd give his incompetent boss two weeks' notice on Monday.

"What kind of business takes people away from their families during holidays?" Her tone sounded like his, when at age twelve he'd let her know he didn't want to learn ballroom dancing.

After he narrowed his two options for his future down to one, he'd announce his intentions. For now though, he'd keep the nature of his business to himself. No use getting the family excited that he planned to move closer to home.

"The kind of business good for the futures of both parties," he said.

Mom would dislike Option A if she knew it involved working in the same actuarial firm as Dana. Option A offered the best mental challenge, but was potentially hazardous to his heart. Although Dana had been cordial, she'd made it clear her call about the job opening was strictly business. That was fine with him.

After she'd broken his heart, God's comfort, and hours reading his Bible, had put him back on his feet. That's where he planned to stay. If Friday's meeting with Dana, their first encounter since their breakup, proved he wasn't over her, Option B was a worthy backup.

"Of course we'll entertain Cisney." Mom sounded too cheery, as if she couldn't wait to have Cisney to herself. "Your sister and Allison will want to hit the Black Friday sales. She can join them. We'll think of something else for Saturday."

"Thanks, Mom. I knew I could count on you."

"Don't forget to ask Cisney about the soft drinks. We can't wait to meet her. Bye."

He jammed his cell into his pocket. Last week during his call with Mom to let her know Cisney was coming, he'd told her Cisney was a co-worker, not someone special. Now, her enthusiasm over Cisney's visit sent warning sensations up the back of his neck.

He bit into his burger. It suddenly tasted like an over-processed veggie patty.

Inviting Cisney home probably ranked up with Option A as one of his worst ideas, especially if it started Mom dreaming about gaining a daughter-in-law.

Cisney's face streaming with tears had touched a sympathetic chord inside him. And that was all.

∂∽⌒

Cisney entered the cafeteria.

Nick was sitting at a table by the window with two of his staff.

She turned in the direction of the tray-return station. Her scheme to bump into Nick at the utensil bin as a reminder he needed to tell her travel information was finally underway. Fair was fair. She gave up skiing with her friends. He needed to show her the courtesy of bringing up the trip. It was a matter of principle.

She moved into the alcove housing the swinging doors to the kitchen. With Nick's mind probably on actuarial matters, and not on his guest for the holiday, chances were good he wouldn't wonder what she was doing there, since she hadn't been through the food line yet.

When she peeked out of the recess, his table was in view. The trick was to time her exit to look as if she'd come from the elevators. That required angling to the far wall, and then making a quick U-turn. Making sure no one approached from the elevators, she executed a dry run. It would work.

Cisney craned her neck to monitor Nick's movements.

He stood and carried his tray toward the bins.

She ducked farther into the alcove. A count of five should do it. One, two, three, four—

The kitchen doors whooshed open. A cart rattled behind her and nipped her calves.

"Oh!" She scooted forward and into Nick's tray.

His tray tipped. The plate slid off, skated down her skirt, and broke in half on the floor.

"Cisney!" He gawked at her skirt. "I'm sorry."

Frozen, her hands spread, she took in the damages. One spaghetti noodle clung to a smear of red sauce on her cream-colored wool skirt.

With him staring at her as if he couldn't figure out why she'd exited the kitchen, she had to say something. "Was the spaghetti good?" She laughed. Did it have to come out so loud and high-pitched? She grabbed the napkin from his tray and wiped at the tomato pulp.

"I'd have eaten more if it had tasted better. Sorry."

"Excuse me, ma'am," the cafeteria employee behind the cart said. "I've got to get these lunch plates to a VP meeting." He rolled his cart toward the elevators.

Nick took care of his flatware, trash, and tray. "I'll find a wet rag and someone to clean this up."

People filing to the bins gave her sympathetic

looks. Some offered solutions for removing stains from wool.

Why did she have to be the one to lose face when she merely wanted Nick to own up to his responsibilities as host for what would most certainly be a miserable holiday.

Nick returned with a wet cloth. "Here, this will work better than the napkin."

She attacked the marinara with the dishrag. "I think it's going to take more than a wet cloth."

"Why were you coming out of the kitchen? I hope you're not marketing the spaghetti."

No comeback formed in her mind, and the truth was best left unsaid. She rubbed harder on the smear.

"Can I do anything else to help?"

"No. I'm fine." About as happy as a thief whose stolen cash exploded and covered him in red dye.

Nick headed toward the elevators, and then turned and faced her, walking backwards. "What soft drinks do you like?"

Mid-scrub, she paused, blew hair from her face, and gaped at him. Had he lost his mind? What did her soda preference have to do with a one-hundred-dollar-cleaning-bill stain?

∽∾

Cisney stared at the two open suitcases on her bed. Mounds of wool, silk, and leather extended above their sides. She'd have to sit on the cases to close them. That's what happened when one packed a set of casual clothes and a set of go-to-church clothes needed for four days.

How would she make it through the day on three

hours' sleep? Last night weeping over Jason's choices, worrying over Daddy's reaction to her losing her "real man," and fuming over Nick's failure to call had hit her like a triple dose of caffeine.

She checked her watch. If she didn't leave in the next five minutes, she'd be late to work.

Her cellphone played the marimba. Who would call so early in the morning? Jason? She fumbled in her handbag. Had he changed his mind? She looked at the display and her heart sagged. Nick?

She swallowed back the pain in her throat. "Hello?"

"It's Nick."

"Hi." Now he called—after she'd packed. *Thanks a bunch, Nick.*

"Would you mind bringing your suitcase to work and leaving your car in my apartment parking spot over the holiday? My apartment is three minutes from work, and we can get an earlier start if we leave from there."

He wasn't going to pick her up and haul her luggage to his car? Peachy. Now it would take her ten minutes—ten minutes she didn't have—to wrangle her suitcases to her SUV.

She curbed a heavy sigh and rolled her eyes. "Sure."

"Good. Let's park in the south lot. I'll meet you inside the south door at five-thirty."

"About how long is the drive to your parents' home?"

"Four to five hours."

She mumbled an OK and ended the call.

Five hours! The only way she'd survive the drive and four days with the LeCrones was to earn a notch on her challenge belt, playing best buddy Angela's creation, The Challenge Game. With uncommunicative Nick at the center of her challenge.

Cisney sat on her suitcases and latched them, then pushed and bumped the first down the apartment stairs. At her SUV, she grabbed the case's handle and performed a heft-and-swing, propelling the bottom of the case upward. One set of rollers caught the rim of the bumper. From this position, she put her weight into the bag and shoved it into the cargo area.

She slapped her hands together in a dusting-off gesture. "Ha! Take that Nick LeCrone. I am woman." If traffic was normal, she could make it to work on time.

After using her push-and-bump method to transport her second suitcase to ground level, she rolled it to her SUV and opened the back.

A curly-haired teen with a backpack slung over one shoulder bounded from the stairwell. He pivoted toward her and offered to help just as she performed the heft-and-swing motion. The bottom of the suitcase missed the bumper. She lost control and the suitcase hit the pavement. One latch flew off. The second released. The suitcase flapped open, and her lacy white, her flower-patterned, and her hot pink undergarments sprang out like popcorn and landed at the teen's feet.

"Awesome."

2

Positioned near the south exit, Nick scanned the herd of Virginia National employees funneling through the double doors. Where was Cisney? Caught in a meeting? Anyone holding a meeting on the Wednesday before Thanksgiving should be shot. Now, leaving would be like inching out of the parking lot after a Super Bowl.

An elevator dinged. He craned his neck toward the sound.

Cisney's dark hair bobbed as she hurried off the elevator to join the crowd. She caught sight of him and waved her hand like a determined New Yorker flagging a cab. She reached him, out of breath. No wonder. She'd been hot-footing it on high-heeled boots. Wasn't she tall enough without wearing boots set on railroad spikes?

"Sorry I'm late. Had to fax a ten-page document, and the fax machine ran out of paper."

"Doesn't the department secretary take care of that?"

"She needed to get on the road."

And we don't?

He grabbed her hand and merged into the crowd.

She held on tight as if she feared being trampled.

When they cleared the doors, he released his grip. "Where are you parked?"

She pointed into the darkness. "I park in the back

next to the fence to avoid dents."

Give me a break. He nodded at a beige sedan on the front row. "This is my car. Hop in. I'll take you to yours."

At his building, he lowered his window and pointed to his parking spot. She pulled in her SUV. He parked behind her, got out, and then raised the hatch on her vehicle. Two huge suitcases greeted him, both red, one banded together with a stretchy pink belt linked to one covered in purple rhinestones. What in the world...? Did she think they were staying until next Thanksgiving?

She came around to the back. "What's the matter?"

He opened his trunk and gauged the space.

She stood beside him. "Kind of tight, huh?"

He'd have to stow his carry-on bag and one of her suitcases on the backseat.

"Do you want to take my car?"

"No." He tossed his bag inside the car.

"You're angry."

He walked around her and hefted one suitcase into his trunk. "No. Just amazed."

"No one called to tell me whether Thanksgiving at your home was casual or dressy, so I had to pack for both." Ice capped her words.

"I didn't know your cell took only incoming calls." He deposited her other suitcase on the back seat and opened her door.

She climbed in. "Thank you. But gentlemen—"

He closed the door on her comment. It was going to be a long four hours, and an eternal four days. When he plugged in his seatbelt, she touched his coat sleeve.

"Sorry, Nick. I'm a little cranky after only three hours' sleep last night. Can we start over?"

In the glow of the complex's streetlights, her hazel eyes looked huge, beautiful, and sincere. The faint scent of her exotic perfume made her apology all the sweeter.

He started the engine. "Sure."

She nestled into her seat. "Good. I hate conflict." Strange, coming from a woman who seemed natural at creating disorder.

"Want to grab a quick burger before we get on the highway?"

"You mean, a fast-food place?"

"Yes, the key word being fast."

She wasn't going to insist on an order-from-the-menu meal, was she? The family would be up past midnight waiting for them.

She shifted in her seat. "That would be fine. Do they serve salads?"

"Yes. I think most do." He angled his head toward her. "You've never been in a fast-food franchise?"

"Not in a while. I avoid grease." She emphasized the word grease. "And Jason always wanted steak."

Near the interstate interchange, he pulled into a fast-food restaurant. "You can order a salad, and tell them to hold the grease."

❧❧

Once they were back on the road, Cisney studied Nick from the corner of her eye. He'd spoken less than seven words over his flip-it-and-serve-it meal, and four of them had been, "Let's hit the road." Well, four and a half words counting the contraction. She'd had to carry the whole conversation. And if he was so hot to get on the road, why hadn't he ordered their meals to go? He could have draped napkins on his lap and stuck one in his collar to catch the glops of grease and catsup dripping from his messy hamburger. As soon as he'd entered the car, he switched on the radio and listened to doo-wop tunes from the seventies, or some such decade.

She could use some calming classical strains about now. Funny, last night, she'd gotten the heebie-jeebies over spending Thanksgiving with Nick. What started as a niggling feeling inflated to fear that he invited her to take advantage of her vulnerability over her breakup. It wouldn't be the first time a guy used unusual circumstances to lure a woman into his clutches. When he'd grabbed her hand as they left work, her inner alarm had vibrated like a rattlesnake until the crush of the crowd made hanging on necessary. But now, her alarm had shut down. The luggage incident proved he was no infatuated male on the make.

He tapped his thumbs on the steering wheel in time to the music. So, actuaries could keep a beat. Did he dance with actuarially sound feet?

What would she and Jason talk about on a trip like this? Their jobs, of course. Or he'd give her a blow-by-blow description of one of his games. Jason always monopolized conversations. A hard thing for her, as much as she liked to express her thoughts; but unlike now, at least someone talked.

Why had Jason ditched her? What made her so undesirable? After Daddy learned of her failure to hold on to Jason, he'd gladly list her shortcomings. She wanted to know them, but not from Daddy. Talk about a knife in the heart.

Her back ached. No wonder. Since they'd left the

restaurant, she'd worked her way down to a slouch. She pressed her hands against the seat cushion and straightened her posture. Thinking about Jason and Daddy had to stop. It depressed her.

If Nick would talk to her, she could rise above this glum moment. Should she ask him about work? That hadn't gone well over their meal. She could start a debate. What controversy would get Nick talking? Sports, most likely. *So, Nick, what's your position on salary caps for professional athletes?* After a few minutes of that discussion, thoughts of Jason and Daddy might be a welcome change.

She leaned against the headrest. Here beside her sat a man ranking in the lowest quadrant on the social ability scale. A perfect specimen for Angela's The Challenge Game.

The game, of course. Working on her challenge would lighten her mood. She'd always liked tests of her skills and creativity. Hadn't Daddy instilled in her a competitive spirit?

Nick could benefit from her skill in bringing out even the most unsocial people. Daddy had taught her a trick or two, but it was mostly a gift. God made Nick a man of few words, but wouldn't he be happier if over the long weekend she helped him feel freer to communicate?

While Nick had ordered their meal, and she'd wiped grease and condiments from a table, the Nick-challenge had taken root in her mind. But to make it an official challenge, she needed to share her idea with accountability partner Angela, who right now was in the air with all their friends flying to Colorado.

Cisney peered down at her tapestry handbag at her feet. The yellow sticky reminder to call Angela that she'd jotted in the restaurant was still plastered to the leather strap.

Hopefully, Nick would someday appreciate her efforts. He was the authority with numbers, but she was the expert with relationships—well, OK, her own romantic attachments were outliers.

Her task would be to hold a conversation with Nick that lasted fifteen minutes. Any pause in the dialog that stretched longer than a minute ended an interchange. And to up the stakes, she had to accomplish her goal before midnight Friday.

To hide her smile, she turned her face to the window. For the next couple of days, she'd create her own entertainment while the LeCrone actuaries got out their mortality tables and debated who was scheduled to die next.

She stifled a yawn. If she counted the green mile markers on the shoulder of the highway, maybe she could drift off for a while. It wasn't like she was by herself and could sing show tunes to pass the time.

&∞⊱

Shock of all shocks. Cisney was quiet and seemed content to listen to the music. While she'd picked at her salad and told him about hiring another assistant, she hadn't been boring, but he didn't talk work on his time off.

Did she ever eat a full meal? Probably not, as slim as she was. She looked nice in the sweater with the big whatever-it-was-called rolled collar against her long neck. Her skirt, covering the top half of her ridiculous boots, showed off her great figure.

She lifted her hands like goal posts.

He startled. What did that gesture mean?

"OK," she said. "I've planned torture methods to get you to talk. I've counted eighteen mile markers, and I've tried to sleep, but now certain thoughts about a certain person are making me sad. I refuse to be gloomy."

He smiled. No, the woman wasn't boring. "You want to talk about it?" Had he really opened that door? Great. Let the Jason lamentations begin.

"OK. Sometimes the mile markers seem as if they're more than a mile apart, and sometimes they seem spaced less than a mile. Do you think Virginia saves money by not hiring civil engineers? Do road workers just take a stab at when the next mile has been reached?"

He laughed, and she giggled.

She pointed at him. "Made you laugh."

"So, you weren't having morose thoughts about a certain someone?"

"Yes, I was. Thanks for bringing him back to mind."

He'd just reopened the door for a sob story. What gave with him, anyway? He rarely spoke rashly, but twice in a row? He looked over at her. "Sorry. That was dumb."

"I didn't think actuaries were ever dumb."

"We aren't. I was trying to be tactful in my apology."

She crossed her arms. "You want to hear the truth?"

"About what?"

"About actuaries."

"I've heard it all, but go ahead."

"People in Marketing, Accounting, IT, Provider

Reimbursement, Claims, Underwriting, Human Resources—"

"I get it. The whole company."

She held up her finger. "No, not in Maintenance. But anyway, I've heard many people say actuaries are arrogant, negative know-it-alls, and weird."

He arched his eyebrow toward her. "And what do you think?"

"I think I'd better be tactful too, since your family populates half the actuarial profession. But I will admit you aren't as weird as some I've worked with."

So, he was weird. Just less than most of his fellow actuaries. "How about a pit stop?"

"Did I go too far?"

"No, we have, and I need a pit stop."

"Good." The dash lights revealed her smile. "We can pick up where we left off after our break."

Great. He'd choose actuary bashing over Elton John every time.

☙❧

Cisney left Nick inside the gas station paying for his drink and sipped her tangy diet orange soda on the way back to the car. His keys dangled from her fingers.

She unlocked the car and slid inside, removed her handbag from her shoulder, and placed it on the floor. Her yellow sticky to call Angela was missing from its strap. The fugitive note probably littered her path somewhere between the slimy restroom and the car. She moved her pearl solitaire to her left ring finger. The gold band against her skin cried, "Alert. Foreign object." That should remind her to call Angela.

As Nick pulled back onto the road, Cisney checked

his GPS. Two hours and twenty minutes to go. Their conversation before stopping had lasted about two minutes. Far from earning a notch on her challenge belt, but two minutes without morose thoughts were still worth it. Hopefully, they could resume their bantering.

By now, Jason probably had arrived in Charlottesville with his new girlfriend. How were his parents receiving her? Would they privately ask Jason about his ex? In their six-month relationship, Cisney had grown fond of his dad. His dad came across a notch gentler than Jason and two notches milder than Daddy.

Her stomach tightened. Every hour brought her closer to a Thanksgiving call with Daddy. Why couldn't she enter the Witness Protection Program just for the holiday to avoid the phone call with Daddy? What was so great about Jason that Daddy latched on to him for her future spouse, anyway? Heaps. Daddy admired Jason's go-getting attitude. Relished their one-up-man-ships. Thirsted for their dog-eat-dog debates. How was she going to find another Jason?

Nick fiddled with the zoom feature on the GPS. He had no idea how much she needed him right now to talk to her. Maybe the stop had revitalized him, and she could push him into a dialog lasting longer than two minutes.

She took a cleansing breath and mentally recorded the time on the GPS. "Tell me something about yourself."

He canceled the zoom and looked at her. "The torture begins."

She smiled and nodded. She felt better already. "Yes."

"My mother's name is Ellen, and my dad's is Roger."

"Should I call them Mr. and Mrs. LeCrone?"

"Mom would be disappointed."

"Then, Ellen and Roger it is."

"Mom would be disappointed."

"Why?" Wouldn't calling them Mom and Dad be a little presumptuous?

"Mom goes by Ellie."

"Hey! Who's torturing who?"

He chuckled and shrugged. A dimple formed on his cheek when he laughed.

She liked that. Wanted to make it appear again. "Go on."

"My sister's name is Nancy. She's an elementary school teacher."

"Nick and Nancy. Cute. I'm glad to have the heads-up on these names. Any others?"

He updated her. "My dad, grandfather, and Aunt Sandy are also actuaries. That about sums it up."

"Can you tell me something that none of your family or your actuarial colleagues knows?"

"Hmm."

She glanced at the time and pressed her lips together. Just over one minute. Had he entered one of his long thinks? If his pondering lasted more than a minute, she'd have to restart the session. *Come on, Risk Man. You can do it.*

"I keep my kitchen garbage can under my sink."

"Ha! Smarty-pants, you—"

He chuckled, producing the dimple.

"What's so funny?"

"My mother calls me that all the time. Smarty-pants."

"In the children's thesaurus, smarty-pants is a synonym for arrogant."

He grinned. "Probably."

"What I was about to say, is, you told me something personal about yourself. I know you don't have a relationship with anyone in your department. If you did, she'd know where you keep your kitchen trash can."

He cocked his eyebrow at her. "Oh, you're good." His words dripped sarcasm.

She'd hit a nerve. Dare she push it? "Are you dating someone, and she doesn't know the location of your kitchen trash can?"

"My love life is off limits."

She'd pushed too hard. Yet, he didn't have to be so harsh. "But my love life's within limits?"

"I don't remember introducing that topic."

Heat flared up her neck to her face. He was right. Why hadn't she excused herself from her office last week, instead of sobbing her woes to Nick after Jason crashed her world? If she had, she'd be with her fun friends now, instead of embarrassing herself with Mr. Smug.

She reached over and snapped on the radio. "Listen to your doo-wops."

࿇

Nick glanced at Cisney. Didn't she know doo-wops were more of a fifties or sixties thing? These tunes were classic seventies.

Her eyes were shut, but he'd bet she wasn't sleeping. Did she think she was the only one who'd been dumped? He didn't want to talk about Dana any more than she wanted to bring up Jason.

He flicked another glance her way. Had he hurt her? That wasn't his intention. Maybe he should apologize, even though he hadn't been the one to pry.

She sat erect. "Oh-oh-oh."

He looked in all mirrors in quick succession. "What?"

She pointed at the time on the GPS screen. "We hit the midway mark for the trip five minutes ago. It's milkshake time. My family always stops for milkshakes when we're halfway to our destination. It's Daddy's tradition."

He drew his brows together. "We're running late as it is. Don't you still have some of your soft drink left?"

She picked up her cup and sucked on the straw until the loud slurping sound screeched, *empty!*

Shakes would put them behind at least another fifteen minutes. "Are you really thirsty?"

"No." She sighed theatrically. "It's just a very special tradition I've never broken...until this trip."

So, if he didn't stop, he'd look like the bad guy again. What would two more hours on the road being judged an ogre feel like?

They approached an off ramp, and he looked for the sign announcing the food choices. "This exit has a couple of fast food options. Can you tolerate a shake from a fast food joint?"

"Sure."

He took the exit.

❧

Cisney scooted through the door Nick held for her.

Wouldn't shakes lift both their spirits? Heal the rift over her insensitivity to his love life? She gave him her cheeriest smile. "This ice cream shop is better than a fast food place. Look. They have peppermint shakes. Usually peppermint ice cream doesn't come out until after Thanksgiving."

He stood with his hands in his pockets studying the menu above the service bar. His demeanor seemed neutral. That was good. Right?

A young woman with a voluminous ponytail approached the order station. "What can I get you?"

Cisney pointed at the menu. "Does the peppermint shake have bits of peppermint in it?"

The ponytail flopped up and down. "Yes, and bits of chocolate, too. You'll need a spoon, it's so thick."

Cisney turned to Nick. "Isn't that great?"

He shrugged his brows and continued perusing the menu.

Cisney turned back to the eager server. "I'll have the peppermint shake with extra chocolate bits."

"And you, sir?"

"Vanilla."

"Cone, cup, or shake?"

The man couldn't even communicate what he wanted in an ice cream parlor. Cisney lifted her face and locked her gaze on his eyes. Was he getting her message to order a shake for the sake of tradition?

Nose-to-nose, and without taking his gaze from hers, he said, "Shake."

A tingle surged through her. Recovering quickly, she pulled on her big thank-you smile, honoring his support of tradition.

He chuckled, his dimple appearing.

Since when did a man's simple announcement of

an ice cream choice thrill her to her toes? It was all in his delivery. And those eyes. And that dimple. Who'd have thought ice cream with an actuary required a surge protector?

Jason would have chosen the cone to nettle her. He was like Daddy that way. Daddy seldom chose what Mom preferred. Unlike the usual males in Cisney's life, Nick was kind—when she wasn't overstepping his boundaries—as if he had nothing to prove.

Cisney accepted her shake from the server, who leaned over and inspected her pearl ring.

The ponytail wagged from side to side. "What a cool idea for an engagement ring. You two make a great couple. Opposites attract, and you two are definitely opposites. Peppermint with extra chocolate pieces versus vanilla." She smiled as if she'd discovered the poster couple for the perfect match.

Cisney and Nick exchanged quick glances, his gaze dropped to her ring, and then he frowned.

She put her hand in her coat pocket. "I'm—we're not engaged."

"Oh, sorry. You certainly fooled me."

Cisney thumbed her ring on her concealed finger. Her elegant solitaire with its large pearl set in a raised Tiffany mount could be mistaken for an engagement ring.

They left the parlor with their milkshakes and headed toward his car. He opened her door. "I don't remember you wearing that ring on your left hand."

Was he accusing her of trying to give the impression they were engaged?

3

Nick pulled the car into Mom and Dad's driveway and killed the engine.

Cisney slept, her back against the seat and her head resting on her folded coat jammed against the window. Her legs were drawn up onto the seat.

While they'd consumed their shakes, she'd given him the silent treatment, for exactly what, he wasn't sure. Refusing to talk was a poor choice of weapon for an expressive woman like Cisney. It turned on her and bit her. For him, silence was a gift for pondering. For Cisney, it was a gap that needed filling.

Before she'd finished her peppermint and extra bits, she'd relented and amused him with a couple of stories. He enjoyed listening to her. That didn't mean fireworks were lighting the sky, though.

He leaned forward to see her face in the light from the porch. Her relaxed facial muscles made the usually spirited Cisney look innocent and vulnerable.

"Cisney, we're here." He spoke softly.

She tucked her knees in closer to her body.

Should he touch her shoulder? He didn't want to scare her awake. He notched up his volume. "Cisney, we've arrived."

She dropped her legs to the floor and sat up. "Sorry, I didn't mean to drift off." She stretched and looked out the windshield toward the garage. "Oh, we're here. Why didn't you wake me?" She rummaged in her purse and produced a brush and a lipstick tube.

"You look fine."

"What do you know about first impressions?" She snapped the visor down, took stock of herself in the lighted mirror, then brushed her hair and smoothed on lipstick.

A woman like Cisney looked good even if she dragged herself in from a storm wearing combat boots.

Mom and Dad were in for a treat. They'd had difficulty relating to reserved and quiet Dana, but Cisney would dazzle them with her electricity. Now, if they'd enjoy her for the holiday, and not fall in love with her, he'd be safe. He wasn't in the market for a woman, much less one who lived by self-adhesive notes.

❧

Cisney raised the visor. The front door of the mansion-sized house opened, and a couple emerged onto the porch. The woman wore a my-baby's-home expression, and the man's build and features replicated an older Nick. Ellie and Roger.

Nick climbed out of the car, raising his hand in greeting. "Hey."

His parents waved.

He skirted the hood of the car and opened Cisney's door. Lowering his head level with hers, he said sotto voce, "I'll bring in your wardrobe later."

She scrambled out, stuffing her brush into her handbag. Not a great first impression if his parents thought she'd waited for him to open her door. "Hi!"

Ellie beamed. "Hello!"

On the porch, Cisney held back while Nick

embraced each of his parents. Her eyes misted. This would be her first Thanksgiving away from Mom and Daddy.

Nick turned to her. "Mom and Dad, this is Cisney Baldwin."

She blinked and angled her face away from the nearest porch lamp. Anything to prevent them from noticing the moisture in her eyes.

"We've looked forward to meeting you." Ellie stepped forward and took Cisney's proffered hand into both of hers. "Please call me Ellie."

Ellie's husband extended his hand. "Hello, Cisney. I'm Roger."

Nick's father had aged well. If Nick was as fortunate, he'd attract starry-eyed actuarial analysts—if such a breed existed—when he someday rose to chief actuary.

Heads poked out the partially opened door like bristles on a brush. Curious grandparents, aunts, uncles, and cousins, no doubt. So, this was what a lone flying fish felt like as it swam toward a school of hungry tuna.

"Come in. Everyone wants to meet you." Nick's mother put a hand on her back to usher her inside. The older woman leaned close and tickled Cisney's ear with whispered words.

"I'm sorry. What did you say?"

Ellie tried again, a little louder. "Why do you have a note stuck to your back?"

Cisney's heart sank. This flying fish's face would be crimson in less than a second. So much for first impressions. She eyed the hungry tuna at the door. "Does it say, 'Call Angela'?" she whispered back.

Ellie nodded, her eyes wide with curiosity.

Which did she want to do first? Chastise Nick for not telling her in the ice cream parlor that she had a yellow sticky plastered to her back, or explain to Ellie—and to Roger and the family tuna—that she didn't use her back as a bulletin board. She opened her mouth to explain.

"Cisney adheres little notes in unusual places," Nick said.

That did it. She'd lambast him later in private. For now, she smiled and addressed her audience. "I stuck the reminder to my handbag strap, and it must have transferred to my back when I slung the straps over my shoulder at a gas station." She made the note disappear into her handbag. Out of sight, and with great hope, out of mind.

Ellie mumbled something to Nick behind Cisney as the tuna parted to let her inside.

He answered, "It'll be OK. Trust me." Was he assuring his mother he hadn't brought a deranged person into her home?

While she shook family members' hands in the foyer the size of a ballroom, she caught Ellie's wrinkled brow and pinched lips. Now what faux pas had she committed?

She continued grasping hands, associating each person's name with identifying words she could remember, a memory trick Daddy had taught her. Aunt Sandy's hair was the color of sand. *Sandy-hair.* Nancy's glasses made her eyes look small. Nearsighted. *Nan-cyted.*

When she reached the end of the reception line, Nick took his turn up the queue. Hugging welcoming relatives—and, oh—a kissing cousin. The last woman, Allison, had coined her own alias when she pulled away from his embrace and attacked his lips with a big smack. *All-on-son*.

Laughing, Nick steered *All-on-son* to the room off the foyer.

Cisney followed the family into the huge formal room. In the far corner stood her dream piano. She halted. The LeCrones owned a Steinway concert grand piano!

While she forced her jaw and mouth shut, members of the LeCrone clan found seats on the tasteful sofas, love seats, and armchairs interspersed around the room.

Grandpa LeCrone moved to her side, his hands buried in his pockets. "I see The Old Girl has stunned you. Do you play?"

"I do. But I've never played on such a Steinway."

"You'll have to give The Old Girl a jingle or two."

The Old Girl? Couldn't they have named the ebony piano something more elegant than The Old Girl? Only actuaries would name this magnificent piece of art something so crass. How irreverent.

Grandpa nodded toward Nick's parents. "Ellie and Roger inherited the piano when Grandma Thelma's arthritis would no longer allow her to play. Ellie is the next best pianist in the family, even if she is an outlaw." He winked at his daughter-in-law.

"That's what Grandpa calls in-laws," sister Nancy said.

Grandpa ushered Cisney to the loveseat where Nick had settled. After she sat next to Nick, all tuna gazes locked on them.

Nick turned toward her, maintaining the space between them. "I'm impressed you play."

As her gaze volleyed among family members, she

muttered through her clenched-teeth smile, "Let's drop it."

Grandma Thelma clasped her gnarled hands. "Please play for us, dear."

"Yeah," Nancy said, "we're tired of conversation, and no one will play charades."

Nick's sister appeared to be in her mid-twenties, as did Allison, who lounged beside Nancy on one of the sofas.

College-aged Fran and Fannie, Nick's fraternal twin cousins, chimed in, begging for something lively.

Two minutes inside the house, and the family wanted her to exhibit her skills? Her toes curled inside her boots. Maybe it was a test. If she was cultured enough to play the piano, they could overlook that she wore reminders on her back. "I haven't played in a while."

Nick nodded at the Steinway. "Go on. You know you want to hear how The Old Girl sounds."

She stood and smoothed her skirt. "I only perform one piece in public. You're going to laugh, but I've played it so much it's the only piece my fingers know by heart." She swept her hand toward the twins sprawled on a sofa. "I guarantee it's lively." Her stomach tightened, and her heart played its own concerto while her boots clicked her closer to the nine-foot instrument. She eased onto the bench and looked up at her waiting audience. "Do you mind if I just take her in for a moment?"

Chuckles sounded all around.

Her fingers caressed the keys. She closed her eyes and drew in a breath through her nose and let the air seep out through her pursed lips. She shook her hands and wiggled her fingers. "I warn you it's not your normal parlor tune. So feel free to laugh." She launched into Rimsky-Korsakov's "Flight of the Bumblebee." Her fingers flew over the keys as they thankfully found the right ones.

After she finished the piece, the room erupted into applause, catcalls, and whistles.

She stood and curtsied. Test One passed.

Aunt Sandy, the twins' mother and the female actuary in the family, called, "Encore! Encore!"

Crinkling her lips into a humble smile, Cisney held up her hands, palms out. "No. I've enjoyed The...um...Old Girl...more than enough. Thank you for letting me experience heaven." She turned to Ellie and beckoned. "You come play, Ellie."

Ellie riffled through a batch of scores stored in the magazine rack flanking her chair. "Have you played Rachmaninoff's Opus 11: number 4 waltz duet?"

"In a recital in junior high. Well, it was mostly a solo."

Eyebrows rose.

Why had she elaborated? Now they wanted more. "A little mishap befell my partner." She scanned her audience.

Their brows inched higher.

She hoped her forced smile communicated something happier than her desire to crawl inside the Steinway. "Fluffy's dander on my skirt became airborne and launched Rodney Coleman into a sneezing fit." She shrugged her shoulder. "I didn't know what to do. It wasn't as if I could pound him on the back or yell, 'boo,' to make him stop. So I played on."

Nancy chortled. "It was a duet of a different flavor—staccato sneezes punctuating a fluid piano melody."

Family members laughed, except Nick. His gaze focused on the ceiling and his head shook slightly. Had she shared something too…too what? Dumb?

Ellie wrestled music sheets from the batch, glided to the piano, and laid the score on the music rack. She slid in next to Cisney.

Like Ellie, Cisney suspended her hands over the keys with her fingertips barely touching ivory. *Please, Lord, don't let me mess up.*

They began.

Ellie's shoulder-length hair swinging in Cisney's peripheral vision distracted her. Cisney clamped her lips between her teeth. *Focus.* She narrowed her eyes. Her gaze latched onto the score and traveled the horizontal staffs like a locomotive racing along steel tracks.

The music flowed.

After they played their last notes, Ellie high-fived Cisney, and then hugged her. "What fun!"

Family members stood and applauded.

Cisney nodded to the various groups, mouthing her thank you. The younger generation whistled and howled catcalls. Grandpa hugged Grandma Thelma. Roger, his gaze on Ellie, beamed with pride. Aunt Sandy and Uncle Bill called for encores.

Nick sat with his arms crossed over his chest, nodding. Somehow, his quiet response portrayed stronger kudos than if he'd stood on a chair and whistled.

She tingled.

Nick's gaze drifted from the cheering bunch toward the windows. Had she been wrong? Had his nod expressed smugness instead of approval? What had she done to warrant that?

∂∞⬠

After the clapping and whistles died down, Allison drifted to Nick. "I'd better get home. It was good seeing you." She leaned in close. "Cisney's a keeper." She turned to the group. "'Night, all."

Nick dropped his chin to his chest. For prowling matchmakers, he needed to wear a T-shirt saying, "I'M SECRETLY MARRIED."

"How about some decaf?" Mom said, still flushed from playing the duet.

Cisney, now beside him on the loveseat, shifted her gaze from Mom to him, and then back to Mom. "It's been a long day. If you don't mind, I'd like to turn in."

Mom directed a worried gaze toward Nick.

He mouthed, "It will be fine." He faced Cisney. "I'll get the luggage."

"Need some help with that, son?" Dad said.

Sure, if Dad could rustle up a luggage cart and an elevator. "No, I've got it, Dad."

Mom laid her hand on Cisney's arm. "Sleep in as late as you like." She gave Cisney a motherly hug. "I'm so glad you're here."

Nick stared at his feet. Would Mom be online until after midnight, looking for the best place to hold a wedding rehearsal dinner?

Cisney said her goodnights to the others and followed Nick to the front door.

He shrugged into his coat. "Wait here. I'll show you to your room as soon as I bring in your suitcases."

"I'm not lame. Let me help."

38

"You can get the door."

He hefted one of her suitcases from the car while she watched him through the glass storm door.

She'd done it. His greatest fear had occurred. Mom loved her, and if Mom fell for her, Dad would follow. Everyone liked her, even Allison, the self-appointed defender of the LeCrone offspring since childhood.

He wanted to blame his growing predicament on Cisney. He wanted to think she'd schemed the whole love-me act. Concocted the note-stuck-to-her-back thing in order to sink the hook. Reeled them in with her awe of Mom and Grandma Thelma's prized piano. Flopped them on deck, playing "Flight of the Bumblebee"—perfectly. She didn't stop there. No. She had to scale and fillet them, with her "solo" story and playing a duet with Mom, which no one else could do, now that Grandma couldn't play. But he had no case against her genuineness. Cisney had done nothing to hook them, except be herself. By turkey-sandwich time tomorrow, everyone in his family would sizzle on Cisney's grill.

He should never have invited her. He'd never fall for a woman's tears again. Isn't that what he'd liked about Dana, she never resorted to tears at the drop of a...boyfriend? Best not go there. He wrestled the second suitcase from the backseat.

He could keep Cisney occupied away from the family where she couldn't charm them with her sparkle. Maybe take her for long walks, out on fishing trips, and to daily movies. No way, though, could he keep her from them twenty-four-seven. Besides, everyone, including Cisney, would think he was interested in her if he gave her that much attention. And anyway, she'd have plenty of time to wow his family while he was gone for his interviews. He'd just have to let all their hints and winks roll off his back.

For now, his problem was to get her settled in a room she might reject.

Inside, with his carry-on tucked under his arm and the handles of her suitcases gripped in his fists, he led her up the stairs. Without stopping, he climbed steps until he reached the landing. He dropped the luggage at the foot of the stairs to the third floor and sucked in gulps of air. "I need...to get out...and run more."

"Your parents' house is beautiful. I love all the wood on the staircases." She ran a finger over the cherry banister and then looked up at him. "Until she went home, I thought Allison was the twins' sister."

He rested his hands on his hips and took in another breath. "She's Nancy's best friend. A graphic designer." He drew in more air and raised his finger in a spiraling motion. "That whole kiss thing when we arrived...I dated Allison briefly in high school, and the greeting kiss is just a carryover..."

Her smile looked calculated. "I think she'd like to pick up where you left off—" She slapped her fingertips to her lips. "Sorry. Forget I said that. Your love life is off limits, and I respect that." She stifled a giggle beneath her hand.

Fine, let her laugh. As long as she stopped prying.

Her curved lips flat-lined, and her eyes drilled him. "I take that back. I'm not sorry. Why didn't you tell me I had a yellow sticky on my back when we went in for milkshakes? Did you think it would make a good joke at my expense? The old kick-me—"

He put his finger to her lips. "You'll wake up Great-Grandma."

Cisney cringed. "Oh, Nick," she whispered. "I'm

so sorry."

"Good, you're back in reasoning mode. There is no Great-Grandma."

She jabbed her finger at him, and rasped, "You weasel…"

He held up his palm. "Calm down. And listen to me for a change."

She gawked at him.

At least he had her attention. "When you went into the gas station, was your coat on or off?"

She thought a moment. "Off."

When you went into the ice cream place, was your coat on or off?"

Her brow wrinkled, and then her eyes widened. "You didn't see the yellow sticky on my sweater because of my coat. And I left my coat on until I used it as a pillow in the car. Then, my back faced the seat."

He hefted his load again, leaving his bag on the landing. "I move to dismiss the case of the offending sticky note."

"Nick! You have a sense of humor."

He gave his of-course-I-do look. Four days of Cisney infiltrating his family would require a heavy-duty sense of humor, unless he died first of a heart attack from climbing two flights of stairs with a hundred pounds of luggage.

She stayed him with her hand on his arm. "I apologize for jumping to conclusions about the yellow sticky. Really."

He grunted his acceptance and climbed stairs.

Cisney followed. "Way up here, I'll feel as if I'm on top of the world."

"Hold that feeling." On the landing, he set down the suitcases and wheeled them toward two doors. He eyed the door that was about a foot and a half shorter than a standard door. Would she balk when she saw the room? He opened the other door. "Your bathroom. Small but functional."

She stuck her head inside. "Cute."

He stood with his back to the shorter door, whose top jamb reached the bottom of his chin. "I have to tell you something. Mom is worried about you having this room."

"Is she afraid I'll break something?"

"Cisney, just listen to me. It's simpler that way."

She crossed her arms over her chest and theatrically cocked her head.

"You know you were a last-minute invite. Mom would have given you my room, but I'll be sharing it with my cousin, Tony. The twins' brother. He had to work tonight and will arrive around midnight. Mom said Nancy's got a school project spread all over her room. So this is the only room left. Mom was surprised at how tall you are, because..."

He swung the door open.

The ceiling at the doorway started at five and half feet and graded to seven at the apex. He'd measured it after he'd bumped his head while he and Dad remodeled the room. At the pinnacle, a twin bed rested opposite a curtained window. Mom made the curtains to match the bedspread and added a brightly painted dresser on one of the short walls. Nancy re-covered two stuffed armchairs and faced them toward the window. The chest at the foot of the bed held family photo albums.

Cisney laughed. "Fun! It's like a little dollhouse room decorated so adorably. Or a princess tower." She lowered her head and moved inside the doorway. "I'll manage fine."

He let out a slow breath. Mom would be relieved. "If the fire alarm goes off in the middle of the night, you've got to remember to duck your head."

"No problem."

"How tall are you?"

"Five-nine."

"So, right about here," he stooped and touched the ceiling inside the room a few feet from the door, "you'll need to lower your head when you exit. Of course, with those boots, it's about here." He moved his finger farther up the ceiling.

She walked to that point and the top of her forehead met the ceiling.

He backed to the doorway. "Do you think you'll remember that, or should Dad check his homeowner's policy?"

She planted her hands on her hips. "Gracious me, you're so caring about my well-being." She grinned. "Tell your mother I love it."

"Thanks. That'll put Mom at ease." He wheeled her suitcases inside the door. "Can you take them from here?"

She nodded and bumped her head on the ceiling.

He turned toward the stairs. "Dad," he said in a singsong voice, "get out your homeowner's policy."

❧❦

Cisney hefted the suitcase bearing her nightwear onto the bed, and then dug her cell from her handbag. If she called Angela now, would she catch her and the gang still at dinner rehashing their trip to the resort? Probably. Colorado time was two hours behind.

Nick's family was nice. They had genuinely welcomed her. Why had Nick seemed perturbed when everyone else enjoyed her playing the amazing Steinway? Was he jealous of the attention they'd heaped on her? Unlikely. Nick wasn't the jealous type. Had she embarrassed him? Going on about the junior high duet? Maybe. Or could he be upset that his family liked her, because he didn't?

She flopped onto the bed next to her suitcase and slumped. What a terrible thought. Strange, too. Near the end of their trip, she'd been congratulating herself for winning him over. Had he laughed at her stories out of politeness? His responses seemed authentic enough, so much so she lost interest in her challenge. Even the fingers of her left hand no longer begged her to call Angela. Or to remove the intruding pearl ring she'd put there to remember to call.

Cisney lifted her left hand toward the glow of the ceiling lamp. The lustrous pearl encased in the high Tiffany setting definitely could be mistaken for an engagement ring. She rippled her fingers in the light. Would she ever wear a diamond on this hand? As Daddy reminded her often, her old-maid clock was ticking. Jason, in taking six months to decide to dump her, had gobbled up precious time to land her forever man.

Talk about a depressing thought. She laid her crossed arms on her suitcase and rested her head on them. She would have to go through the hunt, the insecurities, the wondering if this was the right guy, all over again. Her lungs weighed heavily against her ribcage as if they were filled with sand. Starting over from a broken relationship was like a computer crashing and her having to recreate an entire six months' worth of work. All because she failed to save.

This was not helping anything. She pulled herself erect. Time to claw her way out of this hole before she sank any deeper. She'd call Angela for a dose of encouragement before her confidante and the others hit the slopes tomorrow morning.

After dragging her suitcase off the bed and finishing her nightly routine, she plugged the cell into her charger next to a vase of yellow roses on the bedside table. Were they real? She touched a petal. It was moist and alive and gave off a faint rose scent. How sweet of Ellie.

See, life had its little blessings. Wouldn't it be appropriate to list them in preparation for Thanksgiving tomorrow as she drifted off to sleep?

She crawled into bed and folded her hands over her midriff. Of course, she was thankful for Mom and Daddy. Her stomach clenched. The dreaded call would come tomorrow. After she related the news about Jason, Daddy would load her with pointers on how to get Jason back. *You finally got yourself a real man. Don't let him get away, Cis.*

For the hundredth time posing the questions—without Daddy's help—was she too overbearing, too talkative, too flighty? Was that why Jason and his predecessor, whose name she wouldn't even think, dumped her?

Lord, please transform me into someone a man can love for a lifetime. I want to make You and Daddy proud.

Yes. That's what she wanted. To change. The next man—her forever love—would cherish her for eternity. She snuggled into her pillow. This was the perfect weekend, away from family and friends, to work on her character flaws and become the new Cisney.

Composed, serene, and quiet.

༺∞༻

Cisney woke refreshed and hungry. She stretched her arms high above her head, her smile spreading. The first day of her new self was here.

She took a shower and chose the skirt and sweater from the three outfits she'd laid across the bed. The royal blue cashmere sweater and gray wool skirt were dressier than the slacks outfit but more casual than the red dress.

Ready for the day, she gripped the drape rods and whooshed them apart. A huge body of water lay in Nick's backyard. She closed her gaping mouth, but it fell open again. The LeCrones lived on an honest-to-goodness lake. She sank into one of the armchairs situated for viewing the stunning scene from the large circular window. Why hadn't Nick told her? It was gorgeous.

Traces of the early morning mist wafted over the water. Autumn reds, oranges, and yellows, still evident among the deep greens of the firs and pines, graced the areas surrounding the homes that looked like miniature dollhouses on the far shore.

She leaned closer to the window and looked from one side to the other to gauge the span of the lake. It rounded bends in either direction without ending. Was the boundless lake a sign that great new possibilities were opening up for her?

She dropped her gaze to the lawn between the house and the boathouse, where Nick sat on a bench, reading. She raised her fist to rap on the window, and then stopped, doubting he would hear her from up so close to heaven.

She unplugged her cell. Wait until Angela heard that Nick the Actuary had a Steinway and lived on an enormous lake. She selected her friend from favorites and stood at the window, where the ceiling reached its highest point. While Angela's phone rang, Cisney watched Nick.

"Hi, Cisney," Angela said. "Sorry, I can't come rescue you from boredom. I'm forced to ski on ten inches of new powder!"

Cisney pictured Angela's auburn mass of natural curls bouncing in her excitement. "Thanks for wishing you could, though. What is it, seven o'clock there?"

"Yeah. First lift goes up at eight."

"Only you could be skiing in Colorado a week before your wedding. I'm surprised your mom let you go."

"You know Mom. She wants to do it all. She'd say the vows too, if I let her. Enough about me. How are you?"

"Amazingly, it's not that bad here. Nick is uncommunicative Nick. I had to open my drapes this morning to find out his parents live on a mammoth lake. It's breathtaking."

"I'm glad it hasn't been a total washout. Did you know Nick isn't on Facebook?"

"Why did you look for him there?"

"I wanted to see if he might be boyfriend material for you." Sheepishness tinged Angela's voice. "So shoot me. I think he's good looking, in a serious sort of way. I'm sorry he's the same old drag outside of work that he is inside."

"Actually, he's cooler away from work—even has a sense of humor." Why was she defending Nick?

Especially after his grumpy behavior during the unexpected concert last night. No matter. Today, she'd let nothing stand in the way of creating her new image. "Oh, I played 'Flight of the Bumblebee' on their Steinway. Not just any Steinway, but a grand. It's a dream."

"A lovely lake and a grand piano. I'd say things are looking up."

"Looking down is more like it."

"What do you mean?"

"They put me in an attic room that affords me an awesome view. Anyway, I originally called you because I needed you as my accountability partner."

"Ah, ha. Another challenge. I have one for you, too. I'm going to ski down a black diamond trail before we leave, if it kills me."

Cisney laughed. "It probably will."

"The pun's been good for several laughs around here. Tom complains he doesn't want a fiancée with a broken back. He wants to know how I'll be able to wait on him with a damaged spine after we're married. But making it to the bottom of a black diamond is my challenge. What's yours?"

"I have to maintain a fifteen-minute dialog with Nick, with no pauses over a minute, or I have to start the clock again."

"I'm talking black diamond, here, and you're talking fifteen minutes of conversation? If you want a notch on your challenge belt, make it a half hour."

"I've sort of lost interest—"

A guffaw sounded in the background of Angela's phone.

Every cell in Cisney's body went rigid. "That laugh! I'd recognize it anywhere."

4

Cisney pressed her cell against her ear. "What's Jason doing there with you?" She grasped the top of one of the armchairs to steady her trembling legs.

"Making breakfast." Angela's voice squeaked. "Aw, Cis, I'm sorry. He sort of invited himself along at the last minute."

"Is *she* there with him?"

"She's a beautiful doormat, nothing like you at—"

"I can't talk anymore." Cisney dropped her cell. It landed on the cushion of the armchair. How could Jason betray her using her friends?

She dug her fingers into her hair and paced the length of the window. Her lungs labored to pull in air, and her chest ached. Did the rat know her friends were planning a skiing trip before he dumped her? Did he get rid of her so he could take Miss Beautiful Doormat skiing instead of her?

Cisney punched her fists upward. Her knuckles scuffed the inclining ceiling. Rubbing her chaffed skin, she dropped into an armchair and rocked. Her forehead knocked on the cold window glass with each forward sway. This was not happening. This couldn't be happening.

Below where Nick sat reading by the lake, he turned a page of his book. How could he be so nonchalant down there when she'd been stabbed in the back up here?

She threw herself backwards against the chair. *I*

can't do this—can't go downstairs and play gracious guest. I need to go home.

Yes. Home. By herself. She shot to her feet and looked for a phone book in the drawer of the bedside table. It housed a Bible and a small box of tissues. She pitched the Bible on the bed and peered behind the box. Nothing. She snatched several tissues and wiped at the tears drenching her face. The trunk at the end of the bed held only photo albums.

Stop! Why are you looking for a phone book? She grabbed her phone, identified her current location on Maps, and bought an online Greyhound Bus ticket leaving from Statesville, a city about twenty minutes away. In the direction of home.

縶❧

Nick looked up from his Bible and out over the lake. A great blue heron flew overhead. He'd missed his quiet times by the lake. *Lord, You have comforted me today.*

Since Dana had called off their relationship, God had faithfully directed him to Scriptures that furthered his healing. What a merciful God. His Lord had not only taken care of his sins for eternity, but He cared about his daily scrapes.

Nick ran his finger over the Scripture in Second Corinthians…*Who comforts us in all our troubles, so that we can comfort those in any trouble with the comfort we ourselves have received from God.*

Was he ready to move forward? *Lord, did you guide Dana to call me last week? Please lead me away from Option A if it's not Your will for us to work together.*

No thoughts or Scriptures spoke to what he

should do about Option A. God's focus today seemed to be on comfort and not on guidance for employment options. He'd just let the job situation play out and stay alert for God's nudges.

The heron landed near the shore by the boathouse. What a perfect day to paddle around in the rowboat, or maybe take out the canoe for some exercise. His huffing and puffing up the stairs last night, carrying Cisney's complete wardrobe, proved he needed to get into some kind of workout routine.

Was the sleeping beauty up yet? Would she enjoy going out on the lake? No need to entertain her—the family would line up for her attention as soon as she came downstairs—but he'd like to take her out and show her the lake.

He looked up at the round window of her room. The curtains were open. She must be up. He'd finish reading the Second Corinthians passage, and then— she passed by the window. He removed his glasses. Was she dancing, or practicing karate moves?

$\approx\infty$

Cisney threw her phone onto the bed and shot her fists above her head. "Give me strength! And a ride to the bus station." Images of Jason and his new girlfriend in trendy ski outfits snuggling on the ski lift broke into her mind. "Lord, why is Jason torturing me?"

She wanted to throw something. A pillow wouldn't satisfy. She beat her thighs and shook her head. That helped. Didn't she have the right to act like a mad mongrel in the privacy of her room?

A picture of Jason introducing what's-her-name to Cisney's friends snapped into her head. What was this?

A slideshow of "Jason Betrays Cisney"? "Oohh! Why can't the creep just disappear from my life?"

Cisney stomped to the bathroom, ducking her head where the ceiling slanted. Why didn't Daddy see what a jerk his choice for her future was? In one sweep, she collected her toiletries, returned to the room, and then flung them into her suitcase. Couldn't Jason be content with knocking her down, without trampling her face into the muck?

Nick had better agree to take her to the bus station. Cisney didn't care how long she had to wait on a sticky bench surrounded by candy wrappers. In this state, she had to get out of here now, before people in holiday moods started being thankful. She slammed the suitcase closed, wrestled it to the floor, and strode to the door.

Wham!

She staggered backwards from the sloped ceiling, her hands going to her forehead. The back of her legs connected with the upright suitcase. She lost her balance and sat on it. The suitcase rolled back. She slid off and landed hard on the carpeted floor. Stunned, she sat a moment, and then made sure nothing hurt unreasonably, other than the bump surely forming on her forehead.

Calm down before you kill yourself.

She needed to get to Nick while he was still alone.

In double-time, she crawled to the landing outside her dwarfed door, stood, and listened for sounds of movement on the second floor. Handling nice people was out of the question. Detecting silence, she crept down two flights of stairs. When she reached the foyer, words drifted from the kitchen and intermingled with the conversation emitting from the living room. She stealthily made a tight turn around the staircase newel and headed down the hallway toward the back of the house.

When she reached a butler's pantry, which opened into both the dining room and the kitchen, she scooted past, but not before making out Nancy's voice coming from the kitchen.

"Did you see Cisney's pearl engagement ring? They're engaged! Did she think because her gem is a pearl we'd be fooled?"

"I hope you're right," Ellie's voice said. "She's perfect for Nick."

Cisney clamped her hands to her head and dug her fingers into her hair. Pain shot to the pulsing lump on her forehead. Huffing a cry through her bared teeth, she scurried from the chatter of the gullible women. What next? Could anything else go wrong?

She escaped through the mudroom door, trudged toward the lake across the trimmed lawn—her two-inch heels aerating the grass—and planted herself in front of Nick. She dropped her gaze to the book on his lap. He was reading the Bible? Nick read the Bible?

Stay focused.

He looked up. His dimpled smile formed, and then disappeared. He studied her with sober concern.

She paced the lawn in front of him and flapped her hands. He probably thought she looked like an agitated duck. She clasped her hands in front of her. "I know this is a bad time, right on Thanksgiving Day, but I have to go home."

He removed his glasses and stared at her. Good, he didn't interrupt her with an inane question like, "Who died?"

Her face crumpled and tears overruled her will. "I

can't do this. I don't want to pretend in front of your wonderful family that everything is all right. I don't want a notch on my challenge belt by getting you to dialog for fifteen minutes. I just want to go home. I want to be alone." She curbed an escaped wail. "I'm sorry, I don't mean for this to sound as if it's about you. It's about Jason." She stopped and faced him. "He—he is with all my—my friends in Colorado." She punctuated her words with chops from her open hands, hiccupping between phrases. "They are *my* friends. I—I—I introduced him to them, and now he's wheedled his way in on their ski trip and brought along his new girlfriend."

Nick stared at her like a stunned bird. How could he not react to Jason's treachery?

She clutched her handful of tissues to her face to stifle another wail. Gritting her teeth, she pulled herself together and glanced at the yellow sticky attached to her phone. "My Greyhound bus leaves at ten fifty-five this morning from Statesville. Will you take me there now? I'm all packed. You'd be back within an hour." *Please, please don't argue.*

His gaze flicked toward the house, and then back to her. He laid his Bible and glasses on the bench, stood, grasped her hand, and pulled her toward the lake.

Hadn't he heard a word she'd said? Was he going to throw her in the lake to stop her hysterics? "What are you doing?"

"I'm saving you."

Save? Like baptize her in the lake? She tried to free her hand.

His grip tightened, and she double-stepped to avoid falling.

"Hey, Nick! I want to meet your lovely lady!"

Cisney looked over her shoulder while trying to keep up with Nick. A barefooted man wearing black dress pants and an unbuttoned oxford shirt revealing his undershirt stood on the grass near the back patio, one hand in his pocket and the other raising a glass of orange juice.

"Later, Tony!" Nick stopped at the boathouse next to the pier.

A rowboat, whose bow bobbed a foot from shore, was tethered on the opposite side of the pier.

Nick pointed at the craft. "Get in the boat."

"Wha—"

Tony strode toward them.

She spun to Nick. Tony's approach seemed to infuse urgency into Nick's escape from the harmless-looking young man. She drew the bow of the boat onto the grass. No way was she water-staining her black kid pumps. She climbed inside and, sliding her hands along the wobbly boat's edges, moved to the back and sat. Nick took the pier steps two at a time and drew oars from hooks inside the boathouse.

Tony had covered half the distance to the pier. "Hey, man. I just want to meet her!"

Nick descended the pier's steps and tossed the oars in the rowboat. He unfastened the rope from the pier, shoved the boat into the water, gracefully hopped inside, and back-paddled the small craft with one oar to deeper water.

Once away from shore, she caught sight of a pontoon inside the boathouse. Couldn't Nick have chosen the stable vessel for their getaway? He could forget her using her pumps to bail water from the rowboat.

At the shoreline, Tony stopped and spread his hands. "I'll button my shirt!"

Nick rowed. "Tell Mom we'll be back in about an hour."

After Tony turned and trudged up to the house, Nick helped her wobble to the forward seat as he balanced the boat. Once she sat facing him, he took the seat in the stern and secured the oars in the oarlocks.

She fastened her gaze on him, but he avoided her eyes while he turned the boat.

His maneuver completed, he looked at her and shrugged mid-row. "I didn't think you'd want to meet Tony when, you know..." He released an oar and made little circles with his hand near his hair.

Oh, no. Where could she hide in an open rowboat? Her head-thrashing fit in her room could only mean she looked like a cavewoman. She raked her fingers through her hair, and pain exploded from her forehead. She winced.

Nick's hand dropped to his eyes, and then down to his lips. He shrugged sheepishly.

She pictured smeared mascara and lipstick all over her face. She used her handful of tissues, now a soggy ball in her fist, to wipe under her eyes and around her mouth.

He nodded toward her. "That swelling on your forehead is turning an angry red. Looks as if you were moving at warp speed and forgot to duck. How'd the ceiling fare?"

Certainly he jested. Could her forehead have dented the ceiling?

"Now you see why I need to go home." She hadn't meant to sound so whiny.

"Take out your cell and cancel your bus ticket."

"I can't face your family. Please understand."

"You need my family, not a three-day pity party by yourself in your apartment."

"What would you know about dealing with a relationship gone bad—really bad? I don't need your...philosophical...advice. I need a ride to the bus station."

Was he going to make her miss her bus? She peered over the side. The water looked a little deep to walk to shore.

He ceased rowing and cocked his head upward. Any moment, he would say something profound from his wealth of inexperience. He resumed rowing at an easy pace. "May I ask you a few questions? You don't have to answer them out loud."

"As long as I don't have to answer them, go ahead and knock yourself out."

"Do you read the Bible?"

Oh, brother. Here came the sermon. Maybe she could head him off his track. "Yes. I don't read my Bible as often as I should, but I've read through it in Sunday school over the years." That should at least thwart him from starting at Creation.

"First question..." He swept his hand to include the whole lake. "Who created the earth—all this?"

Stating her Bible credentials hadn't done the trick. At this rate, she'd miss her bus. A fish jumped, radiating concentric circles on the water. Admittedly, this monstrous lake did represent a beautiful piece of God's work. "God did."

"Does God make promises?"

"You mean, like His promise never to leave or forsake us, or like His covenant promises to Abraham and to Moses and to the Israelites and to all people?"

He hadn't tripped her up yet.

"Like both. Does God keep His promises?"

"Yes, the best being that He sent His Son Jesus to die on a cross to make a way to save us from our sins. Is this going somewhere?" Anywhere?

"Yes. Has God prophesied great historical events?"

"Yep." *A-plus comin' at 'cha.* "God prophesied the Israelites' exile to Babylon. The Israelites were exiled. He prophesied that Cyrus from Persia would later free them and allow them to return to the Promised Land. In God's prophesy he called Cyrus by name. One-hundred-fifty years later Cyrus freed the Israelites, and they returned to the Promised Land." She was on a roll now. "And, of course, the no-brainer, Jesus's coming. We know Jesus will return because God promised that, too." Maybe Jesus could come again now and put her out of her misery.

His head jerked backwards as his eyes widened. "I'm impressed. I'm not sure I'd have come up with the example of Cyrus so quickly. That's a great example of God's sovereignty."

Did she really look like an idiot? Well, maybe now, since she looked like a wild woman. But did she, usually?

He pulled the oars up to rest on the edges of the craft and let the boat drift. "Did God merely know these events would happen?"

"No. He planned them, prophesied them, and executed them."

"Jeremiah gives another promise from God, 'For I know the plans—'"

"'I have for you…plans to prosper you and not to harm you, plans to give you hope and a future.'" If that was the Scripture he'd been going for all along, why didn't he just say it, instead of all the questions?

"Exactly. So, sum up what all this means about God."

"That wasn't a question." She was being difficult, and probably unfair, but all these questions. What did they have to do with Jason or her need to go home?

He rolled his eyes. "How would you sum up what your answers say about God's character?"

She felt as if she were on stage for table topics at Toastmasters—make that, rowboat topics. "God is the all-powerful, all-knowing Creator and hands-on Promise Keeper, who plans and controls everything for the love and good of His people and for His glory." The glory part should earn her a bonus point.

His jaw dropped a half-inch. "Great summary."

She shrugged.

He captured her gaze. "So, God has great plans for His people, and God promises His plans are for their good, to prosper them and not to harm them, to give them hope and a future?"

She widened her eyes and nodded. Would he ever get to the real point?

"Do you think it's possible marriage to Jason was not God's plan for you? That God planned someone better for you?" He looked away toward the distant shore and plunged his oars into the water and pulled hard. "After the guy broke up with you over the phone, and then invited himself and his new girlfriend on your friends' ski trip, maybe you should thank God for foiling your plans."

Her mind snapped to attention. That was blunt. Blindsiding. No question, she believed God cared for her, but God concerned about her future spouse? How had such a simple concept escaped entering her thoughts? Ever. She let her body go limp. Nick was right.

She raised her gaze. "But it still hurts."

"I know."

She resisted the urge to roll her eyes. Right. He knew her pain...to quote her overdue sister-in-law...*like a male obstetrician knows how a pregnant woman feels a week past her due date.*

ॐॐ

Nick resumed rowing.

Cisney stared at the water, her lips pursed. Then she looked at him. "I'm going to turn around on my seat and enjoy God's creation, and I request that you don't ask me any more questions, or better yet, don't say anything...just row."

She swung her legs around and faced the bow.

He wouldn't have given her the advice if it hadn't been for today's Scripture reading. As much as God's words comforted him, they also had been a heads-up for ministering to Cisney...*so that we can comfort those in any trouble with the comfort we ourselves have received from God.* But had he consoled her, or made her mad?

He forced his gaze from Cisney's slumped posture and took in the ripples in the glassy water formed by the oars. Then he raised his gaze to the ducks flying in V-formation against the perfect blue sky. Maybe he'd get up early tomorrow and throw out a line for some crappie. Grandpa might want to join him. He could fit an hour in before time to pursue Option A. His heart blipped. The brunette in front of him wasn't the only one on the rebound. Tomorrow would be the first time he'd see Dana since she broke it off with him. He'd require the Lord's strength just as much as Cisney needed it.

A breeze ruffled his hair. He regarded Cisney. Her feminine frame was slight for her height. He'd been right yesterday. Her disheveled hair, her smeared makeup, and the bump in the middle of her forehead couldn't render her unattractive, even if she added combat boots.

What was going on in that head of hers? Had he chiseled a hairline fracture in her resolve to leave? Mom would be disappointed if she left—not because Cisney would miss the festivities, but because she had gone home broken.

He looked at his watch. If they left the house in the next ten minutes, she could make her bus. Should he remind her or just start rowing for shore? Or should he let her miss her bus and hope her mood changed for the better? Her leaving was not a good thing for anyone. No doubt about that. But his place was not to play God, and what seemed the right thing to do was honor her wishes. He turned the boat around.

Cisney bowed her head. Was she praying?

Her hand holding her cell tunneled under her mass of hair to her ear. No, not praying, unless she had God on speed-dial.

"Hi. I want to cancel a bus ticket."

❧❦

Cisney plastered her back against the wall outside the mudroom door. "You have to run interference for me. I've got to clean up and change before anyone sees me."

"Sure." Nick opened the door and peered inside. He grabbed her hand.

He seemed to take her hand a lot. Didn't he know a girl might construe he liked her? But not right now. What about her cavewoman look was there to like? Dragging her was more like a control thing. But as long as he got her to her room without anyone laying eyes on her, he could play Mr. Caveman.

With Nick in the lead, they crept down the hall and scuttled past the butler's pantry and kitchen, where chopping knives and clinking pans emitted a cacophony. He released her hand and pointed to the stairs while he moved to check the front room.

"Coast is clear," he whispered. He passed her on the stairs and took the lead again. Mid-staircase, he ducked down.

She dropped to a squat. Muted voices conversed and a door opened. Her heart pounded. What would be worse: seen by a family member in her disheveled state or caught hunkering down like Marines on a mission?

Nick pumped his hand behind him. What next? Would he give a military signal with two fingers to his eyes and then direct them toward the stair rail, motioning her to jump?

"Thanks, Grandpa," Tony's voice said above them, "I've always wanted to wear argyle socks."

"Beggars can't be choosey when they forget to pack socks, son." Grandpa's last words trailed off, and a door closed.

Then another door closed. Tony going into his room?

Nick waved her on. She scurried by him, getting a whiff of his titillating cologne, darted up the first few steps of the second flight, and then stopped and turned. She needed the Thanksgiving dress code.

Nick, standing at the bottom of the stairs, wore jeans and a plaid shirt under his light jacket. If that was his dress for the day, she'd dig out a more casual outfit than the two lying on her bed.

"How should I dress for Thanksgiving?" She whispered.

"Comfortable."

That told her practically nothing. "Are you changing your clothes?"

"Yes. Comfortable slacks and a sports shirt."

She turned to continue climbing.

"Cisney."

She faced him.

"Just so you know, you're the one who cut our conversation short on the lake. Otherwise, you could have carved another notch on your challenge belt."

She cringed and her cheeks burned. Why had she blurted about the challenge during her hysteria? He'd invited her to his home, listened to her rant about Jason, and helped her see a new perspective—God's perspective—on her life. He didn't deserve her insult.

An apology on her lips, she glimpsed his smile. Was that smugness? So, that's how it was.

She leaned toward him, holding onto the railing, and spoke in her most casual voice. "Just so you know, your sister and mother think we're engaged. I overheard them in the kitchen, earlier." She held up her left hand, flashing her pearl solitaire toward him, and fluttered her fingers. That should wipe the smirk off his face.

It did. His jaw dropped an inch.

5

Cisney's attic-room door closed above. Nick stood motionless at the bottom of the stairs. His family thought he was engaged to Cisney? What made people think a pearl ring was an engagement ring? And why hadn't Cisney switched the wretched thing back to her right hand?

He hooked his thumbs on his pockets. This was not good. It was one thing for Mom to like Cisney. He could deal with that. But now with an engagement planted in her mind, removing her notion he and Cisney were made for each other would be like raising the Titanic.

How could he save the family from disappointment, short of giving in and falling for Cisney? Considering the tension in their last exchange on the stairs, he wasn't in a giving-in or falling-for mood, much less holding a civil attitude toward the woman.

She'd amused him when she'd quipped about torturing him to talk during the trip here, but referring to him as a notch on her challenge belt was brutal. Had defending himself against her affront goaded her into declaring war—flashing that blasted pearl ring of hers?

He shouldn't have brought her home.

Lord, I want to call in troops for battle. Please douse my anger.

He stood a moment and let his irritation dissipate.

Cisney's tearstained face while she wailed about Jason's dirty actions plunked into his mind. Cisney was fragile and vulnerable right now. He shouldn't have let her challenge-belt statement get under his skin. Circumstances called for him to remain the adult.

He let out a heavy sigh. No easy solution came to mind to rectify the engagement mess. He'd have to take Mom aside and set her straight. Watch her face crumple as he destroyed her hopes.

With his hands jammed in his jeans pockets, he walked to his room—his and Tony's room for the holiday.

When he opened the door, Tony looked up while stuffing the tails of his corduroy shirt into his slacks. "Hey, Nick. Why so glum?"

That's all he needed—the third degree. "Just thoughtful. Nice socks."

Tony pinched the crease in his pant leg and drew up his slacks to expose his argyle socks. "You know me, I'll try anything to keep in style, plus these were the only extra socks Grandpa had with him. No way was I asking Dad for a pair and taking his ribbing."

"You know where my sock drawer is. Nothing has ever stopped you from taking what's mine."

"Your drawer was the first place I looked. Except for a couple of pairs of sweat socks, it's empty."

"That's right. I cleaned out my drawers the last time I was home. Sorry."

"No problem. I'd hate to have missed out on these jewels." Tony flashed his argyles again. "So, you're engaged, finally. I can't wait to meet Cisney."

Nick raised his face toward the ceiling and forced air through his lips. How long would it take him to gather his gear to camp on the pontoon at the other end of the lake for the next two and a half days? "I'm not engaged to Cisney. She's a co-worker who had no place to go for Thanksgiving."

Tony perked up. "Really?" He stretched out the word. "Because you dragged her away earlier, I couldn't get a good look at her. Is she plain or ugly, or just plain ugly?"

"She's attractive." The kind of attractive that could reel a man in before he got to know the whole package, if he wasn't careful.

"Is she dull?"

Nick unbuttoned his shirt. "Never a dull moment around Cisney." She'd provided an action-packed Thanksgiving morning he'd not forget.

"Does she laugh like a hyena?"

"Her laugh's nice enough." Wait 'til Tony heard the girlish giggle at the end of Cisney's laughter. His cousin would spout off one of his crazy stories to keep her laughing just to hear that giggle.

Tony followed him into the bathroom. "Does she curse like a sailor?"

Nick turned on the shower. "Depends. Do you consider 'gracious me' curse words?"

"Then she's got to be dumb."

"Nope." He curbed a smile, picturing his meetings with her staff. She was always jumping in and translating his mathematical jargon into her team's lingo.

"OK, then, she must have a boyfriend."

"I think she's unattached at the moment."

"Well, man, why aren't you engaged to her?"

Nick laughed. "Until this trip, I've never socialized with her outside the office." Imagine him engaged to the sticky-note queen.

Tony leaned against the doorjamb. "So you're not interested in her, and she's fair game?"

He should have cut Tony off when he asked about Cisney's looks. She didn't need Tony coming on to her. "She's got a lot going on. I think she agreed to come here to relax and get away from it all." He pointed to the bathroom door. "Do you mind?"

Tony sauntered out, a huge grin on his face.

Lord, protect Cisney from Tony.

ॐॐ

After ducking under the sloped ceiling, Cisney sashayed from the bedroom and entered the bathroom. Hot showers were a godsend. Hers had saved her from a morning gone bad—washed away its ugliness. Now it was time to be the gracious guest. Make up for loading her problems on Nick and retaliating against his smugness. Like always, she'd reacted too fast, but she was back on track. She would be the new, serene Cisney.

Dressed in a coral-colored silk blouse and beige wool slacks that covered her low-heeled ankle boots, she buttoned on a cream-colored knit vest that cinched at her waist. She checked her appearance in the bathroom mirror. Her bangs and extra makeup hid the goose egg on her forehead. And compared to her post-hysteria condition, she looked composed.

Back in the bedroom, she picked up the nightstand's Bible from where she'd tossed it on the bed in her panicked state. She'd held this Bible in her hand during the Jason upheaval, yet she'd cast God's words aside and turned to her cellphone and Nick.

But Nick had directed her to God. A stab of pain

radiated through her chest. Talk about smugness. She'd flippantly answered Nick's questions about God's nature. Of course, she'd been distracted by Jason's betrayal. Nice excuse. Would she have been less dismissive if she hadn't been upset?

She sat on the bed and lowered the leather bound book to her lap. Bringing her Bible with her this weekend hadn't crossed her mind, but Nick had packed his. What kind of new Sunday school teacher was she, anyway? At best, she sporadically read the Bible. And then to toss away God's lifeline in a time of crisis. But she'd never thought of the Bible that way. As a resource when trouble happened. Not until Nick had called her attention to what God thought about her situation.

She rifled through the Bible's thin pages. From now on, she'd be an example for her trusting four-year-olds. She'd download a Bible app to her phone so the next time she ran distressed to her phone, it would be to search God's Word. Like Nick, she'd be ready to help someone in need.

Her gaze fell to familiar words. God never tired of reminding His people as He did in Isaiah: *I am the Lord your God.* She read down a few verses. *You are my people.* She belonged to God. How simple, yet profound. Peace swept over her. Her Father in heaven knew what she needed in the wake of Jason's latest blow.

Daddy's face formed in her mind. Disappointment roosted in his gaze and in the set of his lips. That put a damper on her resolutions. After her revelation on the lake, her heavenly and earthly fathers seemed at odds with each other about Jason.

Didn't Daddy have her best interests in his

expectations for her life—out of a father's love for his daughter? He was smart and robust and successful in all he did. Everyone liked Daddy, or at least respected him. Wasn't it good that such a man got his way? Actually, Daddy didn't always prevail. Didn't he back down when Mom stood firm that her children would go to church?

Why was she judging Daddy? She hadn't told him about Jason, yet. Her premature call on his reaction to her losing Jason was unfair. It was possible God and Daddy were in agreement.

A faint scent of the yellow roses on the bedside table drifted her way. She smiled. She should get downstairs and join the family. She closed the Bible and stowed it in the drawer where she'd found it.

As she shut the guestroom door, her pearl solitaire caught her attention. Should she return the gossip-churning ring to her right hand? If she did, would Ellie and Nancy think she was playing mind games with them?

She could remove her ring. But then Ellie might worry that she and Nick had fought and called off their engagement. Maybe offer the truth. Why not? She hadn't purposely listened in on Ellie and Nancy's conversation in the kitchen. For now, she'd leave the solitaire on her left hand and confess the truth when the moment seemed right.

෧৽ঞ

Cisney followed the turkey aroma and passed through the butler's pantry to the kitchen. The enormity of the room stopped her mid-stride. Cherry cabinets, including the one concealing the refrigerator, masses of granite countertops, and at least three ovens and two sinks added up to posh.

Daddy, considered well off, lived in nothing like this house. Although Nick's family lived in luxury, they came across far from snooty rich. Down to earth, gracious, and kind came to mind. They called their expensive piano The Old Girl, for Pete's sake.

While Nancy emptied canned pumpkin into a mixing bowl, Ellie and Sandy worked on a salad. Grandma Thelma formed a lattice of dough strips over apple filling made from fresh apples, evidenced by the peel coils piled on a cutting board. She counted them. Four pumpkin and two apple. Six pies?

Observing this family was a smile booster. Cisney's smile seeped onto her face like melted butter sought every cranny of a waffle. It felt good. "Good morning." She glanced around for a kitchen clock. "At least I think it's still morning."

The women looked up from their work, smiled, and returned her greeting.

They looked so happy. Thanksgiving Day probably wasn't the time to dash their beliefs about Nick's engagement. Was his family the type who took turns sharing what they were thankful for at the dining room table? She could see it now. Ellie beaming and offering her thanks for her only son's upcoming nuptials.

Nick would probably dream up images of taking a hacksaw to his coworker's left ring finger. Ew.

She drew her hands behind her back and tugged on the ring. It wouldn't budge. It never was this tight. Had the hot shower made her fingers swell? Too late to excuse herself and race up two flights to try the soap treatment.

Ellie tore romaine lettuce into a large mahogany salad bowl. "Did you sleep well?"

"Yes. The room is charming. And thank you for the yellow roses."

"That was Nancy's doing." Ellie smiled at her daughter.

Cisney nodded to Nancy. "Thanks for making me feel so welcomed. The view of the lake from my room is spectacular."

"Lake Norman is more than fifty square miles," Nancy said. "It's the largest man-made body of fresh water within North Carolina. Our little town here, Cornelius, is one of several lying on the outskirts of the lake."

Cisney smiled at the teacher demonstrating her zeal to educate. "When Nick took me out in the row boat earlier, I thought we'd entered the Atlantic by mistake."

The women chuckled.

Nancy swept tendrils of brown hair that had escaped from her ponytail from her face with the back of her hand. "Your belief was well-founded. Lake Norman is called the inland sea of North Carolina."

Cisney looked around the kitchen. A job for her had to lie in all the fresh vegetables and fruit covering the counters. Who was going to eat all that? She turned to Ellie. The woman regarded her with a pained expression. Had Ellie found out Nick and she weren't engaged?

Maybe this was the moment to tell them the truth. "Ellie, is something wrong?"

Ellie rushed to her and lifted Cisney's bangs from her forehead. "I knew we shouldn't have put you in that low-ceilinged room."

No. Jason shouldn't have horned in on my friends.

The other women abandoned their tasks to assess the damage to her forehead.

She took a step back. "It's fine. It doesn't hurt anymore." She chuckled. "I hit the sloped ceiling full steam." She smacked her hand against her other. "Even after Nick gave me sufficient warning." Why was she relieved Ellie's angst had been about her bruise and not about a phantom engagement gone awry?

She looked around the kitchen to avoid the women's scrutiny. "Isn't there something I can do to help?"

"Actually there is." Ellie ushered her through the butler pantry to the dining room. "I had the table all set, and then Sandy gave me this beautiful tablecloth." She indicated the elegant cloth edged in autumn colors.

A wicker cornucopia overflowing with fruits, flowers, and vegetables served as the centerpiece.

Ellie smoothed a crease in the cloth. "I have only two tablecloths that fit this monster table and neither are Thanksgiving-like. This new one is perfect. So now, everything on the sideboard needs to go back on the table. Do you mind?"

"I'd love to re-set the table."

Considering the elaborate centerpiece, Ellie didn't seem the type to trust anyone to set her Thanksgiving table. But she had. Or maybe Nick's mom was testing her as daughter-in-law material.

Good thing her waitress training in a high-class restaurant during two college summers would prove her worthy of the daughter-in-law designation—of course, without committing herself to the son.

After Ellie explained the seating arrangement and returned to the kitchen, Cisney took inventory of the exquisite china, crystal, and silver flatware on the side table. Silver place card holders in the shape of turkeys sat in a clump behind the plates. Cute. Name cards, with names penned in perfect calligraphy, were secured in the turkeys' fanned tails. Twelve would dine in the LeCrone home today.

Cisney lifted three dinner plates and examined the subtle flower details on the top plate. Someday she'd have table finery and invite family and friends for Thanksgiving dinners.

"If you're thinking of stealing the family treasures, I'm afraid I'll have to wrestle you to the floor."

The barefoot man with dark curls and the open shirt who'd chased Nick and her to the lake stood in the doorway, now fully dressed.

She laughed. "I don't think you'd chance breaking three plates."

He crossed the room and extended his hand. "I'm cousin Tony."

She placed the plates on the table and shook his hand. "I'm colleague Cisney."

He nodded toward the sideboard. "So, you're going to put all this mess back together." He slipped his hands into the pockets of his trousers and rocked forward on his loafers. "I told Mom she should give Aunt Ellie the tablecloth after Thanksgiving because Aunt Ellie always has the table set by the time we arrive."

"Ellie seems thrilled to display it this year." Using the length from the tip of her thumb to her first knuckle as a guide, Cisney placed the rim of a plate that distance from the edge of the table. "By the way, I like your socks." She stifled a giggle. Grandpa's argyle socks had nearly foiled her covert flight to her room.

"You're not the first they've impressed. I need to invest in a few pairs."

Tony hefted the stack of remaining dinner plates and followed her around the table while she carefully positioned each plate. She wanted the table to be perfect for Ellie's guests.

"How'd you meet Nick?" he said.

"We attend a lot of the same meetings. I got to know Nick better when the chief actuary assigned him as a consultant to my team's marketing projects."

"Lucky Nick."

She lifted a plate from his stack. "I don't think he feels particularly lucky, although sometimes I wonder if he enjoys wielding his power over marketing people in the name of company financial stability."

"You only work with an actuary. I have to live with one. My mother thinks in statistics and risks. Take sitting with her in a movie. Before the show starts, she's graphing the demographics of the audience in her head and calculating the probability she'll like the movie."

"You're exaggerating."

"No, I'm not. She does that."

The plates positioned, Cisney set the turkey card holders on his upturned palms. "Does her calculation work?"

He followed her for a second trip around the table, craning his neck to scrutinize the name cards she positioned at each place setting. "Either her method has high accuracy, or she fits her viewing pleasure to her prediction."

Finished with the card holders, Cisney turned from the sideboard with a handful of knives. Tony was stretched across the table. He lifted a silver turkey and then switched it with one on their side.

"No-no." Scurrying between the misplaced turkeys, Cisney returned them to their proper spots. "Ellie told me where she wants people to sit."

Cisney handed him the knives and scooped up the spoons. Tony had reassigned himself next to her and put Nick next to Fannie. She'd have to watch Cousin Tony, or fail the daughter-in-law test.

Tony eyed his card holder. "I don't want to sit next to my sister."

"You can talk to Nancy on your other side."

"I'd much rather talk to you."

"I'm flattered, but Ellie rules."

While she positioned knives to the right of plates, Tony followed her around the table and handed her spoons. How many times could she get him to follow her like a puppy dog around the table? After her faux pas with Nick about her challenge belt, maybe it was best to lay low on contests for now.

Tony leaned close to her. "What shampoo do you use? It smells really good."

"Are you hitting on me, Cousin Tony?"

"No reason why I shouldn't, is there?"

Cisney made the circuit with the forks, Tony still in tow. The card in Nick's turkey once again read, Tony. She flashed him her face-scrunching scowl. "You scamp!" Holding onto the back of a chair, she reached across the table and snatched Nick's card holder, then thumped Tony's back in its place. "And I actually thought you cared about my shampoo." She shook Nick's turkey at him as if he were a naughty puppy. "Do not touch the turkeys, or I'm going to find a rolled-up newspaper."

He laughed. "You can't blame a man for trying.

And I do like the scent of your hair."

He'd followed her eight times around the table by the time she was ready to place the napkins. She'd let pass that he'd switched turkeys on the seventh round. This challenge-savvy woman would outsmart the naughty puppy.

Holding a corner of an autumn-orange napkin, she snapped it like a high-class restaurant's hostess and released it from its three-fold pamphlet shape. Then she fashioned the napkin into a bird of paradise flower and placed it in the center of a dinner plate. With her head cocked, she studied the setting. Perfect.

Tony held up the flower and examined it. "Cool. You're really talented."

While he was occupied, Cisney pocketed Nick's turkey from Tony's place setting, and then clamped her hands on her hips. "Tony. Put the napkin down before it comes apart."

He obeyed.

She gave the napkin a tap to center it, and then moved to the next plate. Good. He hadn't noticed the missing turkey. For the moment, anyway.

As she worked her way around the table, Tony strolled behind her feigning attacks on her birds of paradise.

She rolled her eyes. "Be a good cousin and tell me about your job that keeps you at work in the evenings."

They stood at Nick's place setting, where Tony's turkey rested next to the plate. Cisney shook out a napkin and, in a flourish of folding another flower, switched the turkeys and smuggled Tony's into her pocket.

Tony rested his hand on the table near the

replaced card holder. "I man the front desk at a downtown Charlotte hotel during the evening shift, and I'm working on an online degree in hotel management."

"I imagine you have some good front-desk stories to tell." And why didn't he tell one now so he'd be distracted when she slipped his turkey back on the table?

"You have no idea."

She moved to the next plate, but he stayed put, his hand still planted near Nick's card. The way her heart was racing, she'd think she was trafficking diamonds.

He slid his hands into his pockets and closed the gap between them.

Another hurdle cleared. She let out a breath. "So tell me a story."

"OK. This story isn't from our hotel, but I heard it from a fellow desk clerk. Early one morning, a middle-aged woman entered the lobby dressed in her nightgown. She walked over to the rack where all the sightseeing pamphlets were stored. She pulled several stacks of pamphlets from their slots and arranged them on the front desk, and then proceeded to the hotel restaurant. There, the woman grasped a coffee pot and went from table to table refilling patrons' coffee cups."

"Was she sleepwalking?"

"That's what the desk clerk thought. She had asked for a first floor room on making her reservation. The manager escorted her to her room, and she went willingly. Later, she checked out like any other guest."

Laughing, Cisney let her last bird of paradise fall to the floor. As Tony bent to scoop it up, she set Nick's turkey where it belonged. She centered the retrieved napkin on its plate and faced Tony, blocking his view of Nick's place setting.

Tony brightened at her proximity. "The next time you're in Charlotte you should stay at the hotel. I could show you around."

"I'll keep that in mind." She inspected the table. Everything sparkled and pleased her trained eye. "Well, we're done here." She crooked her finger while she moved around him. No way was she leaving him alone to switch turkeys.

He rotated, eyeing her curved finger as if it were a dog biscuit, and followed her to the kitchen.

"Tony, get over here and help me put these pies in the oven," Nancy said.

"I'm helping Cisney set the table."

"We're all finished," Cisney said. "Ellie, will you come and take a look?"

Tony followed Ellie and Cisney to the dining room.

Ellie gushed over the birds of paradise.

"I'm glad you like them." Cisney captured Tony's gaze. "Have I gotten the seating arrangement right?"

Ellie looped the table. "Yes. Perfect."

Tony gaped and moved to the card holder at Nick's original spot. He shot Cisney a you-sly-fox look.

"Now, you assigned Nick here, right?" Cisney pointed at Nick's place setting, holding Tony's gaze.

"Yes, next to you." Ellie smiled as if she were a successful cupid who'd surpassed her quota of matches for the month.

"Good. Just checking." Wearing her I-gotcha grin, Cisney lifted her face and peered up at Tony as she drifted under his nose and followed Ellie into the kitchen.

Tony trailed her, hot on her heels. He bent down

and spoke near her ear. "I like your ring." His voice carried a singsong quality.

Her body tensed.

He kept his volume low. "It looks like it could be an engagement ring."

She wrenched her head and looked back at him.

He raised his hands palms out in I-wouldn't-squeal-on-you fashion, but his smile said, *Gotcha*.

6

Nick raised his bowed head. The peacefulness of Dad's blessing turned into a hubbub of chatter and clinking silverware as the family passed serving dishes around the table. Nick held a bowl for Cisney. While she concentrated on transferring sweet potatoes to her plate, he studied her face. Her transformation from the frazzled woman down by the lake into the composed beauty sitting next to him was amazing. The light scent of her exotic perfume mixed with turkey aroma.

He passed the bowl to Mom and took two snowflake rolls from the basket Cisney handed him. "Mom makes these rolls from scratch." He turned one in his fingers. "To die for."

Mom shooed him with a flap of her hand. "He knows his life is safe, because I always make snowflake rolls, and plenty of them."

Nick looked up from buttering his roll. All family members were focused on their meals, their heads bowed over their plates, except Tony.

After each bite, Tony gazed at Cisney while he chewed. And his cousin's interest hadn't gone unnoticed.

Cisney smiled and waggled her fork at Tony, like the two were old friends.

What had he missed while he showered and contemplated how to get out of his bogus engagement?

Grandpa, seated at one end of the table, poured

gravy over his mashed potatoes. "Cisney, Nick tells me you're in the marketing department."

"Yes. Nick is consulting with us on a project."

"Ah, the actuarial policeman, huh?"

Glancing at Nick, she smiled. "Yes. He watches us closely. Doesn't want the company to skid down the slippery slide of financial ruin."

Aunt Sandy looked around Uncle Bill at Cisney. "When I was a young actuarial student, the marketing people taught me a valuable lesson." She sat back and spoke to the group. "I was the only actuarial staff member in a meeting of about five marketing folks and a vice president, who desperately wanted to increase market share in his area of responsibility.

"I sat quietly and marveled at all the information these marketing people eagerly promised the vice president. I bet I heard, 'We can get you that,' ten times. I was impressed with Marketing's resources. I was too green to voice that I didn't think anyone could get some of the data they were guaranteeing to deliver." Aunt Sandy took a sip of her iced tea. "When I returned to my cubical, my phone rang. The highest-ranking marketing person who'd attended the meeting said, 'How soon can you get us the information and the analysis we talked about in today's meeting?' That was the last time Marketing duped me."

Family members laughed.

Cisney chuckled politely, and then concentrated on buttering her roll. Did she feel ganged up on?

"Yeah," Dad said, "our marketing people think we have answers for everything. But they're an agreeable bunch."

"Happily promising executive staff the moon?" Grandpa elicited another laugh. He winked at Cisney.

"Don't take us too seriously. It's not often we actuaries can rib a marketing person. We have to grab the opportunity, you know."

Nick held his turkey-laden fork suspended. "The CEO has awarded Cisney recognition for her creative ideas and running successful marketing campaigns."

Cisney cocked her head toward him as if she were surprised he'd defended her. She wasn't the only one shocked. His words had tumbled out unbidden. A new, and dangerous, experience for him. Why had he championed her? She could handle herself. Let her see that family tests were involved to break into this family. She couldn't skate in on her performance of "Flight of the Bumblebee" alone.

Cisney's shoulders relaxed, and she smiled good-naturedly. Of course, she'd pass the teasing test that Dana had failed. By now they all believed he and Cisney were engaged. The hole he had to dig his way out of kept getting deeper. But it wasn't Cisney's fault.

"Fran and Fannie," Mom said, "where did you girls go today?"

Good old Mom, changing the subject.

As always, Fannie answered for the twins. "We escaped to somewhere as far away from the kitchen as possible." Chuckles sounded around the table. "We went rollerblading over at the high school and met a couple of hot Carolina guys. They arranged to meet us the first day back to classes."

"You two will probably be the first to marry in this clan's younger generation," Grandma Thelma said.

Mom beamed as she looked expectantly at Nick. He held his breath as if that would stop her from blurting out about an engagement. He needed to have a talk with her soon—now. He grabbed the breadbasket in front of him. From the four remaining rolls, he placed two on his bread plate and two on Cisney's, staring down her gawk.

"Mom, do you have more rolls?" He tipped the empty basket toward her.

She shot up from her chair. "Yes. Lots more." She took the basket and headed for the kitchen.

Nick patted his napkin to his lips, excused himself, and followed Mom into the kitchen. She arranged rolls in the basket, her fingertips white with flour.

This woman was a major light in his life. *Lord, please give me the right words.* He leaned against the counter and spoke gently. "Mom, I think you believe Cisney and I have more going on than we do."

She stopped arranging rolls. Wrinkles formed between her eyebrows, and her shoulders sagged. "You're not engaged, are you?"

He shook his head. "Cisney is a co-worker."

"Why didn't you tell us you two weren't dating?"

He kept his voice tender. "I didn't think I needed to tell you all the things we're not. I told you she was a friend from work."

"But you brought her home." Her eyes misted. "That usually means something special is going on…"

"Sorry." He felt like a heel, even though he'd done nothing wrong.

Her face turned hopeful. "But you do like her, don't you?"

"Sure."

"Because she's pleasant and lovely. And talented, too. Did you see how beautifully she set the table with the bird of paradise napkins? And her playing on The Old Girl. That was wonderful."

He grinned. "I think you want a duet partner more

83

than a girlfriend for me."

"Not so, smarty-pants." She stuffed a roll into his mouth. "I don't want Cisney to slip through your fingers. Did you see how Tony has been eyeing her through dinner?"

That he had. "Tony's twenty-four. He's too young for her. She's more my age."

"Twenty-nine, to be exact. Oh, don't look so surprised. Nancy asked her age when Cisney helped in the kitchen."

"So, I'm too young for her." He took a bite of the roll.

"You're only four months younger. And remember, Sandy is two years older than Bill. Look how happy they are."

Mom was not dropping her hopes that Cisney would wheedle her way into his heart. Why hadn't Cisney switched that annoying pearl ring back to her right hand? Was she purposely making it hard for him...making bird napkins and playing the good sport among a room full of actuaries?

He raised the breadbasket piled high with snowflake rolls. "We'd better get these babies back to the family."

Mom gave him her you-know-your-mother-is-right look and marched past him into the dining room.

Didn't he have enough on his plate with Option A and B interviews in the next two days without Mom pushing him toward Cisney? An escape on the family pontoon was looking good for Option C.

Back in the dining room, Uncle Bill's and Cisney's heads angled toward each other. Always quiet, Uncle Bill now spoke animatedly, while Cisney appeared riveted on his every word. What was she? Some kind of magician?

After he eased into his chair, Aunt Sandy interrupted Uncle Bill with a question.

Cisney turned to Nick and leaned close. "I can't eat another bite," she whispered. "Take those rolls off my plate. They make me look like a pig, and when I don't eat them, I'll look like a wasteful guest."

"You could use an extra pound or two."

She hadn't served herself any cranberry sauce when it went around the table. Was she watching calories, or did she dislike cranberry sauce?

He lifted one of her rolls. "They're great with cranberry sauce spread on them." He broke the roll and smeared a clump of cranberry sauce on one half.

She looked relieved that he'd taken the roll from her plate, until he held the portion dripping with the red sauce to her mouth.

Cisney met his gaze with a glare. When he didn't budge his hand, she rolled her eyes and took a small bite. Cranberry sauce slid off the roll and down her chin.

Grandpa, the only one not engaged in conversation, witnessed Nick's act and raised his eyebrows.

Mom turned to Nick and caught the tail end of the scene.

Wiping cranberry sauce from her chin with her napkin, Cisney looked at Mom. "Mmm. Good."

Beaming, Mom turned back to Dad.

Nick brought his lips to the Cisney's ear. "Just so you know, I told Mom we're not engaged."

As soon as he whispered the words, he regretted them. He'd failed to remain the adult. He'd let her get under his skin—again. He shouldn't have taken out on her his dislike of letting Mom down.

Cisney picked up the remaining roll on her bread plate and broke it in two. "Where I'm from..." She piled on a quarter-inch of butter to one half, and then slopped on a spoonful of sweet potato casserole. "We like sweet potato and butter on our rolls." She put it against his mouth, transferring orange mush onto his lips.

He might never want to see a snowflake roll again. A quick glance around the table showed that only Grandpa had witnessed Cisney's counterattack, and Grandpa, the old goat, nodded, his lips trembling, to stifle a chuckle.

Nick grimaced and took a bite of the loaded roll. "OK. We're even," he said, cringing at the heavy butter and sweet potato combination.

"Cisney," Nancy said, "will you show me how to fold the bird of paradise?"

Fran and Fannie chimed in, begging for a lesson.

Mom, Aunt Sandy, and Grandma Thelma cleared one end of the table to make room for folding napkins.

Nick gritted his teeth. Another opportunity for Cisney to charm her way into his family.

❧❦

Cisney surveyed the women's birds of paradise. Not bad. Grandma Thelma had caught on quicker than expected, and despite her arthritic hands, had fashioned a decent blossom. The upswept points on Aunt Sandy's flower sagged, but on the whole, her creation still looked like the exotic flower. Cisney enjoyed the laughter, the ribbing, and the cajoling among the women. Nick was right. She needed his family.

Tony poked his head inside the doorway. "It's time." He disappeared.

Fran and Fannie whipped their heads to face each other. "It's time!" they said in unison.

Cisney glanced from one woman to another. "Time for what?"

Nancy, Fran, and Fannie scooted their chairs away from the table.

"Come on," Nancy said. "You'll see."

The young women led her down the hallway to the mudroom, where they opened a door opposite the outside door. She followed them down a narrow staircase. Would she have to do something embarrassing they could only do in a dark basement, like bob for apples?

At the bottom of the stairs, Fran opened another door and they filed inside.

The space was huge. Cisney sucked in a breath. The carpet and furnishings were done in browns, tans, and caramel. A door near the stairs opened into a full bath covered in travertine tiles from floor to ceiling. In an alcove next to the bathroom, twin beds rested on a tan shag carpet. Clothes slung over the beds, the side chairs, and even the lamps, verified Fran and Fannie roomed here.

Further into the basement, they entered a media area, where leather chairs arranged in a half circle faced a large-screen TV over a stone fireplace. Strategically placed wall sconces warmed the area.

They crossed an honest-to-goodness dance floor to the brightly lit end of the basement. A Ping-Pong table stood on a honey-colored terrazzo floor.

Tony and Nick slapped a ball back and forth, until

Tony undercut the ball and it zipped sideways off the table on Nick's side.

Tony's eyes brightened when his gaze picked Cisney out of the approaching women. "I'll team up with Cisney," he said.

That was fast. Tony had no idea whether she could find the right end of a paddle.

"OK," Nancy said. "It's you and me, bro."

Fannie passed Fran a paddle. "Why do Fran and I always have to be partners?"

"Because apart, you're klutzes," Tony said, "but together you manage to keep the ball on the table more often than not."

"Ha, ha," Fannie said.

Fran whacked Tony's arm with a paddle, and he yelped.

Lesson to remember: Don't cross the quiet twin.

Tony grabbed Fran's head in the crook of his arm and rubbed his knuckles gently over the top of her head.

"Fannie, you can be my partner." Nick said. "This is a friendly competition. It doesn't make any difference who plays with whom."

Fannie rolled her eyes. "Right. Like over the years, you've never fist-bumped your partner silly or thrown yourself into the victory dance." She linked arms with Fran. "Never mind. Remembering how you do the victory dance, I think I'll stick with Fran."

Nick gave Fannie an I'm-hurt look.

Cisney could have worked with Nick for ten years and never seen this side of him.

"OK. So we're set," Tony said. "Team captains step forward for Rock-Paper-Scissors. If two people have the same sign, the third goes first, and the remaining two go again. But if all are different or the same, we'll go again."

"Whoa," Nancy said. "We could be here all night playing Rock-Paper-Scissors. I have a better idea." She broke off straws from a broom she produced from the utility closet. She extended the evened-up straws in her fist to each team until the straws were gone. "Nick has the short straw, so Cisney and Tony play Fran and Fannie first."

Fannie addressed Cisney. "Winners have to do the victory dance. That's the best part of this event."

This event? Did that mean there'd be more activities? Maybe a laundry tub with ice-cold water and bobbing apples lurked in a cement addition, after all.

Tony handed Cisney a paddle. "Partners alternate hitting the ball. Do you need a warm-up?"

"I don't think it would make a difference."

The two teams faced off while Nancy and Nick sat on bar chairs lining the wall near the table. Perspiration threatened to soak Cisney's underarms as she hunched over the table, her paddle at the ready.

Fannie served. Cisney returned the ball and it landed mid-table on their opponent's side. Fran returned it and Tony put away the point.

Tony never missed a shot. All she had to do was bounce the ball to the other side of the table, and Tony made the point on the return shot.

At twenty-one to three, Tony clapped his paddle on the table and raised his fists. "Winners!" He high-fived Cisney.

She laughed, exhilarated by the intensity of the game. Tony had encouraged her when she'd missed shots and had cheered her on when she'd made them.

She'd sensed Nick's steady gaze on her during the game. Why did his interest seem to contribute to her elation? Something to ask herself later.

The match with Fannie and Fran was probably child's play. Her challenge-weighing gut was seldom wrong. The brother-sister team would be brutal. Now that she'd seen the competitive side of Tony, she'd put every ounce of sweat into the match and say goodbye to wearing her coral-colored silk blouse again.

But Fannie had mentioned a victory dance. Knocking her knees together like a running back after scoring a touchdown would have her begging for bobbing apples. OK. Preference shift. She'd be fine with losing, watching Nick execute silly victory moves, and saving the silk.

And yet...was she really the kind of girl who would let Tony down?

Tony collected sodas from the refrigerator under the built-in bookcases and handed them around. Cisney drew long on her soda. Just one more thought; then she'd stop analyzing. Was her heart beating like crazy because she cared less about letting Tony down and more about impressing Nick? Hmm.

"OK," Tony said, "let's find out who will control the victory dance this year."

The men placed their shots strategically and took advantage of the women's lobs to smash the ball, while the women concentrated on returning the plastic orb and getting out of the way of the men's next shots.

Nancy proved to hold the same skill level as Cisney. So, that was why Tony chanced tapping her as his partner.

Nick served to her with the same force that Tony served to Nancy, which was half the warp speed the men served to each other. She returned the ball and Nancy whiffed the shot as it nicked the edge of the table.

"All right!" Tony patted her on the back.

Nick wiped his forehead with his sleeve. "Nineteen to eighteen." He served.

Nancy connected with Cisney's return, and the ball landed on Cisney's corner. Tony lunged and made contact. The ball rose high.

Nick smashed the ball. On the bounce, it hit Cisney's paddle by accident and skimmed back over the net. She crouched to get out of Tony's way.

Nancy returned the ball to Cisney's quadrant.

Tony dove for the ball and then executed erratic footwork to avoid toppling Cisney as the ball hit the floor.

Cisney removed her hands from protecting her head and straightened. "Wow. That was close."

"We can come back." Tony hunched over and twirled his paddle like a tennis pro spun his racquet.

She'd meant he'd come close to killing her, not making the point. Sacrificing her silk blouse for the cause was one thing, but her life? Men.

Nick cupped the ball in his hand and blew on it. Here was not the mild man who sat in her office side chair and remained motionless while he thought forever. He pressed his lips together and narrowed his eyes. Oh, boy.

She squinted, focusing on the ball.

He served to her in his usual easy-going speed and she hit the ball off the table. She dropped her arms to her side. She'd let Nick intimidate her. Nancy and Nick performed fist bumps with both fists.

Tony put his arm around Cisney and hugged her

sideways. "There's always next year, partner."

Sweet Tony bore the loss well. At least she was saved from doing the victory dance. Ready for a soda, a chair, and the show, she pulled her phone from her pocket. A photo of Nick performing the victory dance might come in handy at work.

Fran dismounted her bar stool and extended her hand toward Tony, snapping her fingers. He retrieved a CD from the counter over the refrigerator and gave it to her.

Fannie backed toward the staircase while her sister put the CD in the player. "For the victory dance, Cisney, the runners-up get to pick the dance and the music, and the winners have to be their partners. It's the reward for us losers, who get to watch their performance."

What? She had to perform some crazy dance with Nick? What kind of victory dance was that? "I don't see how this constitutes a reward for the winners."

Tony handed her a soda and popped the top of his. "Just be thankful you don't have to do the chicken dance Nancy chose last year for Nick and Allison."

Cisney chortled. She couldn't help it. She'd have paid good money to witness Nick flapping his elbows.

"What's the dance this year, Tony?" Nancy asked.

"You and Nick have to roll up your pant legs and dance the polka with us." Tony turned to Cisney. "That part—rolling up pants—we don't have to do."

"Do you need a lesson, Nick?" Nancy asked, laughing.

Nick rolled up his pant legs. "No, I think I can handle the polka."

Surprise, surprise. Nick LeCrone had well-shaped legs. After today, it would be hard to have a blasé financial discussion with Nick without thinking of this moment.

Nick straightened, grabbed her hand, and pulled her to the dance floor. This hand-grasping thing was becoming a habit. A dangerous habit, according to the flutters ping-ponging in the fleshy keeper of her emotions.

Clamping her hand in his and stretching out her right arm, he planted his other hand against her back. She giggled—the nervous kind. Did she remember how to polka?

Nancy finished rolling up her pants and accepted Tony's hand.

When Fran started the music, Nick launched Cisney forward. They stomped around the room to the vigorous Vejvoda's "Beer Barrel Polka." She laughed so hard she had to trust Nick to keep them from plowing into Nancy and Tony.

As Nick whirled her on the last refrain, a blur of faces whipped into her quickly changing field of vision. She wrenched her head past Nick's shoulder. That scamp, Fannie. The twin had lured the family down to witness the victory dance.

The music stopped and Nick removed his guiding hand from her back and spun her out so that their outer arms were extended in a theatrical finish. They both gasped for breaths. Applause sounded from the gallery, except from Ellie. Her hands were clasped under her chin, her ear-to-ear smile a speed bump for her tears. A hundred to one, it wasn't their dancing expertise that had elicited her strong emotions.

Nick dropped her hand as if she had cooties. She stumbled to catch herself as he bent to roll down his pant legs. He must have spotted Ellie. OK, so he wouldn't want his mother to get any ideas about their relationship, but with her own heart already shot full of holes, his abruptness spelled rejection. Even Grandpa had blinked in surprise at Nick's briskness, proving she hadn't overreacted.

Lord, please. I need your strength. Lead me not into rejection.

7

Nick stood before his bedroom mirror and buttoned on a clean shirt. He could strangle Fannie. They never invited the older generations to witness the victory dance. Mom's tear-stained face had left no doubt she thought he'd one day add Cisney to the family. But Mom had missed Cisney's coolness toward him on the trip up the basement stairs. Before he could make amends for dropping her hand as if she had the flu, she'd excused herself to take a call.

They needed to talk. If he was honest with her, maybe she'd...she'd what? Stop being herself? At least he could explain how Mom was collecting gems to support her cockamamie idea that he and Cisney belonged together. Hopefully, Cisney didn't have similar ridiculous ideas about their relationship. That would top off the weekend.

Tony entered, stripping off his shirt. "Fannie says we have to leave in twenty minutes. Grandma Thelma, Mom, and Aunt Ellie are working like crazy in the kitchen to have everything ready for the Holiday Blast. Should I head upstairs and let Cisney know?"

"No. I think she's on the phone with her parents. I'll go up in a minute."

Tony went into the bathroom.

Nick combed his hair. How should he approach Cisney? Why was he constantly feeling guilty when he'd done nothing wrong? Well, except for dropping

Cisney's hand. But why wouldn't he act that way, when he had no control over false engagements, everyone loving Cisney, and Mom's tears? At least, Dad seemed to understand boundaries. Why couldn't they all be like Dad?

Was he rationalizing? What was the real reason he'd reacted so rashly with Cisney? So unlike himself. Even shocked Grandpa.

Nick sat on the bed. First off, the family's expectations were pressuring him. But he probably added to the problem, disliking that Cisney's laughter during the polka threatened his resolve to swear off relationships. He sighed. Better get upstairs and grovel.

While he climbed the stairs to Cisney's room, no concrete way to smooth things over formed in his mind. He knocked gently.

She opened the door an inch, her head bowed against the low ceiling. Was the terrycloth material he glimpsed a towel, or a bathrobe?

He leaned a hand against the wall and bent over so she could see him better. "We leave for the traditional Holiday Blast and movie in fifteen minutes. I know how you like family traditions, so…"

She stared at him as if he were a door-to-door salesman. He held his ground and gave her what he hoped was a contrite expression.

She returned a weak smile. "I think I'll pass."

"Was that your parents who called?"

"Yes. We didn't talk long. It's after midnight in Germany."

"Can we talk?"

"I thought we were."

She was going to make this hard. "I mean, can you

put on some clothes and either come out here, or let me in?"

"I'm decent." She drew the door open and stood aside for him to enter.

Her yellow terrycloth bathrobe nearly reached the floor.

He stooped and moved to a place where he could stand. She did the same.

He motioned her toward a window chair, and then sat in the other. "You don't know my mother. She worries I'm going to be a bachelor forever."

Pulling her robe tighter around her, she sat. "She sees me as a last chance."

She understood. *Thank you, Lord.* He plowed on, braver. "She and my whole family love you…"

"But you don't."

He gaped, searching for a response. None came.

"I'm teasing you."

He shut his mouth. "I was a jerk down there—"

"I know."

"Then why are you so forgiving?"

"Because you crawling up here to "talk" is balm to my hurt ego."

He extended his hand toward her. "So come with us—"

She tightened her grip on her bathrobe. "Don't you dare grab my hand and pull me. I need to put some clothes on."

"You'll come with us?" Why did he hope she'd say yes? Maybe he was tired of feeling guilty.

"I wouldn't be getting dressed to mope alone in my room, would I?"

He stood, hunched over, and walked to the door. "Hurry downstairs. We'll want to have lots of time for the Holiday Blast so we can make it to the movie in plenty of time. Fran and Fannie picked the show, so the previews may be the best part. And we're picking up Allison."

∂∽❦

Cisney scrambled to the seat in the rear of Roger's van. Grandpa, Roger, and Bill hurried from the house carrying large paper sacks that they handed off to Tony and Nick, who packed them in the back of the van. Fannie and Fran piled in and sat next to Cisney while Nancy scooted into the middle seat.

Cisney set her handbag on the floor to give the twins more room. "What's going on?"

Fran held a box the size of a medium-sized sheet cake on her lap. "It's our turn to do the Holiday Blast."

Would wonders never cease? The silent twin had uttered words. And her information was about as useful as Nick's normal fare. "What's the Holiday Blast?"

Fannie jumped in. "Many of the elderly in Aunt Ellie, Uncle Roger, and Nancy's church would like to decorate for the holidays, but find it's too hard or exhausting or dangerous. A lot of them have cherished ornaments and other decorations that sit in boxes in attics or basements. So different teams from the church go out and decorate their houses or apartments with their ornaments." She pointed to the box on Fran's lap. "Every year, we add a new ornament to each household."

"That's awesome." Cisney risked Fran slapping her hand and lifted the lid. Colorful Christmas tree ornaments covered the bottom of the box. "I'm glad to see you're decorating for Christmas and not Thanksgiving."

Nancy leaned against the window. "Although, Easter and other holidays are available, our family always does Christmas while we're all here to participate. We go out late like this on Thanksgiving Day so we can take fresh turkey sandwiches, tossed salads, and pie slices to each household. You may not have noticed that Mom had two turkeys cooking this morning. And right before we sit down to eat, Grandma Thelma slides more pies into the oven."

"I wondered why there were so many pies and vegetables." What a good use of the LeCrone's two ovens. "This whole idea is amazing."

"Yeah," Fannie said. "At the homes, we take down and pack away Thanksgiving decorations that another team put up, and then decorate for Christmas. It's been part of our Thanksgiving Day tradition for five years."

"Six," Fran said.

Nick climbed into the driver's seat and power closed the lift-gate. Tony rode shotgun in the front passenger seat.

A few blocks away, if the winding road could be said to have blocks, Nick stopped at a large Tudor-like house and picked up waiting Allison. She offered greetings around and sat next to Nancy.

As Nick drove on, Tony consulted a sheet of paper. "We'll need to split up into three teams. Fan and Fran, do you guys want to take the apartments like always?"

"Yes." Fran spoke over his last words.

Tony turned in his seat. "Who do you want to go with, Cisney?"

She startled. "Whomever. It doesn't matter." But it

did. She'd assumed she'd be sticking with Nick. And wanted to. But Nick failed to jump in and claim her. He remained silent. She felt like the last person standing by herself when team captains took turns calling players from the group to join their teams. She'd never had that experience, but now she could identify.

Nancy snatched the paper from Tony's hand and studied it. "Three of us have to go to the neighborhood near the church, because we have three houses there and need the manpower to get them all done in time."

Tony seized the paper back. "OK. So, Cisney, why don't you come with Allison and me there."

Cisney forced out a cheerful, "Sure."

Was Nick jumping joyously inwardly?

Nancy held up her hand. "Stop. Wait a minute. As much as I love my brother, I think Cisney should go with Nick."

Tony stared at her. "Why?"

"Let's take a vote," Allison said, laughing.

All, except Nick, agreed.

Were they joking? Obviously, yes, but who was the joke on. Nick, or her, or both? Was this payback for leading the family astray with the engagement false alarm?

Head-in-the-sand Nick kept driving as if he were merely a chauffeur surrounded by soundproof glass.

"All in favor of Cisney going with Tony and Allison raise your hand," Nancy said.

Tony's hand shot up. Snickers emitted from the women on all sides, but no arms went up.

"All in favor of Cisney going with Nick raise your hand."

Every woman's hand rose, except Cisney's. Nick

hadn't voted this time, either. More snickering from the women. It hit her. They were cupids wielding their votes like arrows in their bows. They were for her, not against her. She should be honored.

Her lips trembled as she held back from laughing. "I'd be honored to join my gracious weekend host."

Nick spoke over his shoulder. "Nice to hear there's one adult in this sorry gang."

That had been a vote of confidence, of sorts. She'd be satisfied with it.

Nick dropped Tony, Nancy, and Allison in the neighborhood near the church, where their three elderly participants, all widows, lived in homes within walking distance.

Nick lowered his window. "I'll pick you up here in three hours, so we can make the eight o'clock show."

At an apartment complex, the twins scrambled out, collected two ornaments from the box and three paper bags from the back of the van, and headed toward a ground-floor apartment. Cisney switched to the front passenger seat, riding shotgun.

Nick pulled out of the complex lot. "Fran and Fannie will decorate two apartments, one for a couple married sixty years and the other for a widow in her nineties. Are you ready for this?"

Cisney nodded. "I love this ministry."

He looked over at her. "I apologize for my family."

"Not a problem. They're fun. Who's on our list?"

"We have two in this next neighborhood." He made a turn. "Mr. Palmer, a widower, and the Hansons, a couple who used to be very active in the church until he had a stroke."

Mr. Palmer answered the door. He was thin, and his shoulders hunched. "Well, hello, Nick." Mr. Palmer stepped aside. "Come on in. Make yourselves at home."

They moved inside, and Mr. Palmer shuffled to close the door. "And who's this young lady?"

"This is Cisney Baldwin."

Well, well. Nick hadn't clarified she was a co-worker. Gutsy for him to leave the door open for Mr. Palmer to think they were a couple. Was he being kind to her, or was he so low on communication skills that he didn't think to protect himself?

Mr. Palmer returned from taking his sack of food into the kitchen. "Since I had so few Thanksgiving decorations and put them away myself, I'll just show you where I keep the Christmas stuff." Mr. Palmer slowly led Nick down a hallway.

Cisney looked around. By the ruts in the carpet, Mr. Palmer had moved the small table from the picture window to the side of a stuffed armchair. Over in one corner a piano stood away from the clutter of furniture.

She wandered over and rested her hand on the closed piano cover and then inspected several framed photos. Most were probably grandchildren and one showed a younger Mr. Palmer and a woman who was certainly Mrs. Palmer. In the photo, he stood facing his laughing wife with eyes only for her.

Cisney raised her hand to press against her aching throat that had accompanied her misting eyes. Dust covered her hand. She glanced toward the hall, quickly produced a tissue from her handbag, and wiped her palm, then stuck the tissue in a side pocket of her purse.

When she heard the men's voices, she stepped to the center of the room. How long would it be, if ever, before Mr. Palmer noticed her handprint on the piano cover?

Mr. Palmer carried a red and green Christmas tree stand while Nick hefted two large boxes stacked on top of each other. He leaned his head to the side to see where he was going. She strode over and removed the top box and set it on the carpet.

Nick went to work on putting together a seven-foot artificial tree in front of the picture window. Cisney sat on the arm of Mr. Palmer's stuffed chair while he lifted ornaments from a box he'd taken from one of the bigger boxes and placed on his lap. If only she could take out her phone and record his precious descriptions of how he and Blanche had obtained each ornament. But he might feel like Cisney was interviewing him and clam up.

Nick caught her eye and held up dangling lengths of tinsel. He gave her his I-could-use-a-little-help-here look.

She rolled her eyes and bent over to examine an angel made of white feathers that Mr. Palmer said his daughter made in fifth grade.

Nick dusted his hands together. "OK, Mr. Palmer, she's up and ready for the ornaments. You hand them to us and tell us where you want them to go."

Cisney placed a hand on Mr. Palmer's arm. "Does your piano work?"

"I think so. No one's played it in three years, not since Blanche passed. None of the kids took lessons."

"Would you mind if I play some Christmas carols while you and Nick decorate the tree?"

"No. Have at it. It'll be good to hear some music in this old house."

❧✦

Nick and Cisney walked down Mr. Palmer's sidewalk toward the van.

Nick stopped and looked back at the lighted tree. It looked good. He lifted his hand in farewell to Mr. Palmer standing on the porch.

Mr. Palmer returned his wave. "Send me an announcement after you two get married."

Nick opened his mouth to refute the statement, and then clamped it shut and waved again. A snicker came from Cisney ahead of him. Their engagement was a phenomenon that just wouldn't quit. She picked up speed and climbed into the car before he could open the door for her. Behind the windshield, she was bent over laughing. He climbed in, shaking his head, and then gave in to a small chuckle. Probably as much from her giggles as from the absurdness of the situation.

He backed out of the driveway. "We're behind schedule because someone didn't help decorate."

She stuck out her bottom lip.

"But I have to admit that was the happiest I've seen Mr. Palmer."

Her gorgeous hazel eyes grew huge. "Really?"

He nodded. Her little kiss to Mr. Palmer's cheek as they left would cause sugarplums to dance in the elderly man's head for a week. "But no shirking your decorating duty at the Hansons, even if they have a piano."

∞∞

Nick turned the van into the cinema parking lot.

"OK, Fannie, we're here," Tony said. "Which

104

movie?"

"It's the eight o'clock romantic comedy rated PG," Fannie said.

"What? We have to guess which one?"

"I don't care which one it is," Nancy said, "as long as it isn't a shoot-'em-up movie with one chase scene after another, like the one Tony and Nick picked last year."

Inside the theater near the concession counter, Cisney withdrew her wallet from her handbag.

Nick stepped over to her and spoke close to her ear, smelling the fresh peachy scent of her hair. "Put your wallet away. Dad takes great pleasure in funding movie night and would be hurt if you paid for anything. He's just glad he doesn't have to drop us off anymore."

"I'm not part of the family. I don't want your dad paying for my treat."

"Cisney. Put. Your. Wallet. Away."

She made a face and complied. For once.

He stood in line behind her, the popcorn aroma changing his mind to abstain from eating another bite after the Thanksgiving feast.

"How long have you been doing the Ping-Pong and movie traditions?" she asked.

"Since the twins were in first grade, and we went to Disney movies."

"Wow." She moved forward in line. "You have a really nice family, Nick. They're so friendly and fun."

"You think so, after the voting thing in the car?"

"They're just romantics, that's all."

He nodded toward Tony animatedly talking to Allison in the next line. "Some too romantic?"

"Tony?"

"Yeah."

"I like Tony. He's a tease, but he's also a gentleman and seems good-natured."

He couldn't argue with her on that.

"You want to share a popcorn?" she asked.

"Sure. You want butter?"

Her lips tightened as if she tasted dirt. "I don't usually, but if that's the way you like it, butter's fine with me."

"You sure?"

She nodded and advanced to the counter, where the server glanced at the line forming behind them and held his fingers poised over the register. Cisney surveyed the candy behind the glass. "I'll have…" She ran her finger along the display case.

The server shifted his weight, and Nick gave the guy a sympathetic smile.

She jabbed the glass. "I'll have that—no, make it that," she said and pointed. "And a diet orange soda."

Nick ordered a large popcorn, no butter, and a soft drink.

Cisney and Dana couldn't differ more. Dana would have done less chitchatting in line and spent more time contemplating her order. She was no time waster. He'd respected that about her. *Lord, am I crazy for subjecting myself to Dana tomorrow? I haven't sensed your usual pressure that I'm off track.*

As a youth collected the women's tickets, Tony edged over to Nick. "How about letting me sit next to Cisney."

"Sorry, chum, we're sharing popcorn. Besides, I think Allison would be hurt."

"Hey, man, why do you think I have two sides?"

"Well, if Cisney doesn't object, sit on her other

side. Just don't talk during the movie."

Would Cisney babble through the show? Few things irked him more. Dana never said a word after the lights went down. Dating cool, calm Dana held no unhappy surprises...until she broke it off with him.

Inside the theater, the twins chose a row halfway from the back and filed in.

Cisney stepped into the row.

Tony grasped her elbow. "Let Nick go in next so I can sit between you and Allison."

Cisney moved out of the row and pointed at Nick. "Just don't separate me from his popcorn."

Nick sidled in, and then Cisney, Tony, Allison, and Nancy.

Cisney worked on opening her box of candy while Tony and Allison talked. She got her fingernail under the flap but couldn't get the glue to budge. She tried the other end and then went back to work on the flap. The top layer of the flap skimmed back, leaving the box sealed.

Nick stuck out his hand, palm up. She gave him the box, and he opened it.

"My hero," she whispered.

He grinned and tilted the popcorn bucket toward her.

She shook her head. "I eat all my candy first," she whispered.

"But the popcorn's best when it's hot."

"That's OK, you go ahead." She turned to face him and drew her finger across the outside of the bucket halfway up its side. "Stop here, and I'll take over," she whispered.

"The movie hasn't started yet, you don't have to whisper."

"In movies, my family never talked above a whisper, if at all, or Daddy wouldn't bring us again for a long time." Her beautiful eyes widened. "You don't talk during the movie, do you?"

"No." He held up the popcorn container, glad they agreed on one thing. "You do know the bucket is somewhat cone-shaped and half the popcorn is about here." He moved his finger up on the bucket from where she'd drawn her line.

"Shame on you, Risk Man. You didn't take into consideration that they were chintzy on popcorn. The kernels reach a half-inch short of the top. And you didn't take into account that I'm smaller than you and don't eat as much."

He chuckled. *Risk Man?*

She put her fingers to her puckered lips. "Shh."

He had taken into consideration a less than full bucket. But she ate less? He'd let her have her victory. She was something else.

❧

Cisney savored the dark chocolate taste of her candy and the crunchy white nonpareils on top. What could be better than chocolate and holding her own in a sparring match with Nick on the technical aspects of sharing popcorn? In a lot of ways, being around a man who wouldn't make Daddy's list was a relief. No pressure. No trying to figure out what he liked and disliked in a woman. She could be herself.

She gave Nick a sideways glance. He was endearingly cute when he laughed. Did he know that? The faint dimple and the crinkles beside his eyes changed his whole countenance. Nice teeth, too, except right now they chomped on a mouthful of popcorn. Why did all the men she knew do that? Scoop up a handful of popcorn or peanuts and toss the whole bunch into their mouths? She liked to eat one or two kernels at a time to make them last. The same with her candy.

The lights went down.

Tony held his box of chocolate-coated caramels her way. She didn't want Tony to get too chummy during the movie. His teasing personality amused her, but not during the show. But chocolate and caramel? What would it hurt to share a little chumminess? She received two tumbling candies into her palm before stopping him from issuing more. She dutifully held out her box. He shook his head. The man had just earned lifetime chum status.

She mouthed her thanks, and they turned to the screen.

Too bad Tony wasn't her type. He and Allison looked good together. He'd leaned around the headrest in the car, and the two had talked all the way to the movies, had been joined at the hip in the concession line, and giggled non-stop until the lights dimmed. Later, she'd ask Nick why they weren't an item.

The commercials ended, and the previews started. Allison and Tony gave thumbs-up or thumbs-down after each preview and bumped fists if their thumbs agreed.

Cisney smiled and slipped two candies into her mouth. Were her one-on-one dating days over? This night out with Nick's family was fun, and she always enjoyed her own friends, but fewer eligible men in her age group remained in the shrinking pool. She'd be thirty in a few months.

With Daddy's expectations, she couldn't bring home just any man. Forget a guy who stuttered, or loved gardening, or enjoyed musicals. And in go-getter Daddy's eyes, any man who'd ask Daddy for anything, even his daughter's hand in marriage, had no backbone. Did Daddy know how hard it was to find a Christian who met his standards?

At the top of her list, as it was at the head of Mom's and God's, was a man who attended church with her, and loved Christ. Jason had gone to church with her when it was convenient, but she'd deceived herself at first that Jason, the woman dumper and friend moocher, cared about Jesus. The longer they had dated, the less he joined her during worship.

The movie wasn't helping the tack her thoughts had taken. The heroine needed a wake-up slap. Couldn't she see that the guy she drooled over was wrong for her? That the quiet man in the wings was the man who'd love and cherish her forever? Maybe God needed to knock the heroine on the head like He had her earlier about Jason in the rowboat, thanks to Nick.

Now that God had enlightened her about Jason, would He help her find the right guy quickly? She was already a two-time loser. Ron, the prior real man, who'd tickled Daddy and stuck around for five months, had dropped her to take up with a pretty mousy woman.

Cisney lifted her orange soda from the drink holder. Was she stuck in a depressing cycle? *Cisney meets real man—Daddy's happy—Cisney's on good behavior—Cisney beats real man in darts or other game—real man tires of Cisney—real man dumps Cisney—real man finds his dream mouse—Daddy and Cisney are unhappy.*

What would it take to stop the cycle? Where could she find an adoring wingman with backbone? She let her gaze drift to her left, where Tony was whispering in Allison's ear, and then she let them meander to her right, where...Nick had his cell to his ear?

༄༅

Nick listened to the message he'd allowed to go to voicemail. Dana announced she'd pick him up tomorrow at eleven. He'd rather drive himself. How would Mom react if she saw Dana? That wouldn't happen. Knowing Dana, she wouldn't come inside the house. In any case, he'd make sure she didn't.

When the credits rolled across the screen, he stood and stretched. He helped Cisney into her coat. "Well, what did you think of the movie?"

She stuffed her candy box and cup into the popcorn tub. "The heroine was hard to take, at first. She seemed so dumb about the hot-looking jerk. I have to admit, I would never have predicted that both the mild man in the wings and the hot guy could change enough that the movie pulled off the heroine ending up with the hot guy. You don't ever see that. It was an interesting twist."

Did the movie tempt Cisney that Jason could change enough to warrant a second chance in her affections? A guy like Jason needed a heap of change to be worthy of Cisney. The movie hero had taken five years to transform in to a decent guy. From what Nick knew of Jason, he'd need five decades.

Cisney and Nick trailed Tony and Allison down the theater steps.

Allison turned to give Tony a swat at something he said and her heel caught on the step. She went down with a yelp, plowing into Fran and Fanny, who caught themselves from falling.

Tony righted Allison and stepped down a stair. At Tony's beckoning, she climbed onto his back, laughing and moaning. He hooked his arms under her knees and continued down the stairs.

Cisney leaned close to Nick. "They seem perfect for each other. Why aren't they planning a lifetime together?"

"You sound like Mom. They've been close friends a long time. Why ruin it?"

"You're kidding, right?" She leveled her gaze on his. "Don't you think best friends are what a couple should be first?"

Did Cisney hear her own good advice? Were she and Jason best friends first? A best friend didn't horn in on your circle of friends after he dumped you and left you alone for Thanksgiving. She was still raw from the breakup, or she'd see she didn't walk her talk. At least he and Dana had started out friends, and still were, or he'd have turned down meeting her tomorrow.

Cisney kept her gaze locked on him as they inched their way to the double doors.

He sighed. "Yes, I think it's a good idea for a couple to be best friends before jumping into marriage. When Tony grows up, I think he'll marry his best friend. Happy?"

"Yes." She smiled up at him. "I like happy endings."

∽◦⌁

Nick let everyone out of the van and pulled it into the garage. Tony walked Allison home, and Nancy and the girls tiptoed off to their rooms in the quiet house.

Cisney waited for Nick in the foyer. "Today was one of most entertaining Thanksgivings I've ever experienced. You all have made me feel part of the family."

Didn't he know it.

She stepped onto the first stair.

"Cisney."

She turned, her eyes bright. "Yes?"

He rested his hand on the banister. "I have some business tomorrow that will take me away for a few hours. Will you be all right?"

The brightness dimmed. "Sure. I saw a bookcase in there." She pointed to the room opposite the front room. "It looks like a cozy place to read. Or maybe I'll go down by the lake. I'm good at amusing myself."

Yeah, like thinking up ways to put another notch on her challenge belt. "Mom thought you'd like to go shopping with Nancy and Allison on Black Friday."

"They didn't invite me." She poked his chest. "And don't you make them. I don't want to barge in on their time together."

What was the big deal? Shopping was shopping. Not some social event. "They'll want you to go."

"Promise me you won't say anything to them."

"I won't." Why did he feel guilty for leaving her? He'd never promised her twenty-four-seven entertainment. And she'd claimed she could entertain herself. Even so, guilt lay like a river stone on his chest. "All of Aunt Sandy's clan will be leaving tomorrow morning."

She frowned. "I didn't say goodbye. How early do you think they'll leave?"

"Probably around eight."

Her cell played the marimba. She jostled it out of her handbag and checked the screen. Her face blanched. "I better take this."

She hurried up the stairs. "Hi, Daddy."

8

Cisney held her cell away from her mouth, so Daddy wouldn't get an earful of her heavy breathing after she ran up two flights of stairs.

He spoke loudly as if he thought he had to yell all the way from Germany.

Her breathing and heartbeat refused to quiet, and it had nothing to do with physical activity. She'd have to tell Daddy the truth—tonight.

"We spoke so briefly on the phone before," Daddy said, "I didn't get a chance to ask you about your Thanksgiving."

"It must be about four in the morning there," she said.

"I couldn't sleep. How's my man, Jason?"

"I'm not at Jason's." And neither was Jason. The rat.

"What? Where are you?"

"A friend from work invited me home for the holiday."

"But why didn't you go to Jason's? Is he there with you?"

She hated ruining Daddy's vacation. "Because…because he broke up with me." She cringed waiting for the blast.

"Oh, Cis…" He sounded sympathetic. Maybe Daddy could understand that a man like Jason did pretty much what he wanted, and he wanted to date the beautiful blonde doormat. "What did you do, honey?"

"I cried, mostly. I'm sorry, Daddy, I know how you feel about crying, but—"

His volume ratcheted up a notch. "No, I mean, what did you do that made him leave?"

Her jaw dropped. Was he serious? Utterances of disappointment, yes. But what did she do? Well, nothing. If curbing her wants and needs when around Jason was nothing.

"I don't know, Daddy." Shame flowed like hot syrup over her head and down her back.

"Come on, Cis, you must have done something to make the man who's dead-on right for you hightail it."

"I think another woman, a beautiful one, helped whatever it was I did, Daddy." She stuffed the urge to coat her cynical words with a sarcastic tone.

"Ah, a beautiful woman." He sounded like everything was explained. "A man like Jason needs lots of attention so he doesn't stray. Were you making yourself available for his business and social functions? Did you help him entertain clients?"

She heaved a sigh. "I—"

"I did not raise a doormat, Cis. Get out there and fight for your man."

She didn't want to fight for Jason. Besides, doormats seemed his type, so she must be doing the right thing. "Daddy, I'm sorry this is a disappointment for you."

"I just want you to be happy, honey."

"I'll work on being happy, Daddy."

"Good. Why don't you give Jason a call? He's probably in the middle of family, wishing you were there with him. Or...I'd be glad to call him."

"No, that's OK, Daddy. He's not at home, anyway." *He's in the middle of a robbery, pocketing my friends.*

"I'm bummed, Cis. Really ticked off. I thought we'd caught a live one." His breathy sigh left her with no response.

Lord, help me.

"You sure, you don't want me to give Jason a call?"

"Positive." Even bird droppings wouldn't capture how she'd feel if Daddy went to work on Jason, and Jason begrudgingly agreed to give their relationship another shot.

"Well, Mom and I are on an early afternoon flight home tomorrow. We've had a great three weeks with DJ, Jenna, and the kids. I'm glad you had a girlfriend invite you home for the holiday."

Was it lying to let him believe her friend was someone other than a mild-mannered actuary possessing a male chromosome—the type of guy Daddy considered one of mankind's nuisances in the name of progress?

అఈ

Cisney dragged herself downstairs before eight in the morning, dressed and a smile affixed to her face. The smile wouldn't stay put, though. The muscles around her lips kept drooping. No wonder. Prolonged face scrunching had exhausted them while she cried herself to sleep.

Each day, Jason's image faded a little. Thank goodness. He was becoming more and more of an upsetting irritation, or at times, a wistful sorrow, but

Daddy laying the blame on her for Jason's desertion was a wound so raw that no suture held. Daddy wanted so much for her and so much from her.

Her few minutes reading the LeCrones' Bible had calmed her, but now, Daddy-induced resentment, guilt, and doubt seeped back in and brought along sadness and humiliation. They rumbled inside her like planets smashing into each other. Debris shooting from the clashing spheres peppered her paper armor.

She should've never taken astronomy. The analogy wasn't helping her make sense of her confusing emotions. She dismissed the planets to spin elsewhere and went outside to say goodbye to the departing family.

Allison parked off the road in front of the house and walked over to the driveway.

Tony winked at Cisney, and then enclosed Allison in a bear hug, complete with a ferocious growl.

So, after all Tony's flirting, Cisney had to settle for a wink. She could do with a bear hug about now. At least Tony's parting antics breathed life into her smile. Once inside his car, Tony saluted the onlookers and backed out of the driveway.

As the car rolled by Nick, he rapped his knuckles on the hood. "See if you can come up with something better than the polka next year."

Sandy, Bill, and the twins turned their frenzy of hugs onto Cisney. She hoped their kind assaults wouldn't unravel her fragile emotions. Keep her upper lip stiff and her lower one firm.

She was doing well. As Fran approached, she was even able to offer a smile. No threat here. Cisney wrapped her arms lightly around the reserved twin. Fran's warm embrace lingered for a second longer than the others. Not fair! Cisney bit her lips together. If only she could slink home and lick her wounds and wallow in her self-pity. But, no, Nick had foiled that plan, and she had to hide her protective wall's fallen stones and crumbled mortar the best she could, while everyone stood on the lawn and waved the SUV around a curve.

Lord, throw me a rope.

Waving done, Nick strode by her, followed by Roger and Grandpa, and they scrambled into the house. What was the rush?

Nancy fell into step with Cisney. "Don't mind them. It's our tradition for the men to make the day-after-Thanksgiving breakfast." She laughed. "Wait until you see the show. I think they practice all year, because they keep getting better."

Cisney grasped the rope. God was good.

While the ladies sipped peppermint tea at the country table, the men collected ingredients and utensils. The tea soothed Cisney, and the chatter around her offered a breather from the morning's turmoil.

Nick flipped pancakes over the built-in griddle. He turned to the women. "How do you like your pancakes?"

"Medium well!" Nancy and Allison called in unison.

Cisney looked from one to the other, and then laughed.

Roger whipped a second batch of pecan pancake batter. "How do you like your batter?"

Nancy and Allison directed their hands toward Ellie.

Put on the spot, Ellie clamped her hands to her face and looked to the ceiling. Then her eyes lit up.

"Up at bat!"

"Good job, Mom," Nancy said.

Nick turned and gave his mother a thumbs-up.

Grandpa paused in twisting orange halves on a juice reamer. "How do like your orange juice?"

Ellie joined Nancy and Allison in passing the baton to Cisney. She jerked to attention. What had happened to Grandma Thelma's turn? "Ah, ah...face-slapping fresh!"

The family's laughter, Nick's approving grin, and orange and peppermint scenting the air soothed her mood like the best thing since Gilead's balm.

Nick turned a bubbling pancake. "Are you ready, Grandma Thelma?"

She flapped a hand at him. "Leave me out of this. I'm too old to think of a snappy answer."

"Sorry Grandma, you have to answer your question. How do you like your chefs?"

The men turned from their tasks, stuck out their chests, and draped their arms around each other.

"About as much as Moe, Larry, and Curly."

Nancy and Cisney clapped, and Allison stuck two fingers in her mouth and whistled. The men took a collective bow, and then turned back to their duties.

Roger threw his whisk high into the air and caught it behind his back, spraying batter all over himself and Nick. Nick flipped a pancake with such gusto that it stuck briefly to the ten-foot ceiling before plummeting into Roger's bowl of batter. And Grandpa, not to be outdone, juggled three oranges. After his last toss, he stretched out his apron pocket and the oranges fell one-by-one inside.

Cisney struggled for breaths between guffaws. How had she ever considered actuaries frumps?

After breakfast, everyone joined in to clean the kitchen, and then headed in different directions to get ready for the day.

Nancy and Allison had persuaded Cisney to lunch, shop, and go for pedicures and manicures with them at the Northlake Mall in Charlotte.

Nick had grinned and shot her an I-told-you-so look before heading up the stairs.

Deserted, Cisney wandered into the front room and ran her finger over the keys on the Steinway. She strolled to the cozy room across the foyer and perused the novels in the bookcases. Christian suspense and romance dominated the genres. She selected an Amish romance and, feeling like Jane Eyre, settled into the cushioned window seat to wait for Nancy and Allison.

Nancy's voice coming from the front room beamed her out of Lancaster County, where the heroine's family was *redding up* the house and barn for church.

"Mom! Come quick and look out the window!"

"I don't believe it." Allison's tone equaled Nancy's in conveying shock.

Cisney wrenched her head toward the window.

Nick sauntered down the driveway, his hands in his suit-pants pockets. He must have left from another door, or she'd have heard him. What kind of business needed a suit and tie? She shifted her gaze to his destination, an expensive, foreign sedan parked on the street. A slim woman with long, perfectly straight blonde hair sat in the driver's seat. Nick was going on a fancy lunch date with a woman?

Running footsteps pounded the hardwood floors on the other side of the foyer and stopped. "Dana?" said Ellie's shocked voice. "He said he had to take care of business. What business does he have with Dana?" Ellie sounded indignant.

For some reason, Cisney empathized.

Nick climbed into the passenger seat. The woman leaned over, and they briefly embraced.

The book on Cisney's lap fell to the floor.

෴

Nick waited for the familiar ache of loss to spread across his chest while Dana drove them toward I-77. So far so good. His pumper was pain free. No leaks, no regrets.

Then Dana gave him that little smile he'd loved. "How have you been, Nick?"

"I'm fine." Mostly. "How about you?"

"Truth?"

"Of course."

She held up her left hand, where a good-sized diamond sparkled.

His heart rate blipped. "Ah," he said, nodding. "You're happy."

"Paul's a financial planner."

He nodded.

She glanced his way. "I told Mark you're perfect for the job. We need a good health actuary. Why are you considering the position?"

Until her question, he'd welcomed the change of subject. Was she fishing for whether she was part of his decision?

Working with Dana was the only downside to Option A. Something as small as his heart blip, when she'd held up her rock, warned Option A bore dangerous temptations. Could he dispassionately work on client presentations with her and talk football with her husband at actuarial social functions?

He settled his sweaty palms on his thighs. "Three reasons. First, I'm ready for a challenge." A notch on his challenge belt.

"You're smiling. What's so funny about a challenge?"

"Nothing. The second reason...let's just say the second reason is I'm currently performing my job and a superior's. I'd like to pare it down to one."

"His, right?"

He nodded.

"I know what you're not saying," she said. "It's your chief actuary, Joe Walker. I've met him at conferences a few times." She rolled her eyes.

Joe was a genius and a nice guy. But his communication skills were the pits.

Nick's days were interrupted with calls from people in other departments, outside companies, or government agencies. It was always, "I called Joe with a question, and I couldn't figure out what he said to me. I gave up. I'm calling you because I still need an answer." Nick was known as Joe's translator inside and outside the company.

Nick took in Dana's flawless complexion. "Yes, if I'm going to do the chief actuary's job, I want the position."

"And the title and the office, right?"

"Those are icing." He looked at her slender fingers grasping the steering wheel. He missed holding her incredibly soft hands.

"Our open position is a couple of steps down from partner, but Mark's approaching retirement will narrow the gap."

"Yeah, but I'd be competing with you when he retires," he said jokingly.

"That's not a problem." Her small smile formed. "I'd defer to you because, when I have my first child, I plan to take a long hiatus."

Children. That blip again. Unlike Cisney, who planned no further than her next sticky note, Dana had planned out her life. A rationally planned, step-by-step life was good. Dana was so together. But maybe Cisney's more fluid living was what made her seem fresh and alive.

Dana whisked her straight hair over her shoulder and it streamed down the back of her white dress. "You said there were three reasons. What's the third?"

"I'd like to live closer to my family."

She took her gaze off the road and angled her head toward him. "You seem to have forgiven me, but have they?" She returned her attention to the road.

"I think they have."

Dad never held grudges. Forgiveness was part of Mom's life in Christ, but his reconciliation with Dana ranked high on Mom's worry list, which was the reason he'd keep his meeting with Dana to himself.

❧

Cisney sat in the back of Allison's sedan. Her curiosity surpassed her manners. "I accidentally overheard you earlier. Who's Dana?"

Nancy and Allison exchanged glances.

"Nick and I are co-workers," Cisney said. "Nothing more."

Nancy turned in the passenger seat. "Mom and I were disappointed you and Nick aren't engaged. You guys are good together."

Cisney raised her eyebrows and shrugged. After her pearl ring had misled the women, taking a pass on commenting seemed best.

Nancy's voice turned conspiratorial. "Dana is Nick's ex."

Cisney stiffened. Ex, like in ex-wife?

"Ex-girlfriend, that is," Nancy said. "She's from around here and is an actuary with a consulting firm in Charlotte. They met at Georgia State, and then became reacquainted at a Society of Actuaries conference. Nick drove home every weekend for two years until she broke up with him a few months ago." Nancy frowned. "He took the break-up hard. When he didn't answer his cell the day after she ditched him, I drove up and found him holed up for the weekend, unshaven and deep in delivery food, little of it eaten. You have to understand. Nick is Mr. Organized Neatness, when he isn't mourning a loved one. Only recently has he been back to his old self."

Cisney needed a brown bag. She'd hyperventilate any second. How many times in the last two days had she accused Nick of having no idea what being dumped felt like? Her mind raced, scanning her memory for all the snide judgments she'd voiced.

What an idiot. To assume actuaries were too antisocial to have normal crises—or to get hurt. Except for lacking in communication skills, Nick was like any other nice guy. A really good man. He'd cared enough about her pain to invite her to his home, save her from embarrassment when she looked like a cavewoman, and turn her to God's point of view concerning Jason. He didn't have to do any of that. And what had she offered him? To be another notch on her challenge belt?

Lord, how self-centered I've been. No wonder men found it impossible to love her.

"Are you all right?" Nancy asked.

Allison threw a glance over the seat back. "You look a little pale."

Cisney blinked. Nancy stared at her. Could she be selfless enough to avoid ruining Nancy's and Allison's Black Friday?

She flashed Nancy her I'm-just-peachy smile. "I'm fine. What does the mall have in the way of housewares?"

Housewares? That's the best she could muster in a pinch? Daddy would be appalled.

Nick's sister regarded her for another second, as if she didn't buy her peachy smile. "There're several big stores, with plenty of household goods." The bird dog didn't let up her scrutiny. "Are you sure my big brother hasn't wooed you a little? Maybe you're feeling a touch jealous he's out with his old flame?"

"Nancy!" Allison punched Nancy's arm. "That's a bit frank."

Nancy reluctantly drew her gaze from Cisney and turned her narrowed eyes to Allison, while rubbing her arm. "And that hurt! I'm fighting for my brother, here. You know she's perfect for him, just like I do. I teach fourth graders, after all. I should know puppy love when I see it."

Their shared laughter broke the tension. The camaraderie they seemed to be building would be a lot more enjoyable if the news of Nick's breakup would stop nagging her conscience. How was she going to face him this afternoon? Right now, she needed to assure Nick's groupies she was not dealing with the green-eyed monster.

"Your brother is a great guy," she said, "but I assure you, I'm not the least bit jealous. I hope he and Dana are very happy together. Maybe they'll invite me to their wedding." Had she really said that? Invite her to their wedding? Maybe she could find the perfect wedding gift in housewares. *Shut up, Cisney!*

Nancy and Allison exchanged a look, and simultaneously blurted, "She's jealous!"

9

Cisney bought two sets of Christmas tree placecard holders, a hostess gift for Ellie. The noisy miniature jingle bell ornaments decorating the tin trees would thwart Tony from stealthily rearranging card holders at Christmas.

Laden with shopping bags, the women headed for the nail shop. From the nail polish display shelves, Nancy chose Tomato Sizzle and Allison went with Metallic Blue.

Cisney put Heavenly Pink back on the rack. It was too pale. Maybe Crimson Blast. She shook the bottle and held it up. No. It had a violet sheen to it. Ooh la la. She snatched Rose Smooch. The color matched her favorite lipstick. Perfect.

Her manicure done, Cisney rumpled her nose at the scent of her damp fingernail polish as she moved to the chairs reserved for pedicures. Keeping her eye on her wet nails and using her palms for support, she climbed into the chair between Nancy and Allison.

Nancy leaned back in her throne-like chair while the pedicurist removed old nail polish from her toenails. She rolled her head toward Cisney. "What do you like best and least about Nick?"

Cisney regarded Nancy for a moment. "You don't give up easily, do you?"

"She's very pushy." Allison leaned forward and captured Nancy's attention. "I think she should mind her own love life, and leave mine and Tony's alone."

So, Allison also suffered from LeCrone matchmakers.

Cisney blew on her fingernails. "I don't mind answering Nancy's question, if she tells us what she likes best and least about Nick, first." What about Nick would bug his adoring sister?

"Ouch," Nancy said. "OK, I'll take on Cisney's dare, if Allison tells us what she likes best and least about Tony."

Allison shrugged. "No skin off my cuticles."

Nancy rolled her eyes. She tapped her crimson nail against her chin. "I like best that Nick never told me to get lost when we were kids, as some older brothers do. And the thing I like the least is when he kept putting raisins in oatmeal cookies when he knows I dislike raisins." Sweeping her hand in Allison's direction, she passed the challenge to her best friend.

"Touching," Allison said. "OK. Let's see. Tony." Her eyes took on a faraway look. "Every time Tony and I meet, it's as if we pick up where we left off the last time we were together. So I like best that Tony is like my favorite casual shoes. We always walk well together."

Nancy swallowed a sip of her herbal tea. "Or you tread on him."

They laughed.

"And the least?"

"I'm afraid my favorite casual shoes will wear out before he makes a commitment." Allison's eyes misted and her lips crinkled.

Cisney's heart went soft as mush. "He'll come around." She squeezed Allison's arm. "Talk about two people made for each other. I'm envious."

Protecting her freshly painted blue nails, Allison used the balls of her forefingers to wipe tears from under her eyes. "OK, you next," she said to Cisney.

Nancy and Allison leaned toward Cisney.

"I don't know Nick as well as both of you do, but what I like best is that he likes raisins in oatmeal cookies, because raisins rock!"

Allison and Nancy shooed their manicured hands at her.

"Boo!"

"Not acceptable!"

Cisney grinned. "OK, OK."

The younger women leaned in again. They wouldn't let her get away with anything less than juicy.

"What I like best about Nick is that he invited me to come home with him, giving me the privilege of enjoying his family…" She nodded toward Allison. "And his friend. He did that right after my boyfriend dumped me." Uh-oh. Who'd injected her with truth serum?

Nancy and Allison snapped away from her as if they were blades of the same pair of scissors. They stared at her in disbelief.

Nancy's body slumped. "Oh, Cisney, I'm so sorry." She patted Cisney's hand, their polish colors clashing.

Allison pressed Cisney's other hand. "I never would have guessed."

"Being here with you guys—your whole family—has helped keep my mind off the jerk." She looked at each of her new friends. "Did I say 'the jerk' out loud? I meant Jason. Dear, jilting Jason."

Nancy cut short her sympathetic demeanor. "Even

though what you've shared is sad, you still have to reveal what you like least about my brother."

Oh, which option would she choose? When he pronounced her marketing ideas actuarially unsound? His thinking spells—nearly an out of body experience? Or maybe his habit of grabbing her hand and dragging her wherever he wanted her to go? How about making her eat cranberry sauce? Yuk. Or...making her feel like skunk road kill when his "business" turned out to be a lunch date with his ex-girlfriend?

Nancy and Allison waited, gazes laser-like and sharp.

"All right. All right. What I like least about Nick is his woeful lack of communication skills."

Nancy guffawed, receiving a glare from the startled pedicurist, who then removed smudged Tomato Sizzle polish from Nancy's big toenail.

Nancy apologized to the woman and turned back to Cisney. "You nailed it." She fluttered her painted nails and grinned. "No pun intended. Nick's sadly missing the communication gene. Of course, he thinks he communicates just fine, citing how people from inside and outside the company ask him to explain actuarial stuff."

Cisney raised her eyebrow. "Claiming to be the top communicator in the actuarial department is like a worm boasting how smart he is because fishermen dig him. Have you ever met Nick's boss?"

"No."

"Good. Because I think we've degenerated into gossip." Cisney placed her hand over her heart. "Not a pretty picture for a woman who claims to be a Christian. Sorry."

Nancy scrunched her shoulders sheepishly. "Me,

too."

"Guilty. Me, three," Allison said.

Silence hung in the air.

❧⋙

Mid-afternoon, Allison dropped Cisney and Nancy at the LeCrones'. Nancy brought wrapping paper to the attic room for Cisney to wrap her gifts for Ellie and Nick.

Cisney deposited her gift-wrapped presents on the bed. "I hope your mom and Nick like what I chose for them."

"They will." Nancy pulled photo albums from the chest at the foot of the bed.

Cisney dragged the window armchairs together. "I love looking at family photos."

Nancy opened an album across Cisney's lap. "I haven't looked through these albums since forever."

Cisney smiled at Nancy and Nick as children. "Tell me who everyone is and the stories behind the photos."

Nancy obliged.

They reached Nick's college and Nancy's high school years when a light knock sounded on the dwarfed door.

"Come in," Cisney called.

Nick opened the door. He braced his arm against the jamb and stooped. He'd changed into jeans and a plaid shirt. "What are you two up to?"

"Showing pictures of you in diapers and zits," Nancy said. "And, of course, telling Cisney embarrassing stories about you." She rose, gathered the wrapping materials, and sailed toward Nick, clearing the ceiling by a full inch at the door. "I hear Mom calling me." She ducked under his arm and descended the stairs.

"Do you see what I have to put up with because your charm has mesmerized my family?"

What'd he want her to do? Spit in their eyes? "Come here. I want to show you the two pictures I like best."

"If I'm sitting on a potty chair, I'll stay right here."

"No." She patted the seat of the other chair. "Come on over and sit."

He lowered his head and joined her.

She planted an album in his lap and his laughter made her giggle. "They are cute, aren't they?" She pointed to the picture of Nancy and Allison arm in arm when they were ten.

"I'm laughing because you have marked pages with sticky notes. Do you own stock in the company?"

"No. But stickies are the best invention ever, don't you think?"

Nick wagged his head. He crossed his foot over his knee and repositioned the album. "So, which photos have you tagged to embarrass me?"

If she'd wanted to embarrass him, she would have pulled out her phone and snapped photos of him embracing Dana. She turned to the first yellow sticky and touched a picture of Grandpa, Roger, eleven-year-old Nick, and six-year-old Tony sitting in that order on the LeCrone pier, their backs to the camera and the ends of their fishing poles sprouting from their heads.

"Those were the days," he said. His reminiscing smile tugged at her heart.

Who was she falling for, the boy in the photo or the man he'd become? But falling, she was. Wouldn't that please Daddy. She'd chalk it up to a weekend crush.

She tapped the photo. "When this picture was taken, had you already dreamed of being an actuary like your Dad and Grandpa?"

"I think at this time I was going through my stage where I wanted to raise Siberian huskies in Alaska and win the Iditarod Trail Sled Dog Race."

She chuckled and ran her fingers over the photo. "This should be enlarged and hung somewhere."

"Which was the other one you liked?"

She flipped a few pages to the second yellow sticky. Approximately the same ages as in the first photo, Nick and Tony bent over a tangled fishing line, their heads almost touching in a close-up shot. Nick's focus was on the knot, deep creases between his eyebrows, while Tony's wide-eyed gaze was directed at a small lizard on Nick's T-shirt, his forefinger poised to touch the reptile.

"I remember it took me an hour to untangle that mess, and then Tony snarled it again within minutes."

"Did Tony touch the lizard before it bolted?"

"That, I don't remember."

He slipped tickets from his shirt pocket. "I have tickets for a local musical tonight."

Of course, he'd see more of Dana. Cisney's spirits wilted—no, bombed—but she quickly slapped her I'm-not-hurt smile on her face. "No problem. The Amish book I'm reading is very engaging. And Roger and Grandpa said there'd be a Chinese checkers game tonight."

"What?"

"Like I said, I can entertain myself."

"You don't like musicals?"

"They're my favorite." She could belt out Oh-klahoma with the best of them.

"Then why won't you go with me?"

"You're asking me?"

Maybe his luncheon with Dana hadn't gone well. Maybe he'd changed clothes as soon as he got home because Dana had dumped linguine carbonara on his head.

He cocked his head and furrowed his brow. "Who'd you think I was asking?"

Nick LeCrone had asked her on a date, not to a chess match at the local library, but to the theatre for singing and dancing.

"I'd love to go!"

"Don't get too excited. The writer, choreographer, and actors are locals, but I've seen their work before and it's entertaining and well done. It's called *A Way with Waltz*."

"Thank you." She swallowed down emotion, jumped up from her chair, and moved to the bed. With two hands, she lifted a small box wrapped in blue paper covered with stars. "This is for you. Ignore the happy birthday words. It's all Nancy could find, other than the paper for your mother's gift." She moved closer. "A small gift in appreciation for all you have done for me since I fell apart over Jason while you were in my office. The Lord guided you well, and I'm thankful." She handed the box to him and returned to her chair.

"You didn't have to do this."

"Yes, I did. Open it."

He eased his finger under the tape on one side. If he unwrapped presents like he thought about her marketing proposals, they'd miss the show. He picked at the tape from the other side.

She glanced at his face. A smug smile deepened his dimple. He slowly slid his finger under the center tape.

"Nick LeCrone. You're doing that on purpose."

He chuckled.

She lifted her face toward his and crossed her eyes. "Open it."

He gently pushed her face away. "OK. OK." He ripped the paper, shook the box, and removed the lid. "No way." His chuckle grew into laughter.

"I noticed your desk at work lacked one."

He lifted a mahogany sticky note holder, complete with a fresh pad of yellow stickies. "I will definitely think of you every time I look at it."

"I know you believe I'm self-centered for getting you something I like, but I'm not, because I already have one."

"You do? I've never seen it."

"Yes, I do. It's exactly like yours."

"Yours must be buried under a few hundred papers."

"I'm more organized than you think, because I know which hundred my sticky holder is under."

He held up the gift. "Well, thank you." He chuckled again. "Shall we go down for turkey sandwiches?"

୬୦୧

Nick glanced across the kitchen island, where Cisney built her sandwich on make-your-own-turkey-sandwich night. She stood between Dad and Grandma Thelma and looked radiant.

If he'd known taking her to the theatre would help her forget Jason, he'd have asked her to the famous one in Richmond the night Jason dumped her. Then she might have gone on the ski trip with her friends and saved him from his family matchmakers. And from the way Nancy scooted out of Cisney's room, skiing would have rescued Cisney from them, too.

Grandpa added a pickle wedge to his plate. "So is everyone ready for the big Chinese checkers game tonight?"

Nick dropped more turkey slices on his stack and peppered them. "Today, someone gave me two tickets to a musical at The Warehouse. I thought I'd show Cisney what our locals in Cornelius can do in the performing arts."

He cut his sandwich in half. No one responded. He looked up to six pairs of eyes staring at him. "What? We can join tomorrow night's Chinese checkers game."

"Someone?" Nancy said, the word dripping with attitude.

His gut sagged. Which family members, besides Nancy, had snooped out the window and had seen him in Dana's car?

Now, wait just a minute. Where, or why, he went with Dana was none of their business. Neither were the tickets Dana had given him. The luncheon with Mark and Dana at The Palm was a mere formality. They wanted him. And he wanted the challenge they offered. Whether his family liked it or not, he might just take the job where Dana worked.

"Yeah, someone," he said. "What's the big deal? Someone I had business with today couldn't use the tickets and asked if I wanted them. I thought it would be nice to show Cisney something of the Lake Norman communities."

All went back to loading their plates, except Cisney. She held his gaze. Did she know about Dana? Was that why she acted strangely in her room about the tickets? She thought he was going out with Dana?

10

Cisney retrieved her red dress from the closet and slipped into its silky folds. She stood away from the slanted ceiling and spun around before the mirror on the closet door, even though it cut off her head. Her skirt billowed, and then settled around her legs. She smiled. Wearing her favorite dress always lifted her spirits.

The marimba played. Her muscles tightened as her gaze went to her phone on the bedside table. Why hadn't she assigned separate ringtones to the people in Favorites and avoided these moments of not knowing who called? *Please, please don't be Daddy. I want to be happy tonight.*

She grabbed her cell and looked at the display. Jason? Her heart outraced the marimba beat, as she paced and stared at his name. Should she take his call?

She had two more rings before the call would go to voicemail. *Lord, guide me.*

The music stopped.

She halted and let out a long breath. Safe. For a while.

What did Jason want? Had he forgotten the combination to his ski lock? Start at two. Left to ten. Right to thirteen. Or was he bored on the beginner slopes with his new little lady? Or maybe he felt guilty for leaving her stranded for Thanksgiving. Could he want her back?

She dropped to her knees and rested her elbows on the bed, interlocking her fingers under her chin. "Father, you are the God of comfort. Thank you for consoling me through Nick and his loving family. Lord, would you now please ban thoughts of Jason for the next few hours?"

Her heart calmed. She rose, grabbed her black clutch purse, and scooted down the first flight of stairs. She paused on the landing and took the second flight at a pace worthy of royalty.

Dressed in his dark suit, Nick stood at the bottom of the stairs like a handsome prince waiting for his tower princess. She smiled at him.

His upturned lips looked...pained. He didn't like her red dress?

After she descended a few more steps, lights flashed in quick succession, startling her. Blinded, she gripped the handrail and made it to the bottom step, where her sight recovered and she took in the smiles radiating from Nick's family. She hadn't felt like this since prom night.

"You look stunning." Ellie took her hand and positioned her close to Nick.

So, he'd inherited the hand-pulling habit from his mom.

"Come on," Nancy said, extending her camera. "Can't you put your arm around her, Nick?"

Nick narrowed his eyes at his sister.

Digital cameras fired off lightning-bright explosions.

"Nick, honey, you could put your arm around Cisney for the next photo," Grandma Thelma said, her camera at the ready.

Nick grabbed Cisney's hand and whisked her out

the door. Flashes followed them. He opened the passenger door for her, and then jogged to the driver's side, holding his hand out to ward off flashes. "Paparazzi!"

"Have fun, honey!"

"Enjoy the musical!"

"Be home before curfew!" Nancy said.

Laughing, Cisney waved until the family was out of sight. "You have the greatest family."

He kept his eyes trained on the road.

"Why so aggravated, Nick?"

He glanced at her. "Don't you feel the pressure?"

"No. I feel the love."

He wrenched his tie loose. "I need my family to sign a privacy agreement."

Her princess dream fizzled. "We don't have to go, Nick."

He stared forward, and then turned to her, his face softening. "I'm sorry. I didn't mean to spoil your evening."

"I don't want to go, if your evening won't recover."

If she wanted a depressing night, she could have stayed in her room and gnawed her newly painted fingernails over why Jason had called.

ॐঔ

Every time Nick forced his attention to the dancers on stage, his gaze drifted back to Cisney. She looked beautiful in that red dress. A miniature Nancy sat on his shoulder and nagged him. *If you think she's beautiful, tell her.* Reason sat on his other shoulder. Guess who he trusted more. Sorry, Nancy.

Although he recognized his growing attraction to Cisney's genuineness, her affection for his family, her playfulness, and her good heart, did he really want to start something with her?

He could picture it. If he told her how nice she looked, she'd think he was interested and, say, she responded agreeably. Then he'd start calling her, and they'd date, and in the end, he'd take a job in Charlotte, and they'd be in a long-distance relationship exactly as he'd been in with Dana. Only the direction he drove would change. Experience told him that nothing could be dumber than repeating a disastrous scene with a different leading lady.

He drew his gaze back to the stage. The music and the dancing were good.

Cisney was mesmerized, her gaze following the waltzing couples. At least this evening, she could focus on something other than Jason.

Her hands were loosely folded over her little flat purse in her lap. Her fingers were long like Dana's, but stronger looking, as if they had the energy to play "Flight of the Bumblebee." While they'd looked at the photo album, he'd noticed her nail polish was feminine and pretty, not brash like Nancy's.

LeCrone, eyes on the stage.

❦

The musical's waltz tune whirled in Cisney's head while Nick inched the car from the crowded parking lot. The polka had been silly fun yesterday, but to waltz in the arms of a handsome man had to be one of Webster's definitions of romance. Funny, how the more she knew Nick, the more he fit the handsome man.

He looked over at her. "Want to go for ice cream?"

A dark suit and a flowing red dress begged for a dance floor, but the little town of Cornelius probably lacked a place to go dancing.

"Ice cream sounds good."

Nick ushered her into the ice cream parlor minutes before closing. They sat in his car in the parking lot and worked on their treats.

Cisney savored her rich cappucino-blend. "Does Nancy live with your parents full time?"

"Yep." He wrapped his napkin around his vanilla cone.

"Does she have a man in her life?" Nancy hadn't mentioned a love-interest during their shopping trip. She seemed to focus on her brother's love life. Well, in the LeCrone family, who didn't?

"She corresponds with a soldier in Afghanistan she met in the young adult Sunday school class a couple of weeks before he shipped out. They've been writing for about six months."

"I hope things work out for them. I know she thinks a lot of her big brother."

"You know that, huh?"

"Yes. And I hate to criticize you, but…"

He chuckled. "But you will, anyway."

She turned in her seat to face him and tucked one foot under her. Time to draw one of those delightful laughs from him, one where his dimple deepened. "I was shocked to hear this about you, Nick."

"Oh, I'm sure you were." He licked his sugar cone in several spots, keeping ice cream from running down its sides.

Let him play indifference, but inside that head of

his, he had to be wondering what Nancy revealed about him. How long could she drag out the suspense?

She planted her spoon in her frozen dessert and placed the cup on the dash. "I'm talking a serious flaw in your character, Nick."

He cocked his eyebrow toward her. "You mean, that I wouldn't let her drive my car after she got her license?"

"Interesting." She pronounced the word as if she were a lawyer responding to a hostile witness. "But no, that's not the act that has tainted your character."

"Then spill it, before you bust a gasket."

She tapped his arm. "Look at me, Nick."

He shifted his brown eyes to gaze into hers. Her heart flipped. *Focus on the prize, girl.*

She contrived a frown. "Why didn't you make one tray of oatmeal cookies without raisins for your dear little sister, before you put raisins into the rest of the cookie dough for your own self-pleasure?"

His laughter thrilled her. She had her prize. Relishing his dimple, she grinned and snatched her ice cream from the dash.

"I'll defend myself on that case." He cleared the cone of drips with his napkin. "At first, I made oatmeal cookies without raisins. Each batch was for a week's worth of after-school snacks for Nancy and me. But too often I came home from high school to find Nancy and her junior high buddies had polished them off. So, to protect my snacks, I loaded the cookies with the one thing I knew she wouldn't touch. So you see, Miss Smarty-pants, her character flaw reaped her consequences."

She laughed. He played a great straight man for these silly routines.

Cisney scooped up a spoonful of ice cream. "The music and the dancing were enchanting tonight." Enchanting sounded corny, but didn't it go well with the idea of a charming prince and a tower princess? "Thank you for inviting me."

"My pleasure." He stopped working on his vanilla cone, and regarded her. "You look...beau-beautiful."

Had Nick just stuttered? His voice sounded as if a vanilla bean had lodged in his vocal cords. Nick didn't stutter, and Nick didn't give personal compliments. Each pump of her heart stretched its lining to the limit. What was going on?

She dipped her head. "Thank you. You look handsome in the suit. Uh, your ice cream is dripping onto your hand."

He wiped his hand with his napkin and licked the source of the trickle.

They worked on their frozen delights in silence.

She'd pay her whole fishbowl of pennies back home to know what was going on in his head. Well, asking cost nothing, right? "What are you thinking about?"

He popped the tail of his cone into his mouth and wiped his lips with his napkin. "I told you, my love life is off limits."

"You were thinking about your love life?" Of course he was. His lunch date with Dana had to stir up old feelings. Her princess balloon deflated.

"No. I was thinking about how state workers install mile markers."

She punched his arm. "Be serious. What were you really thinking about?"

"Will I have to ask you to get in line behind Mom to sign a privacy agreement?"

She rolled her eyes.

"I told you what I aspired to in my youth," he said. "It's your turn. What did you always want to be?"

No way would she let him change the subject. "I wanted to be a princess who danced with the other handsome prince at Cinderella's ball."

"You're serious?"

"No, but I'm seriously intrigued to know what goes on in an actuary's mind when he's not calculating risk."

"Oh, but I was calculating risk. And I think it's significant."

ॐ✺

Nick held the car trash bag while Cisney stuffed her paper cup inside. She cocked her head, her dark hair falling away from her face and revealing a dangly gold earring. Her arched eyebrow confirmed she was waiting for him to expound on his love-life thoughts.

Somewhere between Richmond and Cornelius an alien had snatched his body. By the hour, it was taking over more and more of him. It spewed words he'd never allowed outside his skull. The creature, not Cisney, brought up his love life tonight. How could he blame her for latching onto the subject? The beast messed with his speech. Since when couldn't he get the word beautiful out of his mouth? Why had the word bumbled forth, anyway?

And now the alien ignored his resolve to avoid getting involved with Cisney. Between periods of feeling guilty through no fault of his own, he enjoyed every moment in her company.

He needed to regain control of his body. His mind.

And his heart.

He fired up the engine. "If we leave now we can get in on the Chinese checkers tournament."

Cisney turned her head toward the window, her heavy exhalation fogging the glass.

Let her huff. She'd thank him later for silencing the alien. She didn't need to know he was glad Dana had found a man she wanted to marry. That he'd learned one person with a penchant to plan out everything, like himself, was enough for one couple. And Cisney didn't need to know he was drawn to her, that she had awakened his lighter side, a refreshing experience.

Reason assured him he could appreciate Cisney's qualities without entangling himself. He had career decisions to make without complicating his life with Cisney Baldwin.

He turned into a curve, and the vehicle rode rougher and rougher.

Great. A flat tire.

⤜⤛

The dashboard lights facilitated Cisney in observing Nick's face as he pulled off the road. If a flat tire had happened to Jason, he'd have blown several blood vessels, and her eardrums. How would Nick handle the frustration?

His hands resting on the steering wheel, Nick turned to her. "I guess we won't be playing Chinese checkers tonight." Standing outside his open door, he removed his suit jacket, laid it over the back seat, and then reached in and turned on the flashers. "This won't take long." He closed the door.

Trees lined both sides of the road. At least someone entering the curve would see their flashing lights.

Nick's reaction to the flat seemed to come from a man who had God's perspective on many things—except maybe on his family's fondness for her. And communicating information. But if she had to share a flat tire with someone, she'd want it to be with Nick.

She got out and walked around to the back of the car. Nick had rolled his white shirtsleeves up to his elbows.

"Stay inside where it's warm." He extracted the spare from the trunk. The upright tire bounced an inch when it hit the pavement.

"You need me to hold the flashlight."

"I can manage."

"That's ridiculous. I'm not a helpless woman. I can hold a flashlight."

"Then get my jacket and put it on."

She grabbed his coat and returned, wrapping it around her shoulders and breathing in his scent. He handed her the flashlight, and she crouched beside him.

No matter what Daddy thought, Nick LeCrone looked like a man, emitted a masculine scent like a red-blooded male, and changed a tire like a member of a race car pit crew.

After installing the spare, Nick wiped his greasy hands on a rag from the trunk. She took one last stealthy sniff of his jacket's cologne-scented lapel. The coat would be too obvious to leave on "by accident" as she climbed stairs to her room. Pity. His jacket, wrapped around a princess in her tower room, would make a divine coverlet for blissful sleep. She slipped it from her shoulders and held it out to Nick.

Only a porch light and the window lamp in the front room lit the LeCrones' house. Nick's prediction that they'd miss the Chinese checkers tournament proved correct. They strolled up the sidewalk, and he let them in.

Her purse. She didn't have it.

"I think—I hope—I left my purse in your car," she whispered.

"I'll get it."

She followed him to the door. "It's a black clutch purse. It may have fallen between the seats."

After she closed the door, she waltzed into the front room, blew a kiss toward the Steinway, and turned off the window lamp. The evening had been fairytale perfect, even with the flat tire. She hummed softly and waltzed around the room lit by a nightlight and the glow of the porch lights seeping through the front windows. *One-two-three. Sidestep the chair-two-three. One-two-three. Miss the love seat-two-three. One-two-Nick!*

Nick's dark form stood in the wide doorway, only the white rims of his cuffs and his collar obvious in the dim light. He slipped her slim purse into his jacket pocket and raised his arms from his sides, one arm bent slightly. She stepped into his arms, her hand slipping into his warm grip. He pressed his other hand against her back, and then took a graceful stride forward, launching them into a slow waltz. A serenade played in her head while her red skirt billowed about her legs.

They glided between the front room and the foyer, her heart beat adjusting to the three-quarter rhythm. *One-two-three. One-two-three.* Each time Nick's face aligned with the nightlight, its glow revealed his gaze on her. If this was a dream, may she never, ever, wake up.

They swirled into the foyer, and an upstairs door opened. Nick brought her to a stop, her back against the banister. They froze in the waltz embrace, his face inches from hers. The bathroom door closed.

Breathless, she looked into his shadowed face, her heart pounding.

He dipped his head closer to hers, his lips a paper-thin gap from hers.

She closed her eyes, her lips tingling. *Go ahead, Nick. Kiss me. You are the godly man I have waited for my whole life.*

The toilet flushed. The bathroom door opened and a soft tread above led to the creaks of a door opening, and then closing.

They remained immobile.

His vanilla-scented breath tickled her lips. Was he waiting for her to close the gap? A gentle softness pressed her lips, lingered a delicious moment, and then moved away.

She opened her eyes.

"Wow," she whispered.

"Oops," he whispered back.

"Where did you learn to waltz like that?" Waltz? Didn't she mean kiss?

He drew his head back. "Do you really want to know?"

"Yes." If it would keep her in his embrace a little longer.

He spoke softly. "One summer, Mom couldn't pick Nancy and me up after our swim practices at the club, so she made us stay for ballroom dancing lessons.

Probably the reason I wanted to raise Siberian huskies in Alaska."

She bit her lip to stifle a giggle. He drew her away from the banister and spun her out. "I guess we'd better go up, huh?"

Was he calculating risk again? Oh, well, his kiss could keep sweet dreams dancing in her head all night.

From Nick's pocket, the marimba played.

11

Nick stood in the foyer at the bottom of the stairs. Cisney's red dress swished from side to side as she hurried up the first flight, her cell to her ear.

The incoming call had broken the spell. Thankfully. He'd nearly drowned in those huge eyes of hers. But that was the alien's plan. He, Nick, was back in control.

She'd gone before he'd had a chance to tell her about being gone a few hours tomorrow, but Mom would take care of her while he pursued Option B.

He removed his coat, slung it over his shoulder, and shuffled up the stairs. He had some serious praying to do. Option A. Option B. Dana. Cisney. Whom he'd just kissed.

When he nearly reached the landing, Grandpa emerged from his room and plodded toward the bathroom. At the door, he flipped on the light and turned to Nick.

Nick paused on the top step. "I hope we didn't wake you."

"No. Grandma did that when she got up. Late night, huh?"

"We had a flat tire."

"Uh, huh." Grandpa crooked a finger for him to come near.

He stepped closer. "No josh, Grandpa, we had a flat."

"Well, Honest Abe, you thinking about starting something with Cisney, or are you thinking of patching things up with Dana?"

"Does the whole house know about Dana?"

Grandpa gave him an are-you-kidding-me look.

"It's my business, Grandpa." Dana's involvement in Option A would remain his business for a while longer. He wasn't far enough along in his career decision to disclose his interviews and get the family excited about having him live nearby. Things might not turn out that way.

"Sure it's your business. But your grandpa wants to save you some heartache, if he can. Promise me you'll think about three things as you drift off to sleep tonight."

"I'll try."

Grandpa raised three fingers. "What circumstances God has put before you in your love life. And which door the Lord is closing." Grandpa dropped his hand and turned toward the bathroom.

"You said three things."

Grandpa faced him. "Ask yourself, 'Which lovely lady do I find myself laughing with more.'"

"OK, Grandpa. I'll pray on it."

"Good. Just so you know, I'm praying, too." Grandpa took a step toward the bathroom, and then stopped. "And Nick?"

"Yeah."

"You better wipe off the lipstick so you don't get it on your pillow and send your mother into a tizzy when she changes the sheets."

Nick grinned sheepishly and wiped his lips with the back of his hand. "We did have a flat tire."

In bed, Nick locked his hands behind his head.

Thank You, Lord, for confirming today that You planned a different husband for Dana. Please bless her marriage. Guide me now about whether we're to work together.

He focused on the ceiling fan barely visible in the dark room. *Lord, is Cisney a hurting woman You put in my path to comfort, or is she something more? She makes me feel out of control—taken over by an alien.*

Was he blaming an alien for kissing Cisney? No. He'd been front and center when he'd lost his battle with temptation.

Life with Cisney wouldn't be easy. *Lord, she's disorderly, fanciful, headstrong, smart, beautiful, gracious, kind, knows You, and...she makes me laugh.* Could he ask God for no more long-distance relationships, or should he trust Him to work things out His way?

❧❦

Cisney lay across her bed, relating her evening to Angela. All, except the kiss. That was private and hers to enjoy.

"Your voice sounds different," Angela said. "Like you're a wound up music box. I hope you'll be all right when the music winds down to a stop."

Cisney rolled onto her back. "Nick's really a wonderful man."

"So, he's Mr. Communicator, now?"

He'd been cryptic tonight when she'd asked him about his thoughts. The connection between his love life and calculating risk was vague at best. But he had kissed her. Wasn't that loud and clear communication for someone like Nick? "He's improving."

"Good. I wish I could say the same for Jason."

The music box stopped, and she scrambled to a

sitting position. How could she have forgotten Jason had called and hung up? "Jason's not talking? What does that mean?"

"He's been in a mood all day. After he put Candy Sue in ski school he spent the morning skiing by himself."

So that was her name? Candy Sue? Amazing no one had said her name until now. And she'd never wanted to ask.

Maybe his mood had something to do with why he'd tried to contact her. "Jason called me earlier this evening, but he hung up before my cell went to voicemail."

"Ah. That's an interesting end to his sulking day."

Why'd she hope Jason and Candy Sue were not on the outs?

"Did Jason and CS have a spat?" Her replacement's name sounded too syrupy sweet to put her tongue around.

"I don't know. I noticed he didn't give her the usual peck on the lips before she fell sunny side up in the snow at the T-bar. Of course, that may have been attributed more to his disposition than to her."

"So you don't know why he called me?"

"I haven't a clue—wait a minute. I saw him on his cell on the deck this morning. His body language said he was ready to mow down any kid on a snowboard who got in his way on the slopes."

That sounded like Jason when things didn't go his way.

"Was his face beet red?"

"Yeah, sort of like your dad's gets when the Redskins are losing."

"That, red, huh."

"Yes. Do you think his upsetting phone conversation had something to do with his call to you?"

"I hope not." That's all she needed. An angry ex-boyfriend calling her. One who'd given a drunk a fat lip for getting too close to her. "Jason could have called me for something as benign as information. My brother used to be a ski instructor there in his free-spirit days before Daddy put his foot down. Maybe Jason called DJ for a list of his favorite restaurants and couldn't reach him, so he called me."

"Then his call had nothing to do with you. Believe me, he wasn't ticked off over getting restaurant recommendations. Jason seems the kind of guy who steamrolls over obstacles for what he wants, and whatever he wanted, he wasn't getting."

And he dropped what he didn't want like a used tissue. What kind of person dumped his girlfriend over the phone?

Angela let out a sigh. "Tonight, Tom and I decided against going to dinner with the group. We chose to soothe our muscles in the hot tub and eat two family-sized bags of chips. So, I don't know how things stand with Jason and CS now."

Only Cisney's friend would understand substituting initials for the new girlfriend's name. "I hope everything's cool between them, and I don't get any more calls from Jason."

"I can imagine only one reason for him calling you, Cis. He wants you back. What man in his right mind wouldn't?"

Ick.

"The more I think about it, that must be the reason. Would you want him back?"

How could she love Jason a week ago and now feel sick that he might want her back? She held her head in her hand, hoping the nausea would abate.

"Cisney? Are you there?"

"I'm here."

"Tell me, do you want him back? I know you're all goo-goo eyes over Nick tonight, and I was rooting for him, but you have six months invested in Jason. Maybe instead of being a creep, Jason made a big mistake. Maybe his sullenness today was pining over you and had nothing to do with his morning phone call. I could run interference for you."

"No!" That must have been loud enough to blow Angela's eardrum. Cisney toned down her volume. "Sorry. No."

"He can be very charming and pleasant, Cis."

Jason could be amiable and fun, when things went his way. "Truth? I'm glad he's gone."

"Tell me you're not being spiteful because, now that he's regretting his loss, you have the upper hand."

"I have no desire to rub his face in his rejection, or his mistake, or whatever you call it. Anyway, you don't really know if he's regretting anything."

Angela had always considered Jason a great catch. He'd captivated Angela as much as he had Daddy—and her, until now. Enough of Jason.

"Did you ski a black diamond trail yet?"

"Tomorrow. I'm warmed up and ready for it." Angela sucked in a breath. "Oh, I keep meaning to tell you, your fitting for your maid-of-honor dress got changed to Monday."

"That's better than Wednesday, which was cutting it close to the big day." She grabbed her pad of yellow stickies, jotted the change of day, and adhered the note to the bedside table. "Don't break your neck. Besides ruining your wedding and honeymoon in Aruba, I need you and Tom working on the presentation we give to the executive staff in three weeks."

They said their goodbyes.

Cisney sat motionless, her phone still in her hand.

This was weird. Downright bizarre. In so many ways. The biggest? She didn't care to know about Jason's bad days. Or even that he might be having second thoughts. When someone broke up with you, it should be a law they had to obey a restraining order. Why should the dumpee be harassed? She knocked her head against the headboard. What would she say to Jason if he called tomorrow begging her to take him back?

❧

Dressed and ready for the day, Cisney opened the drapes on her tower window, expecting to see Nick reading his Bible by the lake, but the bench was empty. The sun sparkled on the water, mirroring her mood.

What would she and Nick do today? Was he looking forward to a day together as much as she was? Maybe they'd walk to the nearby boat access she'd seen during yesterday's excursion to the mall. Might he hold her hand? That'd be a nice change from him grabbing her hand and dragging her someplace.

She floated down the two sets of stairs. Bacon and coffee aromas beckoned her to the kitchen. Ellie, Roger, Grandma Thelma, and Grandpa looked up from their conversation at the table.

She beamed at them. "Good morning. Sorry, I'm late."

Ellie hopped up. "Perfect timing. The scrambled eggs are hot. Tea or coffee?"

Cisney sat next to Roger and across from Grandpa. "Tea, please." If she ever had a kitchen big enough, she wanted a farm table like this one for casual family meals. So chummy.

"Did you sleep well?" Roger held the platter, while she scooped eggs and bacon onto her plate.

"The best sleep I've had in weeks." Which proved a dreamy kiss trumped phone calls from ex-boyfriends every time.

Cisney eyed the toast and cherry preserves. She'd help whittle down the toast stack as long as the cherry preserves in the glass bowl lasted. Talk about a perfect day: a good night's sleep, time with Nick, and cherry preserves. "Where are Nancy and Nick?"

Ellie poured tea into Cisney's cup. "Nancy is in her classroom putting up new bulletin boards." Her lips tightened. "Nick is taking care of some business, and won't be back until after lunch. I guess he forgot to tell you."

A tingling crawled up Cisney's throat, the familiar warning sign that she might vomit at any moment. Yesterday, business meant Dana. Why would it mean anything different today? But he'd kissed her. That meant something, didn't it?

Or had he meant his oops, following her wow, after their kiss? She'd thought he'd been kidding. Blood drained from her head. Right after his oops, he'd called it a night.

She dropped her hand below the table and pressed her queasy stomach. Nick had ended the night because he knew the kiss was a mistake. How could she have misread him? Easy. He had the communication skills of a Neanderthal, and she had the outlook of a fairy princess.

"Are you all right, Cisney?"

She raised her head. Grandpa looked concerned. "I'm fine." *Take in oxygen, Cisney. And smile.* She flashed a smile around the table and busied herself with her napkin, sucking in as much air as she could without making a sound or puckering her lips. It was working. The prickling sensation in her throat abated.

She stared at her eggs. The tingle returned, stronger. She had to get out of there.

"Dad and I are going to the hardware store this morning," Roger said to Ellie. "Can we pick up anything while we're out?"

"Yes. A head of lettuce. Are you going to get the motor running on the pontoon?"

"We thought we'd try."

Ellie's eyes brightened. "Good. We can all go out on the lake this afternoon. Take a picnic."

Say something, Cisney. "That would be fun." *Eat.* She couldn't bear the eggs. She took a small bite of her toast, the cherry preserves now too sweet.

Her phone played the marimba. Her chance to escape. "Would you excuse me? I think I'd better get this."

They nodded. She hurried from the room and answered the call.

Before she could say hello, the familiar voice spoke. "Cisney."

Jason. Oh, no, not now. Should she tell him she'd call him later? *Lord, guide me.* "Could you hold a moment?"

She had to calm down. She climbed the first flight of stairs. Did God want them back together? Was that why Nick's kiss was a mistake? Why couldn't she remember the good times with Jason? Any happy memory would do. One to spark her heart in his direction.

Cisney sat on the top step and took in a calming breath. *You are my strength, Lord.* "OK. I can talk now."

"That was a dirty thing to do."

She startled. "I'm sorry. I was at breakfast with my friend's family. I didn't think you'd want to share our conversation with them."

"No, not that." He sounded as if he spoke to a rebellious child. "What you did yesterday."

She rested her elbow on her thigh and dropped her forehead into her hand. So far, this did not sound like a reformed Jason wanting her back. "Tell me what you think I did yesterday that was so dirty."

Before he could answer, she sat erect. Was this his jealousy talking? Had Angela told him about her feelings for Nick? Feelings Nick did not return?

"I don't appreciate you siccing your dad on me."

"I didn't sic—Daddy called you?"

"Yes. From the airport in Hamburg. That was a low blow."

"Jason, I did not ask Daddy to call you. I emphatically told him not to intervene." At least she'd meant to sound emphatic. How could Daddy do that to her? When would he learn he wasn't God?

"You need to rein him in. It's over. We'd never work."

He meant she'd never work for him. What was so unappealing about her that she didn't work for men?

"I'm not saying I want you back, Jason, but would you explain to me why you don't think we would work?"

His tone ratcheted down. "Really?"

"Yes. Really."

"OK. But remember you asked." He took in a breath. "You're disorganized. I can picture what our house would look like. You challenge my decisions all the time. Your time is all planned up—you work late, you prepare for Sunday school and church stuff, you give kids piano lessons, and make dates with Angela and the girls. With my career, I need someone available at a moment's notice to be at my side for business dinners, or to entertain in a neat house with good food."

Maybe she should've left his reasons for dumping her to her imagination. Trying not to be herself around Jason hadn't worked. Who she was had seeped through her efforts. But in all fairness, she gave only one child piano lessons. Jason was always exaggerating. And she didn't challenge all his decisions. More like he challenged most of hers. She had hostess skills. She could make napkins into birds of paradise. And she needed time out with friends. Being with Jason was exhausting.

"You there?"

"Yes." It all made sense now. "You're right, Jason. We are not good for each other. Thanks for having the courage to break it off."

Silence.

"Jason, I am not being smug. I mean it. God planned different people for us. I pray you find the right woman for you. And I am truly sorry Daddy called you."

"No problem." He sounded tentative, as if he thought she might be baiting him. "So, you're good on everything?"

Other than the fact that his assessment of her still stung, and the man she'd waited for all her life was rekindling a flame with a smart, beautiful, and probably highly organized woman, she was just peachy. "I'm fine. Goodbye, Jason."

She set her phone next to her on the top step, raised her face, and closed her eyes. *Thank you, Lord, for letting me see why Your decision was right about Jason. You didn't let me down. But Nick, Lord? Why'd You let me fall for him?*

The marimba played. Daddy. She heaved a sigh, buried the tongue-lashing he deserved for calling Jason, and answered her cell.

"Cisney. It's Mom. Daddy's had a heart attack."

12

The consulting firm's project director motioned for Nick to take a seat in his office's sitting area. Nick chose the sofa, and John sat in the chair on the other side of the coffee table. They popped the tops on the soft drinks John had bought them from the machines on the first floor.

As they had weaved through the cubicles to reach John's office, Nick had seen no one working during the holiday. For that, Option B earned a point. Nick doubted Option B could top the job he'd interviewed for yesterday, but he'd listen.

They did away with the small talk, and then John fingered one of several self-adhesive notes on his legal pad.

Cisney would like this guy. Nick curbed a smile.

John took a sip from his can and set it on the coffee table. "Even before hearing the headhunter's glowing rundown of your qualifications, your reputation preceded you, Nick. And I plan to move you to Charlotte with our offer. I know the headhunter told you we were interviewing you for the valuation position, but I think I've got a job far more challenging to propose to you."

Option B was looking up. "I'd like to hear about it."

"Health insurance companies need help in getting better assumptions for their five-year financial forecasts in representing the value of hospital negotiated contracts."

Nick chuckled.

"Our negotiators are very territorial and secretive. I know they need to prevent proposed rates from leaking to competing hospitals, but we have to drag estimates from them that are soft, at best, for the overall worth of our hospital contracts." John leaned forward. "We have a unique idea to aid health actuaries in analyzing pending hospital agreements before their negotiators lock into potentially risky multiple-year contracts. The bonus to getting actuaries involved in negotiations with hospitals is that they can capture the information they need to feed their forecasts models." He picked up his soft drink can and sat back. "What do you think so far, Nick?"

"Tell me more."

John filled Nick in on the details. Option B came from behind and took Option A by a length for the challenge he wanted. Seemed as if God had taken care of his concern about working with Dana. Some things needed no mulling over. He accepted the job.

On the way to his car, Nick checked his watch. The interview had lasted about an hour compared to yesterday's two. All the better to get back to his family and the woman who kept creeping into his thoughts, even during his career-changing interview.

❧❧

Ellie pulled onto Interstate 77, heading toward Charlotte.

Cisney interlaced her hands in her lap to stop them from shaking. "Thank you for taking me to the airport, Ellie. I wish I didn't have to ruin your holiday."

Ellie patted Cisney's arm. "You aren't ruining anything. I'm glad I can help. Thelma will let the men know what's happened when they come home."

"I can't believe my father had a heart attack. He's as strong as a bull. He avoids fat, and he exercises. Could a full day of flights home after little sleep stress a healthy heart?"

Compassion filled Ellie's eyes. "You said he's stable?"

"Yes. Mom said he's scheduled for more tests, but he seems to be resting. The doctor assured her that Daddy's treatment starting within an hour of his first pains is good."

Cisney's lips trembled and tears threatened to flow. She pretended to look out the passenger window. Ellie shouldn't have to deal with her falling apart.

Cisney's reflection in the glass--the woman returning her tearful gaze—looked how she felt. Faded. As if she barely existed in physical form. As if an incomprehensible dimension of time held her captive. How could Daddy, at age fifty-four, suffer a heart attack? He was too solid, too in control. No heart attack could take down the man of iron. Maybe the diagnosis was wrong. Doctors made mistakes all the time.

"May I pray for your father?" Ellie's voice seemed distant.

Pray? That's what she should be doing. But every time she tried, her mind drifted to images of Daddy dying. She swallowed. Where was her strength to pray?

Cisney turned to Ellie. "Yes, of course. Please. I can't seem to stay focused long enough to pray. I wish I could."

Ellie glanced her way. "Don't feel guilty. Just keep trying. God hears your groans." Ellie kept her gaze on the road. "Father, You are sovereign. You know all things and are all-powerful. You are in control. You know what is best for each of us. We pray You heal Cisney's father. Let this be a time he draws close to You and depends on You. Please provide peace and comfort to Cisney and her family. We ask these things in Jesus's name. Amen."

Like a vibrating recliner, Cisney's body buzzed for a brief moment midway through Ellie's prayer. Then she calmed. She laid her hand on Ellie's arm. "Thank you, Ellie. Those were the words I needed to hear."

Ellie smiled. "I pray about God's control often. If you haven't already noticed, I fall into the temptation of worrying."

What had that little buzz been all about? "I'm clueless at the moment, but I know God is saying something to me through your prayer." If only she could remember what words Ellie had spoken the moment she'd felt the quickening.

Ellie gave her hand a squeeze, and then focused on her driving, as if she were giving Cisney the time to think. Did Nick know what a gem his mother was?

Lord, I know You're trying to tell me something. What had she felt before Ellie's prayer, besides total confusion? No doubt, there. Fear. Why had Daddy's heart attack threatened her wellbeing?

She thought back over the years. Had there ever been a time Daddy had been absent, physically or mentally, in her decision-making process? She'd always depended on his wisdom. Even when she'd thought he was wrong, she always ended up doing what he wanted. Right down to the men she loved.

Now that she thought about it, Jason and earlier boyfriends were so much like Daddy. No surprise. Didn't a daughter always measure men she dated against her father's character, his stature, and his passion? She'd measured them, all right, and then accepted them as almost as good as Daddy. Who could compare to Daddy?

Let this be a time he draws close to You and depends on You. That was it! The part of Ellie's prayer that niggled her. As far as she knew, Daddy depended on no one. Yet a glitch in his flesh-and-blood heart proved he was a weak human, after all. He didn't sit on the left hand of God. Did she need to see Daddy as fallible more than he did? Why did that revelation hurt so badly? To witness that the mistakes made by her king on her pedestal were as foolish as her own?

Let this be a time he draws close to You and depends on You. Could Daddy humble himself to depend on God?

Lord, please help my father see Your truth, and help me embrace it.

Cisney's tears flowed. She held up her hand. "Don't panic, Ellie. These are a-ha tears."

Ellie looked uncertain. She whipped a tissue from the box on the console and handed it to Cisney.

Cisney wiped her face. "Honest. My father is, let's say, a headstrong man, and I have spent my life trying to please him. Like you inferred in your prayer, he is no match for our sovereign Lord. God wins hands down. I want to love Daddy for many more years on this earth, but I don't have to try to please both God and him—or please every boyfriend who earns Daddy's approval." She dabbed the tissue under each eye. "I'm sad and scared for him, but free at the same time...you know? Free from the pressure. Free to love the person God sends my way."

Ellie gave Cisney's hand a squeeze. "Good for you." She bit her lip. "In your new freedom, could my son be in the running?"

Cisney laughed and applied a second tissue to her wet face. "I think your son has given his heart to someone else." A twinge of sadness dampened her tone.

Ellie frowned, and her contorted face most likely had nothing to do with the slow truck she changed lanes to pass. "I don't know what's going on with Nick and Dana. He's not offering up any information. When I think of the pain he went through after their breakup, and what he could suffer again if he's not careful, I wonder if God forgot to pump intelligence into one section of his brain."

"Your son is a good man, Ellie. Nick is kind and caring." She hesitated until Ellie glanced her way. "Maybe a little light on his communication skills."

Ellie chuckled. "He's like his father, but don't let that bother you if you do love him. His father proved trainable. You saw how Roger told me he was going to the hardware store and asked if I needed anything. Thirty years ago, Roger would have gone off to the hardware store without thinking to tell me, and then wonder why I was upset when I thought he'd been kidnapped. And then, of course, I'd have to make a separate trip for the lettuce." She smiled. "And another thing. Men like Roger and Nick may seldom compliment you when you look nice, but they will never tell you when you don't."

Cisney's heart squished like a poked sponge. Even though he'd almost choked on his words, Nick had already told her she looked beautiful.

The navigational system talked more frequently as they neared the airport.

How was Mom holding up? How had she coped all these years? Had she spent her married life trying to please Daddy, too? Cisney had always thought Mom functioned like a normal mother. Took pictures, kissed boo-boos, drove her to piano lessons, and made sure she was involved in church. But she'd never thought about Mom's marriage having unique struggles. A mother-daughter conversation was well overdue.

Ellie parked in the loading zone outside the terminal. They got out, and the two of them wrestled the suitcase Cisney brought with her from the trunk.

They embraced for a long moment.

"I'll be praying for all of you," Ellie said into Cisney's hair.

"Thank you for everything. I'm glad I've gotten to know you and your family. You were what I needed this weekend."

They separated, and Cisney rolled her suitcase toward the terminal. At the glass doors, she turned and waved. "Don't let Nick forget to bring my other suitcase."

Ellie lifted her hand in farewell. "Ask Nick about the swans."

Cisney cocked her head. "The swans?"

Ellie nodded and climbed into her sedan.

❧❦

As soon as Nick parked in the driveway, the garage door opened on Mom's side. His gaze shot to the rearview mirror. Behind him, still in the street, Mom waited in her car. Alone. Where was Cisney?

He backed out, let Mom drive into the garage, and then returned to the driveway. He collected his suit jacket and got out of the car. "Cisney too wrapped up in her Amish book to go shopping with you?"

Mom joined him outside, gave him an arched-eyebrow look, and headed for the front steps. "I didn't go shopping." At the stairs, she turned to face him. "Cisney's father had a heart attack. I took her to the airport."

A battering ram struck his stomach. "Is he all right?"

She climbed the steps. "He was stable when we left for the airport. She promised me she'd text you when she knows more." She sounded ticked off.

He planted his fists on his hips. "Mom. Stop. Talk to me. You seem angry with me."

She sat on the top step, and he sat beside her.

"I'm not angry with you. More like miffed. You should have been here for Cisney."

"How is she?" How much more could Cisney take, with Jason breaking her heart, and then hanging out with her friends? And now her dad having a heart attack?

"She's brave. Dear. Sweet."

He wished he'd been here. There he went, feeling guilty again. How was he to know Cisney's dad would have a heart attack while he was gone? Mom's appraising gaze suggested she had more bones that needed picking. "OK. What's the real reason you're...miffed...with me?"

"All your secretiveness about business and Dana."

He took her hand. "I can clear that up for you now."

"I'd like that, Mr. Smarty-pants."

"Monday morning I'm calling my boss with my two-weeks notice. I've taken a job with a consulting firm in Charlotte."

She pulled her fingers from his and planted her hands against her cheeks, her eyes widening. "Oh, Nick, you're coming home."

"Yep. I'll come down next weekend to look for an apartment in Charlotte."

Her smile lit up her face. "Having you nearby will be wonderful, honey." Her expressions sobered. "What does a career change have to do with Dana?"

"There you go again, worrying. Dana set up a lunch interview for me with the senior partner at the consulting firm where she works. But I accepted the offer from my interview today at a different firm."

She hugged him. "I'm so excited." She held him at arm's length. "You and Dana are...?"

"Friends. She's engaged."

Mom beamed. Then she put a finger to her lips and her expression slumped. "Oh..."

"What?"

She eyed him as if she were trying to decide whether she should voice her concern.

"What, Mom?"

She raised her eyebrows. "See how frustrating it is when you don't know what's going on."

"I didn't want to tell you anything about the interviews, because I didn't want you, Dad, and the rest of the family to be disappointed if things didn't pan out."

"But disappointment would have been better than all of us thinking things that aren't true."

Thinking untrue things had to do with their choices, not his, but he wouldn't make that point. "So what's your sudden concern over my new job?"

"Not over the job...I'm afraid Cisney thinks you and Dana are back together."

Zoe M. McCarthy

13

Near Daddy's hospital bed, Cisney peered over Mom's shoulder. "Hi, Daddy."

Daddy's eyes fluttered open, and he gave them a weak smile.

Never in her life, even when he had the flu, had Cisney seen him look like this—feeble and vulnerable. Her heart sagged, and she wrapped her arms around her unsettled stomach.

OK. So now, after revelations on the way to the airport, she knew her reaction to Daddy's helplessness stemmed from her misplaced allegiance all these years, letting Daddy rule her aspirations instead of God. But the knowledge didn't stop her fear, disappointment, and, if she was honest, disgust, from plunging forth. She squelched the urge to throw out an excuse and leave the room.

"What time is it?" His voice sounded scratchy. "What day?"

Mom squeezed his hand. "It's still Saturday. Six in the evening."

His lids at half-mast, he shifted his gaze to Cisney. "You made it."

"I've been here for two hours, Daddy." Why'd she need to defend herself, make herself look good in his eyes? Old ways died slowly, but how long would it take hers to croak? She refused to go back inside Daddy's birdcage. Couldn't she just love him with no umbilical cords attached? *Please, Lord, help me rise above these unwanted feelings and be a loving—better— daughter.*

"Good news, honey," Mom said. "The doctor said your heart attack was the least serious type." She turned her head to face Cisney. "What did he call it, again?"

"Unstable angina."

He gave a weak nod and closed his eyes.

"Honey, Cisney and I are going to get some dinner and call DJ again. We'll be back in about an hour."

His nod barely moved his head.

In the corridor, Mom put her arm around Cisney's shoulders. "I think he's more tired from all the tests than from the heart attack."

That sounded reasonable. The tension in Cisney's shoulder muscles lessened.

Mom looked almost as worn out as Daddy. She needed support, too. "The doctor seemed pleased with Daddy's test results so far."

Mom smiled and led the way to the elevators. "Shall we eat here in the cafeteria?"

"You probably haven't recuperated from your overseas flight. Don't you want to eat out, and then go home for some rest? I'll come back and stay with Daddy."

"No. The doctor said the first twenty-four hours are most critical. I want to stay until he's made it through that time."

"OK. Then let's eat here."

The cafeteria was closed.

While they decided what to do, Mom called DJ and Cisney texted Nick. *Diagnosis unstable angina. Least dangerous attack. Dad sleeping. Thanks for your family's hospitality, kindness.*

Nick would be glad he could listen to his seventies

doo-wop songs in peace going home tomorrow. Just a hunch, though. The trip would seem longer without their silly banter. Would he stop for a shake halfway home? She typed another text. *Make sure you stop for a milkshake tomorrow.* Her fingers hovered over Send. Keeping up their friendship would make things harder in the long run. She held down the delete key. *Move on, Cisney.*

Their contacts made, they decided on snacks from the vending machine. Chips and candy bars. Comfort food. They sat on a nearby bench and held hands while Mom asked the blessing.

Cisney's phone bleeped an incoming text.

Mom opened her bag of chips. "Go ahead and check your text."

She retrieved her cell from her handbag. *Sorry about your dad. Wish I'd been here. Praying. Deliver suitcase Sun. evening?*

She focused on *Wish I'd been here.* He didn't have to say that, and the uncommunicative Nick never would have. There she went again, reading what she wanted into his words, spinning her fantasies. As her friend, he'd merely wished he'd been there to help.

Deliver suitcase Sun. evening?

Her gaze drifted to a dent in the vending machine. She could see him tomorrow with a few taps of her fingers. But he could bring her suitcase to work on Monday. If Daddy was doing well, she'd need to go into the office for a few hours and work on the presentation with her staff. Delegate some tasks. She directed her thoughts back to *Wish I'd been here.*

"I see your little smile."

Her gaze flashed to Mom's as if she'd been caught with sinful thoughts. "The co-worker I spent

Thanksgiving with responded to my message about Daddy. I promised his mother I'd let him know about Daddy's condition."

"His, him?" Mom's tired eyes sparkled light.

"Yes. Nick. He's an actuary."

"Is there something you're not telling Daddy and me?" Her eyes softened. "Daddy told me about Jason."

Mom wasn't like Angela, someone she could dump her highs and lows on.

Daddy would expect Cisney to be strong. If she gushed to Mom about Nick, Daddy might hear about it, and the news might do damage to his ailing heart. "No, he's just a co-worker."

The spark left Mom's eyes as she extracted another chip from her bag.

Nice. Her holding back had lopped off the last bit of Mom's hope. "I do like him a lot, though."

Mom looked up, the sparkle returning. Her thin smile encouraged Cisney to go on.

"I don't know if you're familiar with actuaries, but they have a reputation for being extreme analytics, weird, and anti-social. Nick isn't so extreme, but he's nothing like Jason—"

"Good." Mom said the word emphatically.

Cisney's jaw dropped. Her eyes widened as realization hit. She spoke slowly. "You don't like Jason."

"Not much."

"I thought you'd love him. He's so much like Daddy."

"Cisney, I would miss your dad terribly if he was to die. He's my best friend. But you don't like everything about Angela, do you?"

Cisney shook her head. It irked her that Angela

rambled on in meetings.

Mom hesitated then spoke. "Like most young women, I thought I could change the things about your dad I didn't like, so I let him bully me into marrying him. Then I let him browbeat me into forcing his name on DJ. He wasn't honoring a family name. He was putting his stamp on his son." She looked down toward her lap and smiled. "I liked the name Peter Cameron." Her gaze returned to Cisney. "I was glad when your brother later insisted on DJ, instead of your dad's choice of Don Jr."

Big revelation. Mom had opinions. About Daddy. Did she want to hear more of this? It wasn't as if she could cover her ears and utter la-la-la until Mom stopped.

Mom's gaze drifted toward the end of the antiseptic hall. "Your dad and I had some rough first years." She took a chip from the bag and held it.

Cisney stared at the suspended chip. Daddy's heart attack was unlocking tongues right and left today. Hers. Ellie's. Mom's.

Mom went on. "I came to the Lord about that time, and made a choice to love my husband with the Lord's help. And I do love him. Do you understand what I'm getting at?"

Cisney lifted her gaze to Mom's. She did want to hear more. Being an ear for Mom was important, and for her own healing, she needed to listen. "I think so."

"Cisney, I haven't been the best mother to you, but I've watched you and hoped and prayed you'd be all right. I was afraid to upset the apple cart, but now I think it's more important to be honest. So, I'm going to tell you what I see, and maybe you can pray about it. It might help you in some way."

Cisney dropped a chip back into her bag. She searched Mom's eyes. Was Mom going to tell her what was wrong with her character? Hearing her flaws from Jason was bad enough. But from Mom?

Mom took Cisney's now trembling hand in hers. "I'm going to say this as simply as I can." She hesitated. "Daddy raised you to be like him and to marry someone like him. He can't have both. And I've watched you struggle with this dichotomy for too long. You've worked so hard trying to be like him and at the same time do what pleases him. Do you honestly think Daddy could be married to Daddy?" She tugged her lips into a thin smile and rolled her eyes.

Daddy marrying Daddy? An analogy for disaster.

Mom tapped Cisney's hand with her finger. "The good news is that you didn't turn out like him, as planned. And my prayer is that you will marry for love, Cisney. That you find a Christian man whom you choose for all the right reasons God has stored in your heart." She scrunched her chip bag and dropped it into the trash receptacle next to the bench. "I'm truly sorry I didn't speak up sooner."

"Mom, stop berating yourself. You gave me what I needed most. An introduction to Jesus."

Mom's smile untapped Cisney's emotions. Could she spit out what she wanted to say without bawling? She swallowed hard. "I think the Lord planned this whole holiday, Mom." Her voice quavered. "I think Jesus has been working in all our hearts, even Daddy's."

"I'm praying that's so." Mom reached up and brushed Cisney's bangs from her forehead. Her hand froze. "How did you get that awful bruise?"

❧❧

Cisney unlocked the door to her apartment, dragged herself inside, and plopped her keys onto the kitchen counter. If she felt like this, how did Mom feel at age fifty-three?

Scrunched in hospital waiting room chairs, they'd gotten only snippets of sleep through the night. This Sunday had been the longest she could remember, even without church on the schedule. At least, they all could breathe easier.

Daddy looked better and had garnered some orneriness.

The kitchen clock read minutes before six. Every muscle, except her stomach muscles, which growled for food, begged her to forget cooking. She dropped two frozen slices of whole wheat bread into the toaster.

What would Mom eat? She'd ordered Cisney home, promising to leave Daddy's bedside soon. Who was she fooling? Soon meant eight-thirty, when visiting hours were over.

Cisney spread peanut butter and jelly on the toast and replayed this morning's coup. When Daddy mentioned Jason, she'd kissed his forehead, looked him in the eyes, and said, "I believe it's time I run my own love life, Daddy." His injured look stung, and she'd almost caved and hired him as her lifetime matchmaker and manager, but when he saw she wasn't budging, he'd chuckled and said, "That's my girl."

She pumped her arm. "Yes!" Why hadn't she respectfully put her foot down a long time ago? Sometimes a bully needed to see his victim's backbone, before he changed his attitude and became a supportive friend. Like Robin Hood and Little John. Would Daddy become her Little John? There she went again, spinning her fairytales.

She climbed, groaning, onto a bar stool and chomped a bite from her sandwich. Could she have missed an incoming text from Nick responding to hers about the delivery of her suitcase? She checked. No.

Hadn't she learned anything? Why had she given him the option to bring it by tonight or to work tomorrow without typing RSVP at the end of her text? Not knowing what to expect kept her wondering and wishing. So unproductive. Not that she intended to produce anything tonight, beyond taking a shower and going to bed.

Her caller ID showed a missed call from Angela. She selected Call Back.

Angela answered after the first ring. "Hey, Cisney! We're back. Tom just dropped me off."

"Good trip?"

"I made it down a black diamond. Mostly on my backside, but my challenge belt has another notch. How about you?"

"I'm OK, but Daddy had a heart attack yesterday morning."

Angela sucked in a breath. "Oh, Cis, I'm so sorry."

She filled Angela in on the diagnosis, the prognosis, and the prescribed treatment.

"If you can't make the fitting tomorrow, I understand," Angela said.

"I wouldn't miss it."

"Well, Jason's chumminess with CS today showed I was wrong about Jason wanting you back. So, how's Nick?"

"He saw his old flame twice this weekend. I think

that says volumes, don't you?" Why, on her own, without Daddy interfering, did she finally find a forever man, and he had decided to pursue the woman who'd broken his heart? Was she supposed to learn something from that?

"How rude of him."

"He invited me to spend Thanksgiving with his family, not to fall in love with me."

"You must have it bad for him. You're defending him."

She'd shot up prayers every time she thought about Nick, asking God to remove her feelings for him, but so far they remained like leeches having a feast on her heart. "So, was there a reason other than chitchat for your call earlier?"

"Yes. Remember how much you owe me for filling in for you on your last presentation when you had the flu?"

Oh, no. What did Angela want to spring on her on the longest day of her life? "Let me warn you. I'm exhausted and not in the mood for blind dates, or fishing your engagement ring out of the drain again."

"What I'm asking is a breeze compared to those."

"OK. Let's hear it." She licked peanut butter from her finger.

"Tom won't dance the tango for our bride-and-groom dance unless the bridesmaids and groomsmen tango with us. Would you please, please come to tango lessons Wednesday night?"

"You're kidding, right?"

"I thought you enjoyed waltzing the other night. Pretty please."

"Who have you paired me up with?"

"Because of your height, we put you with Tom's

younger brother, Hunter."

"That kid? Will I still walk like an upright primate when he gets done with my toes?"

"You're such a sport. Thank you, thank you."

The bleep of a text sounded. "Gotta go, Angela."

Cisney read the text from Nick. *Entering Richmond. Want your suitcase?*

She appraised the appearance of her apartment, and then keyed: *Sure.*

∂∾⬗

Nick lugged Cisney's suitcase up to the second floor and rang her doorbell. The way she wore her feelings on her face, even when she tried to hide them, he'd soon know how her dad fared.

She drew her door open. For a split second, she looked as tired as he felt, but when her eyes took him in, fatigue fell from her face like a no longer needed mask. "Hello. Come in. You can leave my suitcase inside the door."

Her cheerful welcome surged new energy into his brain cells and muscles. He placed her suitcase against the wall, shoved his hands into his back pockets, and scanned her apartment. A smattering of self-adhesive notes adorned her refrigerator door, a stack of sheet music rested on her piano, and another stack of magazines sat on her black coffee table, but otherwise her home surroundings were nothing like her messy office desk. Nice artwork on the walls.

"How's your dad?"

"His color is really good compared to yesterday. He's made it through the most critical hours."

"I'll let my family know the good news. They're all

praying."

"Thanks. It was such a pleasure to get to know your family."

"Believe me; they felt the same about you." He put his hand on the doorknob. "Well, I'll be heading home."

Mom would be disappointed he hadn't prepared a speech about Dana's engagement and her role in his job interviews. But on the drive up, he'd decided it was only fair to hold off announcing his new job to co-workers until he'd talked to his boss. Tomorrow was soon enough to fill Cisney in on all the job developments, his decisions, and which way his love life leaned.

"Have you eaten?" she asked.

"No, but I'll grab something on the way home."

She swept her hand toward the kitchen. "Please, join me for a bite."

"That's OK. I don't want to put you out."

"You won't. In fact, you don't want to miss what I'm having for dinner."

What kind of home-cooked meal did Cisney make for herself? His curiosity got the best of him, along with his sudden craving to enjoy time with her. "All right. If you don't have to cook extra for me. Thanks."

"I have to cook a little."

"OK. I'm intrigued. What dish won't I want to miss?"

"Peanut butter and jelly on whole wheat bread defrosted in the toaster."

He laughed. "I don't know if I've ever eaten whole wheat bread on purpose."

"My brand is the best." She led him to the kitchen. "Sit at the bar while I slave over the hot toaster." She put two slices of frozen bread in the machine and checked the use-by-date on the milk carton. "Milk or water?"

"Milk." Nick regarded the peanut butter and jelly jars on the counter. They weren't brands he recognized.

"One natural peanut butter and jelly on whole wheat coming up." Flourishing the plate, she set it before him. With equal flare, she snatched a napkin from the pineapple napkin holder, handed it to him, and joined him at the bar with their glasses of milk.

He took a bite. "Not bad."

"See, natural is good."

"I wasn't raving how good it is. It's just not bad."

"It grows on you." She took a bite of her partially eaten sandwich. "So, did you stop for a milkshake at the halfway point on the way home?"

"Nope."

"I understand. It wouldn't have been the same by yourself."

"True."

Her smile said she liked his answer. Someday, he'd confess her company was the exotic flavor that spiced up a vanilla shake.

She sipped her milk. "Tomorrow, I need your numbers for our presentation—"

He put his finger to her lips. "I don't talk business on my days off, and until midnight I'm still on holiday."

She backed her head away from him. "And yet, you spent two mornings while at your parents' house, taking care of business."

She was quick. Now he'd ended up exactly where he didn't want to go in the conversation. He took a bite of his sandwich. "That was different."

She swiveled her chair to face him. "How?"

He grabbed hold of the back of her chair and turned her toward the bar. "Eat."

Her frown brought wrinkles to her forehead. She picked up her sandwich and her pearl ring caught the kitchen light.

"You're still wearing your ring on your left hand."

She swallowed. "Don't you change the subject, Nick LeCrone."

Time to get out of the hot water. He scooted his barstool back, stood, and grabbed his sandwich. "Thank you, for your hospitality."

Her eyes widened. "You're leaving?"

He took her chin in his free hand, dragged his gaze from her lips, and focused on her eyes. "Yes, I am." He returned his gaze to her mouth. Oh, how he'd like to kiss those sweet lips. "I'll see myself out."

❧❧

Cisney gaped, her gaze following Nick until the door clicked shut. What was that all about? She hadn't had a chance to ask him about the swans.

He was withholding something big. Were he and Dana engaged? But if he thought of Cisney as a friend, why did her rock-solid woman's intuition tell her that Nick was a breath away from kissing her before he left? If he was two-timing Dana, forgiving him would be a long time coming.

14

Nick entered Joe's office and settled into a chair facing his boss.

"What's up, Nick?"

"I'm taking a job in Charlotte in two weeks."

Joe stared at him, his eyes round and magnified by his glasses.

The passing seconds said a lot. Joe was clueless that nobody related to him. On several occasions, Nick had told Joe flat out he didn't have time to tag along to Joe's meetings to field the big guns' questions. But Nick's displeasure had never sunk into Joe's thought process that Nick was tired of carrying the chief actuary's job.

The guy broke out in a sweat and ran his hand over his face. "Uh, have you told anyone else yet?"

"No."

A knock sounded on the door, and Phil stuck his head in. "Nick, I've got a guy from the Bureau who wants to talk to you. Seems he doesn't think I'm knowledgeable enough to answer his questions."

A call Joe should handle. Nick cleared his throat. "I've got a meeting with Cisney Baldwin in fifteen minutes, but I'll call him after that."

Joe broke in. "Get me his number, Phil, and I'll, uh, call him after we're, uh, done figuring things out here." He put a finger to his lips as if he were in deep thought. "And I, uh, think...I think you, Phil, can, um, meet with Cisney. Never too late to learn new things. We'll probably need some extra time in here. Why don't you, ah, get up to speed on her project. Right?"

Phil, still planted halfway in the door, frowned. His wheels were probably spinning to figure out what was going on. No easy task when he had to work his way through the way Joe put things.

Joe shooed his hand toward Phil. "Nick and I have serious items to, uh, talk about."

Phil shrugged, backed out, and closed the door.

Joe labored through weak reasons why Nick should stay. When Nick hadn't rescinded his resignation, Joe pressed his lips together, looked away, and tapped his chin. "Well, ah, this puts a chink in the mortar. Of course, ah, I need to talk to...to Jeff, before you say anything to anyone."

What good would it do for Joe to talk to the CEO? If Nick hadn't been worth promoting or paying appropriately before now, why should he be worth more because he said he was leaving? That would confirm they'd been using him. Jeff hadn't taken his chance to do the right thing since it was obvious Joe couldn't handle the job. It was time to move on.

"No fire, right, in holding off a day, right? Could be there's a misunderstanding. Can you do that for me, Nick?" Another of Joe's strange way of putting things. But the guy looked miserable.

"OK. I'll wait until tomorrow to tell my team." He'd have to wait until then to come clean with Cisney, too. Not the best scenario. He glanced at Joe's wall clock. He cringed to think how she'd react in two minutes when, instead of him, Phil walked into her office.

Nick left Joe speed-dialing Jeff. He headed for the

elevators to save Phil and reassure Cisney that Julie was working on her numbers.

"Nick!"

He pushed the elevator button and turned toward the voice coming from one end of the corridor.

Angela from Marketing waved her arms as if she were at the top of stadium bleachers trying to get a pitcher's attention. "I sent you an email! Read it! It's a surprise!"

He held up a hand in recognition and turned to the open elevator.

"Nick!"

He spun in the other direction.

Julie hurried toward him. "Dick Grant from the Bureau is running out of patience. He just called again and says he needs to talk to you now, or he's taking his problem up the ladder."

꙳

Cisney sat with her hands folded on her desk, her proposal draft printed and copied, missing only the statistics Nick would provide. No hunting for yellow stickies today. Nick would see she could be organized.

Phil Dupree knocked on her open door, his red tufts of hair touching the top of the doorframe. If his bony arms and legs weren't so awkward, he'd have tempted many basketball coaches.

"Hey, Phil, what can I do for you?"

"I'm taking Nick's place today."

"What?"

"I'm to get up to speed on your project." Phil looked confused.

"Why?"

Nick refused to talk to her on his time off, and now he refused to meet with her on company time? Was this personal?

"I don't know why, but that's what I was told to do."

Heat rose from her toes to the top of her head. "We have a presentation to the executive committee in less than three weeks. We haven't got time to get anyone up to speed. I need solid numbers today to present preliminaries to the Marketing VPs tomorrow. Do you have those numbers? I need them before noon."

Phil's spine jerked to attention.

How could Nick let her down like this? She'd promised Mom she'd be at the hospital by one.

Phil's thumb clicked his ballpoint pen on and off a few times. "Nick told me last week he wanted me to crunch some numbers for a new project, but we're meeting later today about it."

She rolled her eyes. Actuaries communicated among themselves no better than they did with the outside world. "So, I'm supposed to bring you up to date on three months of work in an hour so that you can crunch numbers for me by noon?"

"I'm sorry, Cisney, I'm in the dark as much as you are."

His hangdog expression punctured her anger. Phil wasn't at fault. She softened her tone. "I'm sorry, too. For barking at you. Come in and sit." She punched the button assigned to Nick on her office phone. Take complaints to the director, not to the subordinate, who is just trying to do his job.

Nick's secretary picked up. "Hey, Cisney."

"Hi, Linda. Is Nick in?"

"Uh…" A pause. "His calendar says he's there with you."

She glanced at Phil, who shifted in his chair. "If the man sitting in front of me is Nick, something has turned his brown eyes blue." She winked at Phil.

"I don't know where he's gotten off to, Cisney. I know the Bureau of Insurance has stirred up some trouble around here. May I take a message, or put you into his voicemail?"

Cisney didn't trust her attitude in leaving Nick a message. "Please tell him to call me as soon as he's available."

She returned the receiver to its base and collected the prepared documents from her paper-covered desk. "How about we do this." She placed Nick's copy of the presentation in front of Phil. "Why don't you take this and look it over. The executive summary will give you a good idea what we're proposing, and the pages with blanks waiting for specific statistics will show you what we need."

She sat back in her chair. "Except for Eric's staff meeting at ten, I'll be here for the next couple of hours. Call me if you have any questions, and if I'm not here, call Angela."

Phil slid the document onto his notebook. He replaced a couple of yellow stickies he'd disturbed back on her pile. "I'll do what I can."

She planted a smile on her face until Phil disappeared, and then dropped it. Her computer clock said she had forty-five minutes before Eric's meeting. Unless Phil was a genius, no way would she have solid numbers by then.

What was going on? It sounded as if she'd lost her project actuary. What was she going to say to her boss when it was her turn to share the progress on her project? *Do you have a pink slip with my name on it?*

࿎

Nick ended the call with the placated government man and went in search of Phil. The actuarial analyst had ducked his head into Nick's office twice while he was on the phone.

As Nick passed Linda's desk outside his office, she shifted her phone receiver to her other ear and waved a While-You-Were-Out slip at him. Probably the same one she'd tried to hand him on his way into his office to take the Bureau guy's call. This time he accepted the note.

Cisney had called requesting an ASAP response. It seemed everyone wanted him today. He made the last turn in the labyrinth of cubicles toward Phil's. The analyst wasn't at his desk. No wonder. The Bureau call had taken over two hours. Phil would be at lunch. He headed for Cisney's office, calling her on his cell.

࿎

Cisney and Mom carried their salads in plastic containers into Dad's room. Cisney's phone played the marimba from her handbag where she'd left it on the corner chair.

"Get that," Daddy said. "Now. It's gone off three times since you left for the cafeteria."

Cisney strode to the chair. "I forgot to put it on vibrate. Sorry."

"Just answer it. It's driving me crazy."

She set her salad on the chair and grabbed her

192

handbag. Whoever from work was trying to reach her could wait. She'd delayed leaving work, hoping to hear from Nick, and now she had less than an hour with Daddy before she had to leave for her bridesmaid's dress fitting. And Phil knew to call Angela with questions.

She reached inside her handbag and thumbed the switch to vibrate. "So, I hear you had more tests today," she said, dragging the chair closer to the bed, next to Mom's chair.

"Yeah." He thrust his spoon into the gelatin cup and dropped them on his tray. "Why do they always feed this stuff to people in hospitals?" He pointed at her handbag. "You should check your voicemails. I don't want your company going under because you're having lunch—a late lunch—with your old man. It was the same ringtone as for the person who already called you twice."

Maybe not. If she did nothing else tonight, she'd assign ringtones to her most popular callers.

"You've got unique ringtones for work, friends, family, and so on, right?"

What was he, clairvoyant? She took in a forkful of lettuce and pretended to read the nutrition information on her bottled fruit drink. "I haven't gotten around to ringtones yet."

"No? I told you to use that feature. Makes it so much easier to know which calls to ignore."

"I'll do it as soon as I get a chance."

"What color is your bridesmaid dress?" Mom asked.

Cisney gave Mom a thank-you smile. "Hot pink."

"You'll look great in hot pink."

"Angela went with long skirts that flow. It's

actually a decent dress, as bridesmaid dresses go. I'm going for a fitting as soon as I leave here."

Mom's eyes lit up, and she chuckled. "I remember one bridesmaid dress I had to wear. It was tan. Can you believe that?"

"Must have been a paranoid bride trying to make sure her bridesmaids didn't outshine her."

Daddy sighed. "Can we talk about something else?"

Cisney turned the conversation to his tests, and he lavished them with details and opinions. Commanding men were such big babies when they were sick. She cooed or wagged her head during his monologue as she contemplated how to make up lost work time. So much for being a better daughter.

❧

Cisney let herself into her apartment. Which should she do first? Get a soda, make a salad, crash on the sofa and sleep, or check her voicemails?

Or multitask. She listened to the first of Nick's three voicemails and grabbed a diet orange from the refrigerator. *I'm on my way to your office.* She'd already left for the hospital.

She tapped his next message. *I have your numbers. All looks good. Sorry about the mix up with Phil. I had Julie working on your project.* She could make a lucrative business out of training actuaries to communicate with each other.

Cisney took a sip of her soda and listened to Nick's last message. *Talked to Phil. He said you're out of the office. I hope your dad is progressing well. I gave Angela the numbers. I need to talk to you.* He needed to talk to a lot of people, including his secretary. At least, she didn't have to worry about the progress of the proposal.

Food. She needed sustenance. She'd call Nick after she had something to eat.

She vacuumed in half a sleeve of crackers while creating her salad. Her phone buzzed on the counter. With hypoglycemic shakes, she fumbled for it. Angela. Her shoulders sagged. She was in no shape to solve work problems tonight. What else would Angela be calling about? Oh, yeah. Her bridesmaid dress. That would be fitting.

Cisney, you're slaphappy.

She answered. "The fitting went fine. Tell me the proposal is in good shape."

"Hello to you, too. The proposal is in good shape. We can start work on the presentation tomorrow."

Cisney shot up a big thank-you to the Lord. "Sorry. I'm sooo tired. But the fitting did go well. Nice dress."

Angela heaved a sigh. "I'm not calling about the presentation, or your dress."

❧◈❧

Nick unlocked the church and set up a classroom for ten people. He placed his Bible and facilitator's manual on the table and headed down the hall to the drink machine. He'd miss this church. In his five years leading the beginner's Bible study, men and women turned to Christ or developed deeper relationships with God. Some were leaders in the church now. Definitely all had become disciples.

He fed coins into the machine. God's timing

couldn't have been better. His current class would wrap up the night before the moving van arrived to pack up his apartment.

He'd look for apartments north of Charlotte. That way he could return to his childhood church. Mom and Dad would like that.

A loud noise sounded from the direction of the church library. He snagged the can from the dispensing well and went to investigate.

Pastor Doug knelt on the hardwood floor, stacking old hardback books. Next to him rested a box whose bottom had given way and another that was in good shape.

"Need some help?"

Pastor Doug looked up and grinned sheepishly. "Yes. Your pastor is preparing to haul these books to the dumpster under the cover of darkness."

Nick picked up a book and flipped through its yellowed pages. "I can see why."

"Why do people bring all the books from their deceased great aunts' attics and donate them to our library? The writing is archaic, the print is small and crowded, and the pages are tea-colored. Tell me, would you pull one of these books off the shelf?"

"Unlikely." Would this be a bad time to tell Pastor Doug he'd be leaving? It might be his only chance. "I have some good news and some bad news."

"Share the good news first." The older man pitched books into the sturdier box.

Nick tossed in more. "I've accepted a new job."

Pastor Doug straightened from his task and shook Nick's hand. "Congratulations!"

"The bad news is the current beginner's study I lead is my last. I'm relocating to Charlotte."

The clergymen's smile sagged. "Our great loss." He placed his hand on Nick's shoulder. "I mean that, Nick. You've been a faithful servant here. Does this change have something to do with you moving closer to a lovely young lady in Charlotte?"

Nick ran his hand over the back of his neck. "That ended."

Pastor Doug's eyebrows shot up. "Oh. I'm sorry, I didn't know."

"It happened while you lay flat on your back after your surgery. You had enough problems of your own without hearing about mine. She's happily engaged, now."

"And how are you?" The pastor searched Nick's eyes.

"I'm good, but I do have a question for you."

Pastor Doug closed the box and set it on a chair. "Fire away."

"What do you do when you feel as if you're falling for someone so different from the women you've enjoyed in the past?"

"Ah. A new—"

"I mean, she's unsystematic, she's intense, she's a red SUV to my beige sedan. On the other hand, she's energy personified. She's talented, creative, and funny. I don't know whether I want to take care of her or tape her mouth shut—" He shook his head. "I didn't mean to rattle on like that." He raked his hand through his hair. "See what she does to me?"

Pastor Doug chuckled. "I love a good romance. It's all about the conflict."

"Maybe from the outside looking in, but I don't want to pursue something that's all wrong for us. We're both on the rebound, and I really don't want another long-distance relationship, traveling between Richmond and Charlotte."

"There's only one thing to do."

"Yeah, I know. I have been."

"May we do it now?"

"I hoped you would."

Pastor Doug placed his hand on Nick's shoulder and they bowed their heads.

ॐॐ

Cisney switched her phone to her other ear and popped a cherry tomato into her mouth. "So what are you calling about, Angela?"

"Are you sitting down?"

"I'm leaning my elbows on the counter and thinking about crawling up on it to sleep. So you'd better tell me your tidbit before my phone falls from my ear and my head hits the granite."

"The scuttlebutt is that Nick quit his job."

Cisney whipped up to her full height. "What?"

"Maybe it's false gossip. I just wanted to give you a heads-up, in case it's a fact."

Cisney plunked down on a counter stool. Dots rapidly connected. His resignation made sense. "I knew it." She whacked the counter, and then shook her hand until the pain subsided.

"So, he told you?"

"No. But remember, I told you he went out with his ex-girlfriend twice over the holiday?"

"Yeah."

"I bet they made up on Friday and he interviewed on Saturday. He must have had it all planned. And now, there's a good chance she's sporting a diamond again. I had a sneaky feeling last night that he's engaged. My guess is he'll be moving back to the Charlotte area."

"Wow. Who'd have thought Nick the Actuary could be so crafty?"

Crafty didn't describe the half of it. Cisney pushed her salad aside, her appetite gone. Nick had almost kissed her last night. She knew when a man had a kiss in mind, and Nick definitely did. Was the caring man she'd fallen for, sweet Ellie's son, actually a two-timing rat in sheep's fleece?

15

Cisney handed Tom the changes she wanted on the presentation graphs. "Are you ready for your big night Friday?" She forced a smile. Living proof she could be civil to any man whose name wasn't Nick LeCrone.

"Oh, yeah. Been ready for a long time. Angela's my one-and-only."

"Too bad more men don't subscribe to the principle of a one-and-only." That had come out harsh.

Tom did a doubletake.

Yes, she was his boss in woman-scorned clothing.

His eyes wide, Tom backed out of her office, raising the marked-up graphs. "I'll get on these right away."

She grabbed another set of graphs and stared at the top pie chart. Her attitude was the pits. But if one more person stopped by to ask if she'd heard about Nick's resignation, she'd grab her handbag and leave for a vacation as far as her bonus miles would take her.

The company scuttlebutt Nick had created and his unfaithfulness to Dana, almost kissing Cisney after he'd already slipped up and kissed her at the end of their waltz, were only two of the things irritating her.

Daddy was not her Little John. He was back to his old tricks, calling her this morning to tell her about "a single doctor with spirit" he wanted her to meet.

She'd firmly reminded him she no longer needed a

matchmaker.

He'd grumbled and hung up on her. Hung. Up. On. Her.

She should have stood her ground. But no, she'd called him back later and apologized. His acceptance was so soft-spoken she'd almost called the nurses' station to have someone check on him.

A knock on her door jolted her. Nick leaned against the doorjamb. Her stomach bounced off the bottom of her heart. Nick standing at her door was the last thing she needed today. Why hadn't she called her travel agent first thing this morning?

She cast him a cursory smile. "We've got everything we need from Actuarial." She shuffled the graphs. "Thanks." *Please go away.*

"Why didn't you return my calls?"

She anchored her gaze on a bar graph. "Your voicemails told me what I needed to know."

"Maybe you'd be less uptight right now if you'd called me. I said we needed to talk."

She looked up. "I thought we were talking."

"I don't want to have a conversation in here. Take a break, and let's go outside."

Part of her wanted to follow him anywhere, and part of her wanted to slam the door on his nose. *Lord, do I really need to hear how he and Dana have rediscovered their love for each other? Do I really need to listen to his apologies for kissing me under false pretenses?* She didn't have it in her right now to play the understanding friend.

He lifted her coat from the hook behind the door and took a step toward her.

She stood. "OK, OK." She snatched her coat from his hand and marched past him.

Angela stood at the secretary's desk, her blue eyes widening at the sight of Cisney approaching with Nick in tow. Cisney gave Angela her eye-narrowing, lip-tightening look that ordered her friend to zip it.

Angela's lips stretched into a grin.

Yeah, this was amusing. A real blast.

In the elevator, she backed into a corner, crossed her arms over her chest, and scrutinized the dropping digital numbers.

Nick leaned his back against the far wall, his hands resting on the handrail, one loafer crossed over the other. She sensed him studying her.

Lord, if I have to listen to his lousy explanations, please don't let me cry.

At the back entryway, he held the door for her.

She breezed past him and headed for the parking lot. As soon as her feet landed on the blacktop, she turned to him. "All right. I'm listening."

He grasped her elbow and rotated her toward the sea of vehicles. "Let's sit in my car, where it's warm."

She wriggled free. "No. My SUV. I need to be on my turf."

"Suit yourself."

She gritted her teeth. "We can't."

"Why?"

"I didn't bring my keys." Her cheeks burned. This conversation was destined to unravel her. *Lord, settle me down and guide me. I'm ready to behave.*

"I'm parked right here." He led her to his vehicle, two cars into the first row.

He thumbed the unlock button on his key and they climbed inside.

Cisney pulled her coat around her.

"Cisney, look at me."

Tears threatened. Great. If the conversation started with tears ready to spill, she'd be bawling by its end. Maybe she should escape now before she made a complete fool of herself. She looked up.

Nick's gorgeous brown eyes leveled on hers. That, and the nagging thought he'd be in Dana's arms in two weeks, almost broke the dam.

He cleared his throat. So, his calmness was less solid than it had appeared in the elevator. In fact, he looked a little green.

Her heart went limp. Maybe she could be a friend. "It's all right, Nick."

"What's all right?"

"Everything. Sometimes the person we break up with is the one God chose for us."

His brow wrinkled, and then his eyebrows shot up. "You've gone back with Jason?" His voice cracked.

She frowned. "No." Where'd he get that idea? "No, I'm over Jason."

He relaxed a little. "Glad to hear it. So what are you talking about?"

She raised her hands and let them flop to her lap. "I'm trying to communicate with an actuary."

His jaw tightened. "People accuse me of not conveying information, half of which is none of their business. But you know what…?" He jabbed his finger at her. "You're not such a great communicator, yourself."

She gaped at him. What proof did he have for such a rash statement?

He looked toward the window, and then back at her. "You didn't ask me about what to wear for Thanksgiving when you easily could have in our meeting before the holiday, and you didn't call me later. Instead, you packed half your wardrobe.

"You didn't return my calls when I—I the non-communicator—asked you to call me so we could do what? Talk. And another thing, you assume a lot, Cisney. You thought I had a date with Dana the night of the musical because you saw me with Dana earlier. And who knows what you're assuming right now, because I'm totally confused." He punched his window button, cracking the window a couple inches as if to dissipate the steam he'd produced. Then, he leaned his head against the headrest.

Cisney couldn't move. Inside, her heart raced, as if she were about to lose the most important thing in her life. But she didn't have Nick to lose, did she? She spoke softly. "Nick, I'm sorry." She tucked her feet under her and faced him. "I will sit here quietly and listen to everything you want to tell me." Even if her heart bled dry.

He raised his head and searched her eyes as if he disbelieved her.

She gave him her most contrite smile, praying her lips wouldn't tremble.

"All right." He placed his forefinger on the steering wheel. "First, I lined up two interviews over the Thanksgiving weekend because I was ready for a change in my job. One interview happened to be with the consulting firm where Dana works. She arranged to pick me up at Mom and Dad's house for a lunch meeting with her boss." He cocked his head toward her. "Just so you know, Dana is engaged."

Cisney's heart slammed to a stop, switched gears, from fear to hope, and ramped up again. She bit her lip to stifle her apology for misunderstanding his relationship with Dana. She'd agreed. No talking while he had his say.

He tapped his middle finger on the steering wheel next to his forefinger. "And second, I didn't say anything to my family, because I didn't want them to get excited I was moving near home, only for them to be disappointed if I didn't take either job."

She clamped her teeth harder on her lip. He would eventually tell her which job he took, wouldn't he? The Dana job, or the Dana-free job. *Cisney Ann. Mouth shut. The suspense won't kill you.* But it might wound her if her teeth broke skin.

Any second his ring finger would join his others on the steering wheel. Was this going to be a ten-point speech?

He rested his wrist over the steering wheel, abandoning the countdown. "As a courtesy, I wanted to tell Joe I was leaving before I told anyone else in the company. When I met with him, Joe prolonged our discussion and sent Phil to meet with you. Then Joe asked me to hold off telling anyone. Obviously, Phil put two and two together, and the rest is grapevine history. I intended you'd be the second to know, but once I left Joe's office, everything went south."

She felt dumb as a yard gnome. "I'm so sorry—"

He held up his hand. "I'm not finished." He hesitated. "Cisney, when we embarked on our trip, the next to the last thing I was looking for was a woman in my life. All I desired was to find a challenging job closer to home. But the last thing I wanted, and still don't want, is a long-distance relationship."

His sword sliced her heart in two. How much clearer could he be? He wasn't interested in dating her.

He closed his eyes and rubbed his forehead.

Here it came. Third—or was it fourth?—he didn't

relish hurting her. And fifth, she was a nice woman, fine for a stolen kiss, but not worth two five-hour drives per weekend.

He opened his eyes and looked at her. "This is so complicated. I'm a little slow, compared to my family, but I like you a lot." But he didn't want to complicate his new life and his new job. "I took the job I interviewed for on Saturday."

The job without Dana. What difference did that make now?

His gaze rested on the steering wheel, as if he needed one of his long deliberations.

She held her breath. Why couldn't he just hurry and get it over with? What difference did it make whether her heart broke or she passed out from lack of oxygen?

"I'd like to get to know you better..."

She startled. If she'd heard him right, she was guilty of...big...major...wrong assumptions. Again. She raised her hand like a first grader.

He rolled his eyes, but his lips tipped into a smile. "OK. I'm done."

"Would you say that again in different words, to make sure I understood you right?"

"Will you go out with me tonight?"

❧

After work hours, Nick sat at his desk in the quiet of the deserted department. He scrolled through his data files, cleaning up his PC, so after he left, his team wouldn't have to weed out unnecessary documents.

His computer clock said he had an hour before he met Cisney at the hospital. When she'd cried after he'd asked her out, guilt had threatened, until her tear-drenched smile clued him in that her sobbing was a positive reaction. Would he ever master how to react to a woman whose emotions changed faster than the speed of light?

His cell vibrated.

"Hi, Mom."

"Are you packing up your apartment?"

"I'm still at work, tying up loose ends. Have Grandma and Grandpa returned to Charlotte?"

"They left this morning. Did you talk to Cisney?"

"Yes."

"And?"

"We're straight."

"How romantic." He could picture her rolling her eyes.

"I'm taking things slow, Mom."

"I see. Because you have all the time in the world before you move?"

"I'm making progress."

"Really?" Excitement tinged her voice.

"I want to get to know her."

"Well, don't wait till you could write her biography before you let her know how you feel."

"I need to get to know her to know how I feel, right?"

"I suppose so."

"Stop worrying, Mom. I've put my love life in God's hands."

"That's good. But when we turn things over to the Lord, we still must do our part."

He'd throw her a bone. "We're going out tonight."

"Wonderful! How's her father?"

"Cisney said his doctor is discharging him

tomorrow. I'll meet her parents when I pick her up from the hospital."

"Great news. Send Cisney my love, and tell her I'm praying." Her cheery tone suggested she'd pray more about his date than about Cisney's father.

∂∙◦

Cisney rolled another lettuce wrap and doused it with one of the tangy sauce choices. "Are you ready for Daddy to come home?"

Mom thanked the waiter for her hot tea and took a sip. "I think so. I just hope he'll rest a few more days before he starts making business calls."

"I guess, Daddy is Daddy. I doubt he's going to change."

Mom touched her hand. "There's hope, Cisney." Her eyes sparkled. "I left my Bible on his bedside table last night by accident. When I arrived this morning, your dad was reading it."

"Really!" Daddy's heart attack scared him more than she'd thought. "What did he say when you caught him with an open Bible?"

"I had my bookmark in Ephesians, and he'd opened the Bible there. He'd just read…" Mom fished a small Bible from her handbag and found the verse. "'Fathers, do not exasperate your children; instead, bring them up in the training and instruction of the Lord.'"

Cisney's heart pulsed like it had when she was a child and feared she'd made Daddy mad. Yes, she was learning at almost thirty to spread her own wings, but she'd lived in Daddy's nest for a long time. Why did that verse have to be the one giving Mom hope? It rang so personal to their father-daughter relationship. She cringed as she pictured him grousing that God had no business telling him how to raise his children.

She eyed Mom. "What did he say?" She held her breath.

"He wanted to know if I thought he had exasperated you." Mom cocked her head and raised her eyebrows, posing Daddy's question to her.

Of course, he exasperated her. But he also spent time at evening meals teaching her and DJ marketing skills. She used many of Daddy's ideas. But it would have been nice to chitchat about their days more, and be drilled less on the ten best ways to sell your ideas or some other such training. And in Daddy's mind, his way of thinking always trumped hers. That hadn't bothered her so much until everything with Jason.

"Well?" Mom waited for Cisney's answer, holding her teacup suspended between the table and her lips.

"What did you say to him? And why did he mention me, and not DJ?" Mom's answer to Daddy better not have been, "You'll have to ask Cisney," or she'd stay clear of his hospital room tonight.

She felt like Peter must have when Jesus knelt like a slave at Peter's dirty feet. Peter refused to let Jesus, his Master, wash his feet. Likewise, she couldn't bear to see Daddy in an inferior role to herself. Daddy was no Jesus, and right or wrong, exasperating or not, the role reversal embarrassed her.

Mom smiled. "I said you loved him. I told him he could trust God to guide you, that through your faith you were growing more confident of who you are and to Whom you belong. Your dad thought a minute and then said he wished he'd been more supportive of you and DJ going to church."

Wow. Was it possible Daddy could understand that redirecting her allegiance to Jesus would allow Daddy and her to have a richer relationship? This morning's calls came to mind. Could it be that she'd called to apologize for asserting herself after he'd read the verse in Ephesians? Had the verse touched his heart, softening his response to a whisper? *That's OK, honey. I'm sorry I hung up on you.*

Cisney bit her lips together to keep from losing it while the server topped off her iced tea. After the waiter left, she took a sip. "I'm glad Daddy is trying, but I don't know if I can watch him learn humility." Her voice squeaked. "It's been hard seeing him as weak as a baby these last few days."

"Well, you'll have to, since I'm going to the hospital, and I'm your ride for the evening until Nick comes to pick you up."

Cisney chuckled. "I could head off Nick in the parking lot."

Mom narrowed her eyes in mock anger.

"I'm kidding. In my heart, I know Daddy submitting to God is good. It's a chance for him to become twice the man he is." She laid her hand on Mom's arm. "Please pray God gives me new eyes in seeing Daddy."

Especially tonight when Daddy met the actuary of her dreams.

❧❦

Cisney stuck her head inside the hospital room. "Hi, Daddy. We're here." She made room for Mom in the doorway.

Daddy lowered his newspaper and smiled. "Ah,

my girls."

"You're chipper today." Cisney kissed his cheek and sat in a chair near the bed. Mom checked the water in his flower vases.

"Yes. They're going to let me out of here tomorrow."

"I hope you rest at home until you get your strength back," Cisney said.

He wagged his head and pushed his body into a more upright position. "Let's not talk sick stuff." He appraised her. "You look very nice after a long day's work, honey."

Mom pulled a wilted flower from a vase and spoke over her shoulder. "Cisney's going out tonight."

Daddy frowned. "Yeah? When?"

Mom had foiled her plan to keep quiet about the brevity of her visit. In case God was working in baby steps to change Daddy's heart, she'd thought having Nick arrive without Daddy expecting him would limit the time Daddy had to come up with a strategy to scare Nick off.

She checked her watch. "In a half hour."

"Half hour! I've waited all day for your visit, and you're spending a measly thirty minutes with me?"

Mom dropped her collection of drooping flowers in the trashcan. "She has a date."

Daddy beamed. "You and Jason made up."

"Daddy!" He'd have abandoned such hope if he knew his interfering call had ticked Jason off. But she'd never tell him.

Daddy held up his hands. "Sorry." He inhaled and exhaled a slow breath. "OK. So who's your date?"

"His name is Nick LeCrone."

"LeCrone. What kind of name is that?"

Mom leaned close to Daddy and whispered, but not so softly that Cisney couldn't make out the words. "Don, I think you're exasperating Cisney."

He shifted in his bed. "Forget I asked. Why don't you tell me about Nick."

"You'll meet him soon."

"All the better you tell me about him now."

Daddy did his homework before he connected with new clients. But Nick wasn't his client. Yet, wouldn't any normal father want to hear about his daughter's date?

Cisney put her finger to her chin. "Let's see. Nick is kind, smart, fun, caring—"

"OK, he's a nice guy. What does he do for a living?"

The time had come for Daddy's biggest test, if he didn't want to frustrate his daughter. Could he hold his judgment of Nick in check?

"Nick's an actuary. An FSA—a Fellow in the Society of Actuaries."

His face looked as if he'd eaten his least favorite vegetable. He turned a pained look toward Mom. She cocked her eyebrow as if warning him to tread lightly. Daddy sighed and worried a loose thread on his blanket.

"I know a few actuaries. One did well financially. Smart fellow." Daddy nodded as he focused on toying with the thread. "The guy bought his work clothes at the flea market. I'd see him on different days wearing different plaid shirts with the same checkered pants." He kept nodding. "He once told me he had a thousand plaid shirts."

A smile crept across Cisney's face. She knew actuaries whose behaviors were almost as strange, but they were the exceptions in the growing actuarial profession. "I assure you, Daddy, I've never seen Nick wearing checkered pants."

"That's encouraging."

"He's also a faithful Christian."

Daddy's eyes widened slightly. "An actuary, huh?"

Experience told her Daddy meant, "An overt Christian, huh?" OK. So she shouldn't have smiled about the actuary wearing other men's shirts, but to imply Nick was substandard was wrong.

She took a breath. "Daddy, that Nick is a Christian is what I like best about him. To me, that's what makes him wise, honorable, and strong. Nick's not perfect, but he's more of a man than any guy I've ever dated."

Daddy looked up at her, and then his gaze darted away. Not the reaction she'd expected.

Mom's gaze followed Daddy's line of sight.

Cisney whipped her head around.

Nick stood in the doorway, his hands in his pockets.

16

Cisney sat riveted to the chair next to Daddy's bed as heat crept up her neck. Nick was early. At what point in her confession to Daddy about Nick's character had Nick arrived?

Daddy motored the bed to a ninety-degree angle and up to full sitting height. Preparing to do battle with the actuary?

Mom swept shriveled leaves from the bedside table into the trashcan and settled on the end of the bed.

Their perfect-family tableau in place, Cisney made the introductions, and the men shook hands.

Daddy motioned Nick to Mom's chair. "So, Nick, I hear you're an actuary."

Not already. Cisney glowered at Daddy. He ignored her, and crossed his arms over his hospital gown.

In the chair next to her, Nick looked relaxed. How long would that last?

As soon as Nick uttered his yes, Mom jumped in. "Cisney told me you've taken a new job in Charlotte."

Daddy talked over Nick's response. "What? No one told me that. You're moving?"

"In two weeks. I took a job with a consulting firm."

Daddy stared at Cisney as if accusing her of perjury. Then he laughed. "Oh, I see. I wish you the best in your new job, Nick. Charlotte is a great city."

Daddy didn't fool her. He thought he had everything figured out. If Nick was moving out of state, either she and Nick weren't serious, or their interest would eventually dwindle with Nick so far away. Daddy thought he'd still have time to work on her for a better son-in-law.

"Nick's from the Charlotte area, Daddy. His parents live right on Lake Norman, and the views from their house are fantastic."

While he kept his big marketer's smile working, Daddy sent her a puzzled gaze. "How would you know, honey?"

"Nick is the friend I spent Thanksgiving with." Certainly Daddy wouldn't carry this protective father routine any further.

Mom laid her hand on Dad's leg. A warning. "We've traveled by Lake Norman on the interstate. It's huge. Do you fish?"

Nick nodded. "Yes. A favorite pastime of mine."

Daddy was not about to be ignored. "In your job you give a lot of advice on health insurance risks, is that right, Nick?"

"That's my job." Nick smiled at Cisney. Probably recalling how he enjoyed exercising or withholding his actuarial stamp of approval.

"You pull data together, look in the rearview mirror, so to speak, and make recommendations to the VPs, right."

"Yes, more or less. We look at trends in the economy, the industry, the market, and the company. And you're right, we pull data from various sources, and with educated assumptions, model the risks."

"Then from your numbers you make

recommendations." Daddy pronounced the word numbers like it was a dirty word.

"Yes."

Where was Daddy headed? Why didn't a nurse come to give him meds or take his vitals? Nurses and aides were always interrupting them. Why not now, when she'd welcome their intrusion?

"That's very interesting, Nick. Do you ever sit down with the experienced marketing guy or doctor or salesman and find out what his gut tells him recommendations should be? I ask because it seems to me the guy who lives it, breathes it, and has his ear to the ground should be given a lot more credence then some bunch of numbers." Daddy softened the punch with his friendliest grin. "Just saying, you know."

"You're right, Don. Probably twenty-five percent of my day is spent in meetings with company experts or on the phone with outside specialists, picking their brains. Actuaries don't just push data through models. We want to know what's happening in the trends we see. That's when we go to those on the frontline. But we can't dismiss observed trends on someone's gut feel. Yet these people can help explain an unexpected trend and help us decide whether it should be universally applied. Actuaries look to you experts to validate the front view and tell us the changes you see coming down the line that would modify trends in our models."

Daddy opened his mouth, and then closed it.

Mom's slight nods toward her cheered, *He's perfect.*

Cisney bit down on a smile. Daddy had picked a fight, but Nick hadn't stepped into the ring.

Daddy shifted positions and cleared his throat.

"Glad to hear that, Nick. Maybe you can tell me something else. Why is it that so many actuaries, present company excluded, aren't just a little different, but downright weird? I mean, some actuaries I know, I'm surprised the company lets them out of their cubicles. They make a bad name for the profession. Let me tell you about this one actuary I met. Pretty funny."

Cisney slid down in her chair and would have kept on going if the gap between the bed and the floor was greater.

∂∾∽

Nick drew Cisney aside to allow a hospital employee to steer an empty gurney by them in the corridor.

She looked up at him. "I'm sorry some of Daddy's comments were pushy."

"It's OK. Your dad doesn't intimidate me."

"I wonder if you'd say that if he hadn't been restraining himself. His comment about actuaries was out of line, no matter how charming he said it."

"Which comment was that?"

They headed toward the elevators.

"When he tried to infer actuaries' formula-based predictions are less dependable than those of professionals who have cultivated a special intuition through their hard-earned experience—like himself, of course. But I guess, considering actuaries' reputations for oddness, it was better for him to make that dig than asking you to share the weirdest thing you've ever done."

At the elevators, Nick pushed the down button. "His comment is partially valid. Often actuaries are guilty of discounting other professionals' theories, sometimes for good reason, sometimes from arrogance."

She smiled and elbowed his ribcage. "I won't argue with that."

They entered the elevator. She studied him.

"Why are you staring at me like that?"

"What part of my conversation with Daddy did you hear when you arrived?"

"Ah. You're curious to know how embarrassed you should be."

"Something like that."

"You said, 'Nick's not perfect, but he's more of a man than any guy I've ever dated.' See nothing to be embarrassed about. It's just the truth."

"Don't let it go to your head. I'm simply learning to stand up to Daddy."

"You were lying?"

She gave him a withering look. "No."

They stepped off the elevator and walked toward their exit.

Her lips formed a small smile.

"What're you thinking now?" he said.

Her smile transformed into a full grin. "You stood up to Daddy really well. I admire your style. It's like you have nothing to prove. I probably shouldn't tell you what else I was thinking."

"But you will."

"I can show restraint."

"Go ahead. I'm intrigued."

"Better not."

"Suit yourself." He'd give her a count of ten to spill her thought. One, two...

She stopped at the exit. "Well, if you must know, I

couldn't help thinking how Jason always took the opposite viewpoint from Daddy and vice versa. They'd debate like they were vying for the state trophy. Like gladiators, they flexed their muscles and jabbed their spears at each other. I'm sure they both got high on the rush, but I didn't enjoy the display."

"But you were OK watching me in the arena?"

"That's just it. Arguing with you was like Daddy was shadow boxing."

"He probably missed the rush."

"Well, I relished the show. And did you see Mom? She almost clapped after your response to Daddy's story about the weird actuary he'd told us about minutes earlier." Cisney imitated Nick's deep voice. "'You're right. Some actuaries exhibit odd behaviors that put people off and blind them to the solid track records of most actuaries' sound advice.'" She chuckled. "Daddy's face went blank for a split second as if he were determining whether he'd won or lost the point."

Nick opened the door to the outside for her. "He tells a good story."

"And you kept up with every sports comment and question he threw at you. You were awesome."

Tempted as he was to earn hero status in her eyes, he'd forego encouraging the present tack. "I hope you're not expecting me to become your weapon against your father as you stand up to him. That would smack of whittling another notch in your challenge belt."

She halted and looked up him, shocked. Had his comment ended their evening before it started? He shouldn't have said anything, even if he was right.

"I think that's exactly what I was doing. Not the

challenge-belt thing, but in trying to get over seeing him as merely human, I was starting to enjoy watching him squirm. I don't want to go there. I want to honor my father, who has raised me in love, even if he does exasperate me now and then."

They wove their way through parked cars to his car. He couldn't have asked for a better answer. Commuting between Richmond and Charlotte sounded better the more he got to know this woman.

He opened the sedan's passenger door. "Are you ready for something different?"

Would she enjoy what he'd planned for the evening, or would she hightail it back to her father, lauding his assessment of actuaries?

❧⚜❧

Cisney had two questions left in playing Twenty Questions to get Nick to reveal where they were going. She'd ruled out a movie, a play, bowling, indoor putt-putt golf, and going for ice cream.

She could do this. "Is it something you think I've never done before?"

"Yes." He looked over at her. "You better make your last question a good one."

If she couldn't win the game, at least she could elicit his dimple. "We're going to a bar to get drunk?"

He laughed.

A win. Whether he'd agree or not.

Nick looked over at her. "By the way, Mom got your thank-you note. She said that receiving a real snail-mail thank-you card was rare. She told me to tell you she loved it."

"I did learn a few things from my mom."

Nick turned the car into the Chesterfield Towne Center parking lot.

They were going shopping? If he wanted her to help him Christmas shop, she'd gladly assist him, but he should have told her up front, instead of letting her think he could be imaginative.

He parked and sat back. "You're quiet all of a sudden."

"I'm trying to think what we could do here besides shop."

He opened his door. "We're not shopping, but we could if you'd rather."

Anticipation crept back in. "No. Unless you were planning to shop for bungee cords, I'm fine on everything else."

"Good. I have to warn you, though. You may think shopping more exciting." He retrieved a tan leather bag from the backseat.

If he didn't tell her soon, she'd explode. She got out and met him at the back of his car and eyed his bag. What could they be doing that was BYOS—bring-your-own-something? He probably wouldn't tell her if she asked.

They entered the mall through the food court doors. Several tables formed the perimeter of a large square, replacing the normal arrangement of tables. Inside the square, a man with a black beard, dressed in a gray turtleneck, black sports coat, and grey corduroy trousers, leaned against a table. He conversed with a bald man sitting in one of the chairs that lined only the outside edges of the square. Did this have something to do with their evening?

Other men, a few youth, and one woman roamed the area, toting boxes or bags similar to Nick's. People coming into the food court from outdoors and from inside the mall stopped and watched the milling box-and-bag people.

Phil from Actuarial came through the doors and headed toward them, carrying his own black pouch. His eyes widened when he saw her with Nick.

"Hi." Phil stepped aside and grasped the arm of the tiny woman who'd followed him. "Nick, Cisney, this is my wife, Natalie."

Doe-eyed Natalie stuck out her hand to Cisney. "It will be nice to have someone to stand with."

Stand with her to do what? Cisney smiled and shook Natalie's hand. "Nice to meet you, Natalie."

The top of Natalie's head barely reached Phil's armpit. How did they have engaging conversations while they walked together? Maybe that's why Natalie followed Phil in. What was the point of her keeping up with his long-legged strides when they'd have to yell at each other to be heard?

The box-and-bag people moved closer to the tables, pulled out chairs, and unloaded their bags.

Chessmen?

Cisney gasped. This cliché was not happening. Wasn't Nick different from the Phil-type actuaries of the world? She raised her gaze to Nick.

He gave her a sheepish grin. "Welcome to the annual simultaneous chess exhibition, in which our chess club members are pitted against a National Master." He indicated the bearded man caged inside the square.

Wouldn't it take hours and hours for that one man to play all those participants? Where were bungee cords on sale? "How fun."

Nick laughed. "Every muscle in your face says

you're—let's say, fibbing."

Natalie's doe eyes brightened. "It *is* fun. Paul was fourth to the last eliminated last year. I thought I'd pass out holding my breath."

Yeah, sounded as much fun as holding her breath watching trees grow. If she'd known the plan, she'd have worn her orthopedics to stand with Natalie, instead of her high-heeled boots. "Won't the mall close before the master plays all those people?"

The three chuckled.

Nick took Cisney's hand and drew her closer to the square, where plastic checkerboards stuck to the tables like cellophane. He laid his leather bag next to a chessboard. "The master plays all of us at the same time. After we make our first moves, he walks around the square and makes his initial move at each chessboard. We have until he returns to make our next move, unless we take a pass."

"Oh." That sounded better, but they'd still be there a long time while the master thought out each of his...she counted the males and added the one woman...each of his twenty-four moves.

Phil folded his long body into the chair next to Nick and arranged his pieces on his board. Natalie squeezed Phil's shoulder, and then backed to stand a few feet behind his chair.

Still standing, Nick set up his chessboard. He turned from his task and looked at Cisney. "Have you ever played chess?"

"Daddy taught me the basic moves, but he gave up teaching me strategy when I fell asleep a couple of times during games."

Nick straightened. "I guess I blew it. You can wander the mall if you like."

"No. I'll stay."

He pulled out his chair and sat.

Feeling like a traitor for not squeezing his shoulder like a chess groupie, she stepped back to join Natalie.

A heavyset man near the tables signaled the participants to make their first moves. Barely pausing at each board, the master strode around the inside perimeter, playing black chess pieces in a snatch-and-plant manner. The players jotted notes on papers next to their boards. Logging their moves?

"Wow, that was fast," Cisney whispered to Natalie.

"Opening moves are usually a no-brainer, especially for a national master."

Cisney craned her neck to see Nick's next move. He lifted his knight and placed it on a white square.

The senior master completed his second circuit as fast as his first. Maybe the tournament would finish before bunions formed on her toes.

As the master made his rounds, the participants, in various poses of thought, seemed to gravitate closer to their boards. The frequency in which participants slouched, forked their hair, or ran their hands over their faces seemed to reflect how well their games progressed.

Cisney observed Nick. He sat erect, his forearms resting on the table. That was her Risk Man. Cool, calm, and confident.

While stopping at the board of a baby-faced man, the master made his final move, spoke a quiet checkmate, and extended his hand, which the man shook. Two boards over, he repeated the pattern with a youth. Cisney's heart went out to the teen while he bagged his chessmen.

After the master removed a white bishop from Phil's chessboard and moved on to Nick's match, Natalie relaxed her shoulders. The master stopped and studied Nick's board while he pinched and pulled on his beard. Then he picked up a black knight, deposited it on to a square, and stepped to the next game.

Cisney exhaled a breath. Had she really been holding her breath? She leaned to the side and studied Nick's face. Total concentration. *Come on, Risk Man, you can make it through another round.*

Several more participants lost to the master in his next two circuits. Cisney counted fourteen players remaining. Now the master lingered at each board, caressing his beard before playing a piece.

The master approached Nick. Cisney jiggled her leg, bit her lip, and clasped her steepled hands to her chin until the master played a piece and moved on. She checked the spectators on either side. Her nervous behavior, more appropriate for a close basketball game, hadn't seemed to distract them.

The master soon reduced the number of contestants to four: an African-American youth, the woman, Phil, and Nick.

Phil's hands slid through his red hair and clenched his head.

Natalie's shoulders sagged.

Cisney turned to the doe-eyed woman. "What?" she whispered.

Natalie frowned. "Phil's in trouble."

Cisney gave Natalie a sympathetic look. She turned and analyzed Nick's posture. His arms remained resting on the table, but his head bent closer to his board. Was he in trouble?

When the master stood one chessboard away from

Phil's, Natalie's hand groped for Cisney's fingers and gripped them.

Cisney startled, and then squeezed encouragement into the tiny woman's hand.

The master studied Phil's board. He took Phil's queen with his piece and sidestepped to Nick.

Natalie let out a breath.

The master planted his hands on the table, framing Nick's chessboard. A black strand of the master's hair flopped onto his forehead.

Cisney's chest muscles froze, trapping air in her lungs.

Natalie increased the pressure of her grip.

The master's fingers hesitated over his black bishop, plucked it from the board and then replaced Nick's pawn with it. He headed across the square to the woman's board. Nick was safe for another round. Cisney sucked in oxygen and gave Natalie her I-thought-I'd-die look.

They released each other's numb hands and shook out the tingles.

While the master eliminated the woman from the tournament, Phil sat back in his chair, dropping his long arms to hang at his sides.

"Phil knows he's lost," Natalie whispered.

"I'm sorry." She truly was.

The master played a piece at the youth's board and returned to Phil, where he took Phil's pawn with his queen. "Checkmate," he said. He shook Phil's hand and stepped to Nick's board. Phil left his pieces where they lay and examined Nick's game.

Cisney clasped her hands together, her palms sweaty and her heart beating double-time. *Come on, Risk Man. You can make it through another round.*

The master stroked his beard and pondered his next move.

Cisney crossed her fidgeting arms to control them.

Nick and the master each had a king, a rook, and a bishop, but Nick had only one pawn whereas the master had two. Why hadn't she paid more attention when Daddy tried to teach her the game? At least she knew Nick down one pawn didn't bode well. Did Nick have a chance? Obviously, his play was a challenge to Mr. Beard-in-the-Hand.

The master moved his rook and walked over to the youth.

Nick's body remained as still as his white king.

Don't let your enemies get your king, Nick.

The master bent over the youth's game. The young man looked about fourteen. Had Nick played against national masters when he was that young? Probably.

The master captured one of the teen's white chessmen and walked toward Nick, but Nick hadn't played a piece. Would he be disqualified? *Move a man, Nick. You know which one. The one that will keep Mr. Beard-in-the-Hand from checkmating your king.*

Nick remained as immobile as he did during his long deliberations in her office. Would he come up with an attack like he often did against her marketing strategies, or was this the end for Nick? Would he concede the game? Knock his king over? Isn't that what losers did, knock their kings over? *Keep your fingers away from your king, Nick LeCrone. Just move a man. Please.*

Nick retreated his bishop.

"Thank you," Cisney said, exhaling. She clamped her hand over her mouth. Her cheeks burned. Turning full circle, she mouthed apologies to the nearby spectators.

Natalie patted her arm. "It's intense, isn't it," she whispered.

Cisney nodded vigorously.

During her faux pas, the master had made his move and returned to the youth's table. Had she unnerved Nick with her outburst? Would he lose because of her? *Please, Lord, let him forget we even came here together. Give him the power to concentrate.*

The master offered the teen a small smile, his first during the tournament, and shook the youth's hand. His eyes focused on Nick's game as he sauntered back to Nick.

Nick took one of the master's pawns with his bishop. That evened the men's pieces on the board.

The master captured Nick's bishop with his rook.

No, not your bishop!

Nick moved his rook. "Check."

That was more like it. She dabbed her perspiring brow with the back of her hand.

The master moved his king, and Nick captured his opponent's last pawn with his rook.

Why was Nick settling for peons instead of going after the master's big guns?

Her phone played the marimba.

17

Heads snapped toward Cisney as she fumbled for her cell in her handbag and stifled the call.

Nick hadn't twitched, but the master gave her a cold glance.

Even Natalie took a step away.

Cisney stood as still as an ice sculpture in a freezer. Further apologies to her fellow spectators were out of the question. The embarrassment was too much. She'd melt into a pool of water at any moment.

The master took Nick's pawn with his rook. That put Nick down a piece. Thankfully, he couldn't blame her. Her phone had gone off after Nick had made his move. So far, he'd played a valiant game. Would he take the loss as well as he'd accepted the flat tire?

The two men danced their pieces around each other's for several plays. On the master's turn, his finger tapping his bottom lip, he lifted his gaze from the chessboard and appeared to assess his opponent. Then he straightened. "I offer you a draw."

Nick shook the master's outstretched hand.

The spectators and all the other players, who had packed up and crowded in to watch Nick's game, applauded.

A grin on his face, Phil clapped Nick on the back. "That was awesome."

Nick swept his chess pieces into his leather bag and stood. Several people crowded around to shake his hand and offer congratulations.

Cisney accepted a hug from Natalie. Obviously, a draw was considered a very good thing.

Nick shook the hand of the African-American youth, and then turned to Cisney. His smile was apologetic.

She scooted to him. "That was so amazing! No horror film has had me more on the edge of my seat. Make that, on the edge of my boots."

He grinned. "I didn't blow it, then?"

"Are you kidding?" She drew Natalie into a side-arm hug. "I almost passed out holding my breath."

Natalie chuckled. She lifted her hand and placed it on her husband's chest. "You did great, too, honey. You were one of the last three this time—that's moving up a place."

Phil gripped her hand. "Thanks, sweetie." He turned to Cisney. "In my five years in the club, I've never seen anyone beat or tie the master."

Nick shrugged. "I think the master got distracted and slipped up."

Cisney winced. "You have me to thank for that."

Nick looked puzzled. "What do you mean?"

"You know, when I erupted with, 'thank you,' and then my phone went off."

"What 'thank you?' Your phone rang?"

"You didn't hear those sounds in the last few moves?"

"No. You can put your conscience at rest. The master got distracted long before the last few moves."

"Yeah, but you took smooth advantage," Phil said.

Cisney touched Nick's arm. "What would have happened if the master hadn't offered you a draw?"

"We'd have kept playing until the fifty-move rule

took effect."

"But the master recognized there was no way you were going to slip up," Phil said.

Cisney regarded Nick while he and Phil rehashed their games. What would life be like married to Nick, taking their children to watch their daddy's chess tournaments?

❧

At Cisney's apartment complex, Nick accepted her invitation to come inside for a cup of decaf. The hour was late, but he'd stay a few minutes.

Cisney turned the key in the lock. "You'll have to excuse my mess. I'm preparing for the Sunday school class I teach."

"Ah, something we have in common. I lead a Bible study."

They entered, and as she'd promised, white computer paper, construction paper in many hues, books, Bibles, cardboard boxes, lengths of various colored material, pots and pans, toy food, and puppets cluttered the sofa, the coffee table, and the surrounding floor. He wandered over to the colorful chaos while she headed to the kitchen.

"What age do you teach?'

"The fours and fives. This is my first year. I love it. I take it yours is an adult class?"

He lifted a red, blue, and yellow velour-like toucan with an orange plastic beak. It perched on a brown plastic log with a switch on the back. He toggled the switch to the on position. The bird didn't do anything. Battery must be bad. He turned it off and placed it back on the sofa.

Zoe M. McCarthy

He lifted Bibles and checked the versions. "Yes. I'll miss this year's group. They're always prepared and don't wander off on tangents like some groups I've led. We've had a lot of rich discussions."

She turned on the coffee maker, and then joined him in the living area. "Most of the items you see there are to focus the children's learning."

"What's the lesson this Sunday?"

"Mary and Martha." She scooped up the lengths of fabric and draped them over the opposite arm of the sofa, making a place for him to sit. She sat on the corner of the coffee table.

He spread his hands toward her arsenal. "You must need a pickup truck to haul all this stuff to church."

"Good thing I have an SUV, right?"

"How do you use all these things?" He raised a bell and rang it once.

She snatched at it, but he pulled it out of her reach. The bell jangled.

She scowled. "Are you trying to get me evicted?" She reached for the bell.

He held it farther from her and feigned preparation to ring it.

She rolled her eyes. "Did you pick up this immaturity from Tony? Until I saw the pictures of you as a child, I thought you were born an adult. Now, I'm not so sure."

He grinned and set the bell on the coffee table. "OK, how do you use this stuff?"

She raised a pot and a wooden spoon. "All the cooking utensils are for opening play while the parents drop off the children. I'm layering the idea that Martha was busy cooking in the kitchen. I'll make a stone oven

232

out of this box." She indicated the empty laundry softener box. "I'll cut a U-shaped hole in the middle, cover it with brown paper, and then use these markers to draw stones." She uncapped a marker. "Smell."

He didn't trust her. One sniff and he'd come away with a brown blotch on his nose. He took the marker from her and sniffed. "Chocolate."

"Aren't they wonderful?"

She delighted in the weirdest things. A trait that made spending time with her pure pleasure. "Isn't making an oven a lot of work for one lesson."

"Oh, I'll save it. One of the other teachers will use it again, or I will."

"OK. The bell?"

She lifted her palm. "Be patient. I'll use the lengths of material, the Bible clothes, the oven, and some of the wood utensils for role-playing the story." She lifted a corner of the tan cloth. "This will be the dirt floor of Mary and Martha's house."

"Where are the Bible clothes?"

"Right here." She grasped a blue pillowcase from a colorful stack. "See, I cut a bowed hole in the end to pull over a child's head, and cut two barely bowed holes on the sides for their arms. Don't you think it makes a perfect biblical-period sheath? The other short lengths of cloth are for headdresses and cloaks."

"Interesting." What a wise God, designing vibrant and creative people like Cisney to teach the children. He'd never look at a pillowcase in the same way again. He'd be sleeping on potential Bible sheaths.

Cisney went to the kitchen and returned with their mugs of coffee. She gave him one, set hers on the table, and placed her finger on the tip of the bell's handle. "I ring this with gusto when a child correctly answers one of the five or six questions I ask after the story. You wouldn't believe how they listen while I tell the story because they want to make my bell ring. Children this age can answer why questions, as well as the who, what, and where questions." Her enthusiasm was catching.

"I'd like to be in your class."

"Sure. Anytime." She picked up the toucan, her finger on its switch. "This week, we'll teach Toukie the Scripture verse and what it means." She held the bird in front of her midriff. "Toukie, let's see if you can say our verse. 'Seek first His kingdom and His righteousness.' Matthew six, verse thirty-three."

The recorder inside Toukie repeated the verse twice while the bird's wings flapped.

He laughed. Good thing he hadn't said anything dumb when he'd switched on the bird. "Learning in your class has got to be fun."

Cisney smiled and related the activities and materials she'd employ during other periods of the morning.

Nick sat back. "I'm impressed. I have to admit I thought the preschool classes were mostly babysitting. Not that I thought about them much. If all teachers prepared and expected as much as you do from the children, the preschoolers would be teaching their older siblings and parents."

"I hope so. Ever since I saw you reading your Bible by the lake, I've been spending time daily in the Word and praying for creativity to teach the little ones under my charge." She raised the bird. "Teaching Toukie Scripture was one answer."

God had used his quiet time with the Lord to witness to Cisney? Unbelievable. "The fruit you're bearing is a great gift from God, Cisney. You're building a good base for those young children's future Sunday school experiences." He lifted her hand and toyed with her fingers. "Go out with me tomorrow night."

"Because I teach Sunday school?"

He squeezed her hand. "Because you're you." And because he was falling in love with her. At a speed too fast for this actuary.

She beamed, and then her smile faded. "I can't. Tom's adolescent brother and I have to learn the tango for Angela's reception."

"How about Thursday?" Was he pushing her? But days to enjoy her company were running short. "I promise I won't drag you to another chess tournament or a symposium on how fuzzy numbers incorporate uncertainty on parameters and properties."

From the pile of puppets, she selected a large sheep that appeared to be made of real wool. "Aw. I like fuzzy." She grinned. "This is BoSheep."

"Cute."

"I'd love to go out Thursday, but I have the rehearsal and dinner that evening."

And she had the wedding Friday night. That reminded him—Angela had sent him an email Monday inviting him to the wedding. A surprise for Cisney. With everything going on, he'd forgotten to send Angela a reply. But he'd already planned to drive home after work so he could spend Saturday apartment hunting in Charlotte.

There had to be sometime they could get together soon. He mentally scanned his work schedule. "Will lunch on Friday work?"

She wrinkled her nose. "I'm taking Friday off.

Angela's mom has all the bridesmaids scheduled for a day at the beauty salon, after breakfast at the hotel. Our nails will be manicured, our skin defoliated, our hair swept up into sculptured curls, and our faces painted with makeup."

He heaved an inward sigh. Time with her wouldn't fit into their schedules.

Cisney's eyes lit up. "How about this? The rehearsal dinner is at five-thirty at Short Pump Mall." She named a popular pizza place. "I'll pass on dessert and join you at seven-thirty." She indicated a restaurant across from the pizza place.

"Are you sure?"

She nodded.

"Then it's a date." He took a sip of his coffee and placed his mug next to hers. "This has been a great evening. Thanks for being a good sport about the tournament. I'd better go."

"No, you can't leave, yet."

18

Cisney cleared the stack of Bible clothes and several puppets from the sofa. Still perched on his end as if ready to dash off, Nick watched her every move.

Had she scared him? Did he think she was transforming into a brash woman ready to attack him? Good. Keep him guessing.

She settled onto her side of the sofa and faced him. "There's something I want you to do."

His eyes widened slightly. He probably thought she wanted him to kiss her. Which wasn't altogether an unwelcome idea. But this was their first official date. No oops or wows this time. They were supposed to be seeing whether they liked each other enough to warrant kisses later. "Can you guess what you have to do?"

He cocked his head. "Are you going to make me play Twenty Questions?"

"I guess not." He made such a good straight man to her schemes. Jason bulldozed over conversations while they were together and never gave her a chance to be playful. It was so much fun. Better than a notch on her challenge belt. "Your mother told me to ask you something. I haven't had a chance to do so, until now."

His eyes narrowed. "My mother?"

"Yes. Just before she left me at the airport."

"She didn't say anything about this to me."

"Of course not, silly. She told me to ask you." And everyone thought Cisney was so transparent with her feelings.

His tightened lips and serious eyes needed no accompanying words. His expression warned he might shutdown and escape like he had after he delivered her suitcase.

She rested her elbow on the back of the sofa and supported her head with her hand. "So. Tell me about the swans."

He flopped back against the sofa and clamped his hand over his eyes. "For crying out loud." He ran his hand down his face. "Do I have no privacy?"

"Not if you want to arrive home before midnight."

❧❦

Nick shifted to a more comfortable position on the sofa and leveled his gaze on Cisney.

She clutched the talking toucan to her chest.

Why had Mom wanted him to tell the story about the swans? To create a touchy-feely moment that would bond Cisney to him forever?

She slid the switch on the bird. "We're waiting."

The toucan flapped its wings. "We're waiting. We're waiting."

Even if he got up and left now, she'd hound him until he told her. He sighed. "If you put the bird down, I'll tell you about the swans."

"Can I hold BoSheep?"

"Yes, if it doesn't talk or baa or flap its legs."

She set the bird on the floor and drew the sheep into her lap. She said in a high, wavering voice, "We're reeeaady."

"You're pushing it."

"OK. I promise, we'll be good."

If she laughed at the swan story, he'd ring her bell until the neighbors called the police. Or maybe he'd just kiss the breath out of her.

He inhaled and let the air out in a long rush. "When I was fourteen, I was invited to a weekend chess tournament at a conference center in Warrenton. In the orientation before the tournament, the activity director told us how three juvenile trumpeter swans were imprinted to follow an ultralight aircraft the previous fall from the Warrenton center to Maryland's Eastern Shore. The experiment to help the trumpeter swans learn to migrate succeeded. All three returned to their flock in Warrenton the next spring."

"That is so cool." She fanned her face with her hand. "That touches my heart."

Crafty Mom knew Cisney would like his story. Could he stop there? She wouldn't know the difference. Mom might find out. He'd better tell her the whole tale. "The activity director went on to say that, contrary to popular belief, trumpeter swans don't always mate for life. Sometimes 'divorce' occurs, particularly following nesting failure. In my fourteen-year-old mind, I was distressed to think the male would leave his mate because she couldn't give him cygnets."

"That makes me sad, too. I always thought swans mated for life. I saw them as examples God provided humans to imitate."

Sheesh. Her gorgeous eyes misted. Nothing like wringing the feelings out of Cisney. This was not his modus operandi. He hoped Mom would be satisfied.

He pushed on. "The director said a pair of swans forms a monogamous pair bond that lasts for many years, and in some cases for life. The cob, the male, may mate with other pens without breaking the social pair bond."

"You're kidding. The unabashed male enters into open affairs with brazen pens?"

"Yeah, I guess. Anyway, I spent my free time watching the trumpeter swans at the center and researching them on the Internet. Their nests lay on the ground near the water. The cob not only helps construct the nest, but aids in incubating the eggs. The director told us one pair of swans at the center was having trouble reproducing. All I could think about when I wasn't playing chess was that the cob was going to divorce the pen."

Cisney stroked the sheep's wool. "That would crush me to know they were drifting apart. Sorry. No pun intended."

He shook his head, but couldn't help chuckling. At least she wasn't laughing at him yet. "To get back to the story, I decided to do something about the unproductive pair's problem. Long story short, I swiped some plastic gloves from the kitchen and located their nest, which most likely contained a set of defective eggs. Since the swans have a clutch of four to seven eggs, I stole two from another nest. Then, from a vantage point in the woods, I waited until the current incubating swan left the nest of bad eggs. When it did, I hurried down and deposited the stolen eggs in among their others."

Cisney's eyes grew huge. "Did it work?"

"The incubation period is about a month and a half, so I never found out what happened. But in my mind, I had saved the swans' marriage." He studied her lips for a hint of a laugh emerging. Bad idea. Now he really wanted to kiss her.

"What a wonderful story. You probably saved their marriage." She slapped her knee. "That's what I choose to believe." She grew thoughtful. "I think your mom wanted me to know how much you believe in commitment."

"Probably. So are you happy now, and I can leave?" Before he took her in his arms and kissed her. He leaned forward in preparing to rise.

"No."

He straightened. "No?" One more no and he'd label her a tease. "Now what?"

"You didn't tell me if you won the chess tournament. Did you?"

He stood and grinned. "Of course."

19

Nick parked near a popular restaurant. The Short Pump Town Center parking lot was less packed than on Friday and Saturday nights, and the normal dinner hour had long passed. Hopefully, they wouldn't have to wait long for a table.

He killed the engine, collapsed against the seatback, and closed his eyes. Getting things in order to leave the company was a bear. And he'd eaten nothing since a candy bar at lunch. Man, he was tired. But a slice of cheesecake would rally his food-deprived body, and Cisney's electricity would infuse his spirit.

Inside the restaurant, Nick took in aromas that spoke food, and his stomach growled. Patrons crowded the entrance area, waiting for their pagers to light up and buzz. No mystery that the entry was full. The temperature outside had dropped significantly in the last couple of hours.

He skimmed the area for Cisney. His scan stopped on the tall brunette leaning against the wall, her gaze focused on her e-book reader.

Nick fought his way through the throng and stood before her, taking in her exotic scent. "Good story?"

Her head snapped up, and her full lips spread into a smile. "Yes." She zipped the e-book reader into its leather cover. "I'm reading an intriguing romantic suspense."

"How long have you been here?"

"About two chapters." She held up the pager. "This should go off any"—the pager flashed and rumbled—"moment." She grinned.

The hostess seated them and left menus on the table.

Nick perused the dessert section. After a moment, he looked up to find Cisney regarding him with her large hazel eyes. She hadn't touched her menu. Was she too stuffed from the rehearsal dinner? "Aren't you going to order something?"

"I already know what I want. When I arrived, I drooled over the offerings behind the glass case."

He nodded and went back to the menu.

As always, she'd order the most bizarre thing she could find.

A slight young woman arrived to take their order. "Hi. I'm Cindy. I'll be taking care of you. What may I get you?"

Cisney rested her elbows on the table and her chin on her interlocked hands. "Tell me about the Mile-High Chocolate Truffle Cake."

"Layers and layers of fudge cake, with chocolate truffle cream and chocolate mousse."

"Anytime chocolate or fudge is mentioned three times, the cake has got to be scrumptious. I'll have that, and decaf."

"And you, sir?"

"I'll have plain cheesecake and coffee."

The waitress collected the menus and left.

Cisney folded her arms on the table and leaned toward him. "Why do you even bother looking through the menu? You always order the basic standard."

"How about you? I thought you'd already decided

on what you were going to have, but you changed your mind, like you frequently do."

"No, I don't. I knew I would order the cake all along. But hearing the waitress describe the delectable intensifies my anticipation."

"Does this mean you'll groan in ecstasy while you eat it?"

"Maybe I will, smarty-pants."

He laughed. "How'd the tango lesson go?"

"Can we talk about something else?"

"That bad, huh?"

"It was OK. I'd climb Mt. Everest to make Angela and Tom's day special, but tangoing with Hunter is beyond a surmountable challenge."

Why did his ears always do a double take with the way she put things? But how she expressed herself was what made her Cisney. And what made her Cisney gave him much to enjoy.

Angela. He still hadn't answered her email inviting him to her wedding. "While you're dancing the tango and eating wedding cake, I'll be driving toward Charlotte."

"Apartment hunting?"

"Yeah. I promised Julie I'd go over her pending projects after work tomorrow, but I hope to get on the road by seven."

Their desserts arrived. He held back wolfing down his cheesecake in two bites.

Cisney scooped a bit of the cream onto her fork, added a little of the mousse, and then slid the utensil into the cake so the cream stuff stayed on top of the cake portion. Her eyes closed as she drew the fork from her mouth and chewed the chunk of her chocolate overkill. Watching her eat was a culinary experience in itself.

He ate his cheesecake to satisfy his stomach, but his gaze and thoughts stayed focused on Cisney's mesmerizing lips. He couldn't fault her for the temptations she was creating. She was merely a woman whose mind was on chocolate.

She laid her fork on her empty plate and snatched the bill from Nick's side of the table.

He startled, and then reached for it.

She yanked it away, almost knocking a plate from the hands of a passing waitress.

He feigned resignation, and then leaned over and grabbed her arm. Ripping the paper nearly in half, he wrestled it from her grip.

She pouted.

He laughed. "Are you as good at tennis as you are at swiping the tab?"

"Better."

He chuckled. Every aspect of getting to know her amounted to an adventure. He helped her into her coat. "You want to walk the mall?"

"Yes. That would be fun."

They exited the restaurant door leading to the massive outdoor mall decorated in Christmas trimmings. Nick zipped his coat against the blast of cold air.

Cisney wrapped her red scarf more snuggly around her neck and linked her arm in his.

Unlike others loaded down with Christmassy shopping bags and scurrying from one shop to the next, they strolled the mall, window-shopping.

Cisney pointed ahead. "A jewelry store is coming up. I love to look at flashy displays."

Why did she like looking at jewelry? She didn't

seem the type to deck herself out in gold and gems. She only wore that pearl ring and gold loops in her earlobes.

He couldn't remember her wearing any other jewelry.

Cisney withdrew her arm from his and hurried to the show window outside the jewelry store. "Look at that emerald necklace. It's gorgeous." She turned her collar up and buried her gloved hands in her coat pockets.

Nick caught up and stood behind her. "Would you wear a necklace like that?"

"No, but I can appreciate it." She raised her shoulders and shivered. "It's freezing." She moved down the length of the window. "Wow! Look at that diamond engagement ring. It's got to be two karats."

He located the one she described. That was one gaudy ring. "I've never understood engagement rings. Wouldn't a guy want to give a woman something he treasured to show how much he cared for her?"

"You mean like his hockey stick?"

"Yeah. His hockey stick that took him to the national championships two years in a row. The guy gives it to the woman he wants to spend the rest of his life with because it's the one material thing he cherishes, other than her. Now she owns it, and he possesses nothing he esteems close to how he prizes his woman."

She turned to him. "That was profound, Nick. Do you believe what you just said?"

"I'm warming up to it." He nodded at the diamond ring. "Would you want something like that?"

"Remember, most married women wear their engagement rings for life. It's important they feel comfortable wearing them. So if a man bought that two-karat diamond ring for a woman with short fingers, she'd probably...love it." Her laugh ended with that little giggle he enjoyed.

"Just kidding," she said. "The huge diamond would look wrong on her stubby fingers. Also, she may not be into flamboyant. But..." She pointed at the ring. "If it was between that flashy diamond ring and his hockey stick, I think she'd go for the diamond. Later, she could have her rock cut down to one karat and have the other karat made into earrings."

"Or sell it and buy a one-karat ring and the earrings. Cheaper that way." He rubbed his cold hands together as she stared at him. "What? You don't think guys buy bigger for status reasons? Which has nothing to do with how much they love their women." He just didn't get the attraction for diamond rings.

"Nick, diamonds are forever. Marriage is supposed to be forever. A hockey stick could splinter when she raps it over his hard head for giving her such an awful token of engagement."

"I still think sacrificing his greatest possession is more romantic."

"What sacrifice? Unless she keeps his hockey stick in a bus station locker, he would still have his prized possession in his house. He could borrow it on the sly when she's visiting her mother. Sorry, I don't think your engagement theory is gonna fly."

He raised his shoulders and hunched into his coat. "Do you want to get out of the cold?"

"Yes. Let's go in that clothing store and buy warm hats." She grabbed his coat sleeve and tugged him toward the shop.

He resisted. "I don't need any more hats."

"Your ears are red. I'll treat."

He might allow her to drag him into the store, but over his dead body would she buy him a hat.

They wound their way around tables of men's shirts to the hats.

Cisney perused the men's headgear lined up on display racks. She snatched a hunting cap, whose flaps hung down. A mischievous grin on her lips, she positioned Nick in front of the mirror and pulled the cap down on his head.

He stared at his ridiculous image, keeping his expression noncommittal. "Is it me?"

She yanked the hat from his head. "No. But this one is." She replaced the hunting cap with a leather fedora, cocking it at a rakish angle. "Perfect." Her eyes sparkled.

"Doesn't do much to warm the ears."

"Don't be such a drag." She returned the fedora to the rack.

A hat in the women's section caught his eye. Time to turn the tables. He grasped her hand. "Come with me."

He stopped within reach of several glitzy hats. He lifted the wide-brimmed black one with a shiny, purple, oversized bow that sprouted reddish, iridescent fuzzy stuff and three black feathers. A rhinestone brooch anchored the bow. He set the outlandish hat flat on Cisney's head and grinned. She'd have to agree he'd selected the most absurd hat.

She turned to the mirror. "I love it. It's a Victorian hat, and it's worn like this." She tilted the brim to one side, positioning it low over one eye.

He flipped over the tag. "It's called a Rembrandt." And it cost about as much as an original Rembrandt.

"Perhaps that's because its fashioned after the black hat Rembrandt wore in his self-portrait." She cocked her head, setting a pose. "Is it me?"

She was gorgeous. His grin weakened. Was there nothing, not even a silly hat, which could spoil Cisney's attractiveness? Probably not. Her beauty shone from within.

He renewed his smile and crossed his arms over his chest. "I think you could wear any of these hats and it would be you."

She blushed and removed the Rembrandt. "Your words are precious because I'm told by a woman I trust that analytical men, like actuaries, don't often express compliments, even if they think such lovely words. So, thank you."

"You're welcome." If she was referring to Mom as her source, they'd sure gotten chummy fast while he'd been on his interview. Mom must have been a busy little bee, pollinating Cisney's ear with the ways of analytical men and his childhood incidents worth mining.

She replaced the hat on its stand, and they wandered to the winter headwear section.

Somehow, after his protests and against his resolve, they left the shop wearing new stocking hats, his black, and hers red with an orange and purple knit flower on the band.

Cisney linked her arm in his and laughed. "You could have at least let me buy you the blue hat with the red stripe."

"I like black."

"Cisney."

They swung around toward a man's voice.

"Jason."

જ્જ

Nick regarded the fool who'd dumped Cisney. A big guy. Muscular. Ruddy complexion. A little taller than himself.

While he sized up Cisney's ex, the guy returned the favor, and then locked his baby blues on Cisney. The jock approached her as if he planned to kiss her cheek.

She stepped back. Her arm, yoked with Nick's, drew him with her.

Jason hesitated, and then retreated a pace. "You look great, Cis."

Cisney's body tensed.

Had the guy used the nickname to mark his territory?

Cisney raised her face to Nick's. "This is Jason Disney."

Cisney Disney? She had to be kidding. The name should have been their first clue they weren't meant for each other.

She returned her gaze to Jason. "This is Nick LeCrone, a friend from Virginia National."

Why had she added the friend modifier? She hadn't introduced Jason with any description. *Jason Disney, the jerk who dumped me.*

Jason flicked a glance at Nick, so brief it reeked of putdown. Then the muscleman turned sideways, extending his hand toward a store window. "Cis, can I talk to you for a minute?"

Cisney's arm, still hooked in Nick's, stiffened. "No thanks. Nick and I were just leaving."

Was Cisney still influenced by this guy? Her

edginess showed that Jason still aroused her emotions. Anger? Fear of coming under his magnetism? If she was over Jason, wouldn't she be less jumpy?

Jason's eyes pleaded with Cisney. "I need less than a minute." He swung his gaze to Nick, his stare cold and condescending. "You can give us a moment, can't you?"

Nick shrugged. "It's up to Cisney."

Cisney tightened her grip on his arm and tugged. "Let's go, Nick."

Right decision.

Jason dropped his outstretched arm and planted his fists on his hips, his face flushed to an angry red. "Expect a call from me, Cis."

"Please don't, Jason."

Had a hint of uncertainty notched her voice? Maybe he was reading things into her tone. But no question, her words hadn't issued a command.

Their linked bodies turned from Jason in unison, but for him, and maybe for her, the seemingly intimate rotation was a mechanical means of ending the encounter. Cisney and Jason's reunion had proved more eye opening than he wanted.

They walked a few yards. She twisted and looked back at Jason.

A bowling ball dropped in Nick's stomach.

20

A cold gust blew a white fast-food bag across the parking lot. Cisney snuggled against Nick. What had Jason wanted to tell her? Probably that he and Candy Sue were history. And Jason was lonely.

She looked up at Nick. "I'm sorry about the scene with Jason."

He looked straight ahead, his expression stone-faced. "Yeah."

Was that all he had to say? Yeah? Maybe she should let go of his arm. Reciprocate his coolness. But succumbing to hurt feelings would ruin the already tainted evening.

She should be thankful Jason hadn't made a scene. When she'd told him she wished him well in their last call, she'd meant it. And at first, he'd seemed contrite in the mall. Then the way he looked at Nick had raised red flags. She knew too well what could boil beneath his so-called forgive-me charisma. Why had she put up with his manipulative charm for six months?

"Where are you parked?" Nick said.

He sounded detached, as if the encounter with Jason hadn't happened. Hadn't he seen how red Jason's face was, or heard his threat? *Expect a call from me, Cis.*

If only Nick knew how relieved she was to see Jason head in the opposite direction after they'd turned their backs on his bravado, then maybe Nick wouldn't be so dispassionate.

Jason had several pounds on Nick, all muscle. He'd shown what he could do when another man made advances toward her. Like the black eye he'd given the overly friendly drunk a few months ago.

"My SUV's over that way..." She released Nick's arm and pointed, then retracted her finger and surveyed the cars. "No. I think I parked closer to the other end."

Nick stopped. His heavy sigh created a cloud in the night air. "So, which is it?"

Withdrawn a minute ago, and now gruff. Was Nick jealous and taking it out on her? If so, bumping into Jason revealed a side of Nick she'd hoped he lacked.

She swallowed her hurt. "I think it's toward the end there, and a few rows back."

They walked in silence until they reached her vehicle.

She pressed the unlock button on her key fob. He opened her door, and she slid onto the cold leather seat.

He looked at her, hesitated, and then leaned down and captured her gaze. "I'm sorry, Cisney. I shouldn't have been brusque with you. You've done nothing wrong. I'm angry with myself."

"Why?"

"Because I should never have pursued you. I didn't realize how unready for a relationship I am until I saw how attached you still are to Jason."

"What do you mean? I didn't leave you standing in the middle of the mall and have a side conversation with Jason. If you remember, I refused to talk to him." This wasn't happening.

"I said you did nothing to disappoint me...consciously, anyway. I'm frustrated with myself. Period."

She scanned her actions since Jason had stopped them. What had she done to indicate she cared for Jason? Was Nick making something up to get rid of her? She felt like her lungs weren't pulling in enough air. With or without oxygen, she would not cry. "Tell me one thing I did unconsciously that made you think I care for Jason."

He caressed her cheek. "You looked back, Cisney. You looked back at Jason."

He turned and strode away.

21

Curled up in the corner of her sofa, Cisney hugged BoSheep and wept. All her past relationships had been disasters, but the growing one with Nick had seemed so promising. For once in her life, she'd ignored what she thought Daddy prized in a man and had followed her heart. And, she'd chosen a man who loved God and who encouraged her faith.

But she'd been unrewarded for doing the right thing. She didn't exactly blame God, but…OK. She did blame Him. Pretending otherwise didn't fool God.

A new flow of tears dripped off her jaw. She yanked tissues from the nearby box and wiped her face. She needed to stop crying and go to bed. Black circles under swollen eyes were the last things she wanted to wear on Angela's big day. No way would she let on to Angela tomorrow that Nick had broken her heart.

"Lord, I love Nick." Her words came out in a wail.

She'd never dreamed the actuary she'd known for a year as a colleague could capture her heart, but in two weeks he had. She'd even thought God's hand was in it. Wasn't a godly man like Nick someone the Lord would want her to seek for a lasting marriage?

"Oooh!" She whipped tissues from the box until a pile grew on her lap. What did God want her to do? *Lord, I thought You were on my side this time.*

Her gaze settled on her Bible on the coffee table. Oops. Hadn't she promised God, after the

Thanksgiving Jason fiasco, to run to His Word when trials arose?

She placed BoSheep on the sofa and lifted her Bible, still open from this morning's reading. The day's passage came from John's Gospel, relating the day Jesus fed five thousand people on a remote country hillside. Jesus had accepted a boy's offered lunch of two fish and five loaves of bread and fed all the hungry people.

The boy brought his meager resources to Jesus to help solve the problem, and then Jesus did His part...the impossible part.

"Lord, what can I offer to help eliminate Nick's misconception? He's hurt so badly, and he's so bullheaded that he's right, he won't believe I looked back at Jason for Nick's protection. How do I prove to Nick I'm worth the risk?"

A plan entered her mind as clear as spring water. Its radical nature and possible ramifications put much of what she had at stake. Could she trust the Lord with her offering? That she wouldn't end up in worse trouble?

She shoved off the couch in search of her laptop. She'd do her part.

❧❦

Cisney watched the morning sky grow pink outside her apartment window. She closed her Bible. Today, if she did nothing else, she'd trust God. The day already held its blessings.

Angela's mother had taken responsibility to transport the bridesmaids' dresses to the church. Hallelujah.

Cisney packed her undergarments and satin pumps in her I'm-a-Sunday-School-Teacher bag. She regarded the thin stack of envelopes containing the documents she'd worked on until after midnight. Her heart took a few irregular beats as she slid them into the bag. *Lord, I trust You.* She grabbed the bag and her coffee from the kitchen counter and headed for her SUV.

According to Angela's instructions, Cisney parked in the lot across the street from a magnificent old hotel. Inside, her red ballet flats padded the marble floor as she hurried past the enormous faux marble columns to the restaurant.

She hit the dining room threshold five minutes early, but of course, the last person arriving would be considered late. The mothers of the bride and groom, the bride, and her four other bridesmaids sat at a round table covered in a white tablecloth, laughing and sipping orange juice. Was the empty chair next to Angela reserved for her because she was the maid of honor? If so, how sweet.

She hugged Angela, and then Angela's mother. She smiled her greetings to the other women, whom she barely knew, and slid into her seat of honor.

Angela nudged Cisney with her elbow. "How's Nick?"

She paused before opening her mouth. A first. How could she avoid talking about Nick and her as a couple? "He's driving to Charlotte after work to hunt for an apartment tomorrow."

Angela's face fell.

Why did Nick's departure from Richmond disappoint Angela? Cisney searched her friend's eyes. "What's the matter?"

Did Angela know something about their situation? Impossible.

Angela hesitated. "I guess no harm in telling you now. Monday, I emailed Nick an invitation to our wedding, as a surprise for you. Although he didn't answer my email, I hoped he'd come."

Cisney hid her disappointment and placed her napkin on her lap. Wouldn't Nick's presence tonight have been the perfect answer to her prayers? After the wedding, she could have given him the envelopes and watched how God used them. But Nick's fast-approaching relocation had to get in the way. *Sorry, Lord. I trust You.*

She had to say something. "You look radiant, Ange."

The bride grinned. "I thought this day would never arrive."

Sidetracking Angela from a conversation about Nick was too easy. The wedding day promise must have mellowed her tenacious buddy.

Cisney perused the menu. The poached eggs sounded good, but so did the omelet. She'd go with whichever popped into her mind when the server came to take her order. She closed the menu and chatted with her breakfast companions.

Halfway through Cisney's omelet, Angela's toothy childhood friend, Lucy, clinked her fork against her glass. Lucy waited for the conversations to cease, her face glowing with eagerness to deliver her announcement.

"Angela, we have a surprise for you. I sent an email to everyone here…" She turned to Cisney. "I'm sorry, we didn't have your email address, and we didn't want to ask Angela for it, or it would ruin the surprise."

Cisney smiled and waved away Lucy's concern. She was one hundred percent behind whatever activity would make this day special for Angela.

Lucy closed her mouth over her large teeth, but her lips open again. "Anyway, Angela, we've all agreed to devote our entire day to you without any interruptions, as good attendants should. So..." Lucy wrinkled her nose, donned a squinty-eyed grin, and vibrated her fists close to her chest.

Cisney caught herself holding her breath.

Lucy motioned to the portly woman named Amy, who produced a flaccid pink velvet bag with a white satin drawstring.

"So," Lucy said, "we will cast our annoying cellphones into this bag, and it will not be opened again until after the reception tonight." She directed her hand toward the pink pouch. "Ladies, your cellphones, please!"

On cue, Amy lifted her cell high with a two-finger grasp and dropped it into the pouch.

Cisney gaped at the velvet bag, her one-hundred-percent support plummeting like the dial on the gauge of a siphoned gas tank. How would Nick call her? If God nudged her to call Nick on the way to the beauty salon, how would she comply? Stop at the first nearly extinct pay phone she passed?

Amy traveled around the table, collecting the devices.

Lucy lifted her finger as if testing wind direction, her eyes sparkling. "And, the mothers of the bride and groom have agreed to chauffer us to the salon and to the church. We will leave our cars here at the hotel so we won't be tempted to stop en route to borrow a phone or to take care of business, because Angela, serving you is our concern today. We have hearts only for you."

The women nodded and clapped.

Cisney rotated her head toward Angela. Surely, Ange would roll her eyes and refuse to accept such silliness.

Angela beamed.

Cisney's heart sank. If she spotted the wedding-day bug, whose stinger had injected sappy sentimentality into her feisty friend, she'd squash it with her bare hand.

Amy stood next to Cisney, smiling and extending the now bulging pink sack. Cisney raised her face to Amy's. Which look should she give her—her pleading pout or her defiant scowl? She went with the pout.

Amy pinched her lips and shook the pouch.

Cisney shrugged, offered her fake smile around the table, and produced her cell. But the weight of her phone in her hand awakened second thoughts.

She raised hopeful eyes to Amy. "Maybe I could just step out for a moment and make one short—very short—call. And then my heart is all Angela's." She looked at Angela, who, under the influence of the wedding-day bug's toxin, seemed to be rethinking her choice for her maid of honor.

Cisney returned her gaze to Amy.

The puffy-faced woman glowered at her and rattled her cache of cellphones. Cisney hesitated, and then dropped her cell into the pink bag. *Lord, I—*

The ladies gently cheered.

Even Amy's grimace relaxed, and she patted Cisney's shoulder as if she were a sponsor encouraging an addict who'd made the right choice.

OK. She was back in the good graces of her companions and no longer under their scrutiny. What was going on here?

Lord, wasn't my part to prepare the documents and *present them to Nick? If so, how can I, if I'm cut off from the man?*

22

The day had been full of activity, and Angela had beamed through the ceremony, but Cisney's mind had wandered to Nick non-stop. She'd surveyed the guests in the pews more than once, and when she'd failed to spot Nick, she'd kept watch on the church's entrance, hoping he'd show up at the last minute, but he hadn't.

Now, with the vows, the photo shoot, and the ride to the reception hall over, Cisney sought a moment to herself in the restroom. The clock in the plush room read seven o'clock. By now, Nick would be on the road to Charlotte, his false notions about her rambling around in his head…if he thought of her at all.

Observing her image in the mirror, she fiddled with her dark curls.

Perhaps this day, Angela's day, was not the right time for God to clear up Nick's misconceptions. God would be faithful. He would take care of reuniting them. Or He would lead her in a new direction. Comforting her wounded…totally crushed…heart. That was pathetic. Didn't she know better than to try to sway God's will? *I trust You, Lord.*

She shoved the envelopes aside in her bag and located her lipstick. She was beginning to think God had given her the task of creating the documents as a test of her obedience, rather than to actually present them to Nick. He'd probably think her labor of love silly, anyway.

Her lipstick refreshed, she exited the restroom and headed for the ballroom. For now, she had other things to trust God with. Like getting her through the tango with Hunter.

She joined the bridesmaids and groomsmen surrounding Angela and Tom. The emcee, dressed in a blue sequined jacket and black tux slacks, moved to the dance floor, attaching a microphone to his glinting lapel.

Cisney combed the wedding party, seeking her dance partner. Hunter was not among the men in black. In a moment, the emcee would announce the bride and groom's dance.

She leaned toward Tom. "Where's Hunter?"

Tom searched the area. He frowned. "I'll strangle him."

Cisney placed a calming hand on Tom's arm. "No. Angela won't want to spend her wedding night alone while you're in jail for fratricide."

Angela sidled to them. "Where's your brother, Tom? It's almost time for the tango."

Cisney donned a brave smile. "It's all right, you guys. Hunter will be here." She rose on her tiptoes and scanned the guests. Wouldn't he?

The emcee shared humorous snippets about Angela and Tom, and then the fast-talking announcer chuckled. "Usually, the bride and groom start off the dancing with the groom sashaying his bride around the dance floor for all to behold. But tonight, folks, Angela and Tom have planned a special surprise for you."

The bridesmaids and groomsmen paired up. Tom led Angela to the center of the dance floor. He shot Cisney an apologetic look. Angela looked at her over his shoulder, emanating sympathy vibes.

Rising above her fear of looking like a jilted lover, a part she played so well, she smiled at her friends and waved off the problem.

The other couples took their positions on the outskirts of the dance floor, leaving a gaping hole where Hunter and Cisney had been choreographed to stand.

Cisney scanned the onlookers for Hunter. Guests nodded toward her, whispered, and searched their ranks, obviously distracted by the maid of honor short her escort.

Please, Lord, send Hunter. Don't allow Hunter and me to ruin this dance for Angela and Tom. Take eyes off me and turn them to the bride and groom.

Her prayer went unanswered. No red-faced Hunter fought his way through the stirred-up spectators.

What should she do? Fill in the open spot on the floor and tango with an imaginary partner? Wait out the dance in the ladies' room?

The first strains of Zade's "Tango" invited the couples to take their stances.

Cisney's heart raced. *Lord, tell me what to do?*

Through a break in the crowd, she glimpsed the black coat sleeve of a man progressing toward the dance floor. She let out a heavy sigh. Hunter was on his way. Her heart calmed as she turned and located a vacant spot on the floor. She spun back to Hunter.

Nick!

Nick stood tall and handsome in his black suit. He stood on the sideline of the crowd, one arm extended in her direction, his expression contrite, but expectant.

She inhaled a joyous breath. Everything in her

wanted to run into his arms. But this was Angela's moment, not hers. Staying put, she waited for Nick to cover the distance. Or did he not know how to tango?

Nick made no move toward her, yet his gaze beckoned her.

She sidestepped Amy and her dance partner in mid-promenade and glided to Nick, her hot pink dress fluttering against her ankles.

He took her into his open embrace and guided her flawlessly into a gap among the striding couples. An audible sigh of relief oozed from the crowd. Glimpsing Nick's handsome face, Cisney's heart beat like a teen's on a date with the class hunk.

Nick promenaded her between two couples, and then initiated her into a turn. She snapped her head and rotated to face him. Their staccato steps moved in unison. *Slow...slow...quick, quick...slow.*

Angela caught Cisney's attention and grinned. She lifted her hand from Tom's shoulder and pointed at his head.

Tom held his bride in a rigid embrace while he walked her through the steps. His gaze remained on his patent leather shoes while his lips mouthed T ... A ... N, G ... O.

Angela rolled her eyes.

Cisney stifled a giggle.

Angela shifted her gaze back to her man.

Cisney made her turn and snapped her head. She tried to maintain the aloof expression that added to the tango's drama, but Nick's presence, God's faithfulness, and the forever-love a wedding promised weakened her resolve. She couldn't stop smiling.

Lord, Your part is awesome!

Nick leaned in close. "Don't look now, but

according to people's stares, I think we're upstaging the bride and groom."

"We should stop."

Nick aimed for a narrow opening in their audience and promenaded Cisney to the alcove off the lobby, where the restrooms and coatroom were located. He brought her hand to his side and captured her gaze.

If she shifted her eyes away from his, would he disappear as suddenly as he had materialized? Was he one of her fairy-princess dreams?

A waiter exited the men's room, giving them a knowing look. Nick pulled her closer to the unoccupied coatroom, where the lighting shone less bright.

Always pulling her. With the tingles his warm hand sent through her, she'd forgive him this time. "What sent you to my rescue?"

"When I arrived in the parking lot, a young man in a tux was absorbed in tying aluminum cans to Tom's car, while a couple of teenage girls wrote just married and other sentiments on the windows. I wondered if the tango would be performed minus the young groomsman."

"Why didn't you ask Hunter about his tango duty, or send him inside?"

Nick's sheepish grin, coming from a diehard actuary who strived never to err, gave her goose bumps.

"It's a long story, but I think Hunter's preoccupation was the Lord's second ambush."

"Ambush?"

He fingered one of her curls. "Do you remember the story where God tells King Jehoshaphat that the battle against the king's enemies is His alone?"

"God's people were only to take up their positions and watch God win the battle."

"Yep. God set up ambushes against Jehoshaphat's enemies."

"So, if you had sent Hunter inside you would have ruined God's ambush?"

He nodded.

"You said Hunter in the parking lot was God's second ambush. What was the first?"

"I thought God planned to go to battle for me after I returned from Charlotte, but as usual, it's futile to second guess the Lord. I was a half hour into my trip, when the traffic came to a stop. I sat for fifteen minutes with nothing more than the bumper sticker on the truck in front of me for entertainment."

"I imagine you were listening to your doo-wop tunes."

He chuckled. "We need to have a talk about the definition of doo-wop music another time."

"OK. Back to the bumper sticker."

"You know the sticker that says, God Allows U-turns?"

"Yes."

"This sticker said God Expects U-turns. So at my first opportunity, I turned around and headed for home to change into this get-up." He flicked his lapel. "Then I waited on the fringe of the dance floor, hoping God had won your forgiveness for how coolly I treated you last night." He took both her hands in his. "Cisney, will you forgive me? I know you looked back at Jason last night, but I don't care—"

"I looked back to make sure he wasn't coming after you to pulverize you."

"What?"

"On another embarrassing occasion, Jason gave a guy a black eye on my behalf."

"Oh."

His glazed-over stare said he was processing all her moves last night with this new information. She waited. For the first time, she was comfortable giving him time to think.

Over the coatroom's half door, she surveyed the coats. Where'd the woman who owned the black and white checkered designer jacket, cinched at the waist with a red patent leather belt, shop?

He cleared his throat.

Her gaze zipped to his.

"I am so sorry, Cisney."

"I forgive you. But you could have saved me a lot of work last night, if you had allowed me to explain, instead of walking away."

"What work?"

"I have a bag full of résumés addressed to companies in Charlotte."

"To prove you would leave Jason?" He moved closer. "You don't have to leave your job or your parents. I don't mind making weekend trips."

Her smile took an elevator from her heart to her lips. "Some physical distance from Daddy might be a good idea."

"Look." He stepped back and reached into his suit coat pocket.

He held up a ring.

Cisney's heart stopped.

Nick's hand lay in the shadows of the alcove's poor lighting. She shifted her shoulder to allow the ceiling light behind her to illumine the ring.

Where a gem might sit on the wide gold band—

split on the underside, so one size could fit all—was a round plastic disk. Etched in the disk's gold center was a symbol for the planet. Five circles lined the top arc of the disk. She made out what looked like a leaf inside one circle and three lightning bolts in a second. The other symbols were lost on her. Embossed in capital letters under the world emblem was: Captain Planet.

Her virtual romantic-memories scrapbook snapped shut. She raised her gaze to his.

His eyes were wide with excitement. "When I was eight years old, I esteemed Captain Planet more than anyone. Who wouldn't? Captain Planet did everything to save the earth. Because of him, I wanted to grow up to be a scientist in the EPA."

"Was this before or after you planned to raise Siberian Huskies?"

He captured her chin between his thumb and finger. "This is a serious moment, Cisney."

She snapped her satin heels together and brought her shoulders to attention. Maybe this moment could still end up in her scrapbook memory.

He lifted her left hand. "This is my most prized possession in all the world. I want you to have it."

He moved her pearl solitaire to her right hand and slid the Captain Planet monstrosity—which she would cherish forever—onto her left ring finger. "God won the battle to open my heart again by placing you in my life. I think I can take some credit for falling in love with you, though. Will you accept this token of my love?"

She rotated the plastic ring on her finger, her heart bolting like the lightning bars on the ring. She raised her face to his, grinning. "Yes. I will. I like it so much better than a hockey stick."

❧❦

Cisney gathered what she needed for her presentation to the executive staff.

Angela strolled in and sat in Cisney's side chair. "Hi." She set her presentation packet on the end of Cisney's desk. "Are you ready?"

Angela's tan from lying on sunny beaches in Aruba had long faded, but her newlywed glow still gleamed.

"Yes. We'll dazzle the VPs like we did with our presentation before Christmas."

Angela nodded at Cisney's hand. "Are you going to wear that in the meeting?"

Cisney wiggled her left ring finger. "Of course." The VPs hadn't discounted her last proposal because she'd worn Nick's Captain Planet ring.

"I hope Nick appreciates how you wear that hunk of plastic everywhere. Is he coming again this weekend?"

"No. I'm driving down to Cornelius this time."

"Those four-hour trips have got to get old. I don't know how you guys do it."

"Well, you know Nick. He misses his Captain Planet ring."

But Angela was right. A long-distance relationship was hard. The trip both ways cut into their weekend hours together. Except for time at Christmas, they seemed to spend more time talking over the phone than being with each other. She couldn't enjoy much of Sundays because she dreaded Nick's late afternoon departures, when it felt like part of her heart ripped from her chest and drove away with him.

They stayed at Mom and Daddy's house when Nick was in Richmond, which meant she had to share him with them—mostly with Daddy. The men had worked out a relationship.

Daddy's jabs at Nick were less frequent and more benign. Every weekend, he sat by the window and kept an eye out for Nick's arrival.

Mom adored Nick. She hummed as she made him cookies for the weekend and his trip home.

"Cisney?"

"Hmm?"

"You were off gathering wool."

"I hate long-distance relationships."

❧◦❧

Nick paced between the Steinway and a sofa in the front room, keeping his eye on the window.

Mom came in from the kitchen. "No sign, yet?"

He stopped pacing. No need to incite Mom into worrying. "Not yet."

"Nancy has Grandma Thelma on the phone. She and Grandpa want to see Cisney. Do you want them to come up for lunch Saturday or Sunday?"

"It'd be nice if we could have a family lunch here tomorrow."

Mom nodded and went back to the kitchen. He heard her relay his message to Nancy.

Dad said something about a Chinese checkers tournament.

Where was Cisney? She was now twenty minutes overdue and she didn't answer—his cell rang.

Cisney.

He took a relieved breath. "Hi."

"I'm just turning into the neighborhood. I thought I could make up time to hide my slip up, but I couldn't."

"What slip up?"

"I stopped for my mid-trip milkshake and, in talking to the server—remember the one with the huge ponytail, at the place you accused me of trying to appear engaged with my pearl ring?"

He pinched the bridge of his nose. "Yes. But I didn't accuse you of anything."

"Anyway, I left my cellphone there and had to go back to get it."

"How'd you manage to forget it?" He walked out onto the front porch, hunching against February's cold. Her headlights should appear at any moment.

"I put it down to show Sally my Captain Planet ring. And, you know, with all her gushing at how beautiful it is, I forgot to pick my cell up when my shake came."

He chuckled at her little dig about the ring, his breath forming a cloud. He couldn't believe she wore his ring everywhere she went. He liked that.

Headlights appeared.

As soon as she parked, he opened the passenger door, tossed her handbag into the backseat, and climbed inside. He wrapped her in his arms and drew in her exotic scent, the one that stayed on his clothes after he left her each week and made him miss her all the way to Charlotte.

He pulled away. "I wanted to talk to you before the family pounces on you."

"Should I leave the car running for heat?"

"Yeah."

She looked so beautiful in the glow from the

garage floodlight as she turned in her seat to more fully face him. Nerves rattled in his stomach.

He took her hand and toyed with the Captain Planet ring. "Cisney, I know we've been together—sort of—for only a few months, but even before we started dating I admired how hard you worked, how creative your ideas were, and how you never used worldly, dishonest tactics in your marketing strategies."

"You...admired...me?"

"Yes. Then. *Now*, I love you."

She swallowed. "Back then, I pretty much thought you were an arrogant actuary who looked for ways to judge my strategies too risky. By the way, Julie is doing a great job in supporting my area."

He touched his finger to her full lips and grinned. "Are you going to let me talk?"

She caressed his jaw. "I love you, Nick."

"In that case," he said, "do you still have those résumés you prepared?"

Her beautiful eyes widened. She nodded.

He leaned to the side and wrangled a black velvet box from his jeans' pocket, and then looked into her eyes. "Will you marry me?" He opened the box.

She stared at the diamond twinkling up at her. Tears let loose and flowed.

He'd give it a ninety-five percent chance they were tears of joy. He held the box poised in front of her. "Well?"

She swiped away tears, but more replaced them. "Do I have to give the Captain Planet ring back?"

He lifted her chin with his free hand and kissed her. "Yes."